Over 100 Great Novels of Erotic Domination

If you like one you will probably like the rest

New Titles Every Month

All titles in print are now available from:
www.onlinebookshop.com

Electronic editions of all titles can be found at:
www.adultbookshops.com

If you want to be on our confidential mailing list for our Readers' Club Magazine (with extracts from past and forthcoming titles) write to:

SILVER MOON READER SERVICES
The Shadowline Building
6 Wembley Street
Gainsborough
DN21 2AJ
United Kingdom
or
info@babash.com

or leave details on our 24hr UK answer-phone
08700 10 90 60
International access code then +44 08700 10 90 60

NEW AUTHORS WELCOME
Please send submissions to
Silver Moon Books Ltd.
PO Box 5663
Nottingham
NG3 6PJ
or
editor@babash.com

The Initiate first published 2003 Silver Moon Books
ISBN 1-903687-30-6
© 2003 Miranda Lake
The right of Miranda Lake to be identified as the author of this book has been asserted in accordance with Section 77 and 78 of the Copyrights and Patents Act 1988

THE INITIATE

BY

MIRANDA LAKE

All characters in this book are fictitious, and any resemblance to real persons, living or dead, is purely coincidental.

THIS IS FICTION - IN REAL LIFE ALWAYS PRACTISE SAFE SEX!

1.

The Lady Hysena Macarydias aged 17, daughter of Barca IX, Lord Protector of the Southern Roads, and Lissa, Princess of the Kingdom of Argo, shuffled her sore feet and tried to fight off the surely heretical yawn than was threatening to disgrace her.

Holy Father Tarrip had been droning on for what felt like days in his monotonous voice, not missing a single word from the Novice Initiate ceremony. Hysena knew she had to go through this; indeed, she had been tutored for this very moment almost from the cradle, been told that as a daughter of the aristocracy of Qalle this day would be the greatest of her short life. But no one had warned her how mind- numbingly boring it would be. She stood with the other six initiates and almost wished that she was back at home.

The rich robes that had made her squeal with excitement and awe when she first saw them were threatening to smother her. They covered her completely: even her eyes were concealed by a strip of gauze that allowed her to see, but not well. Beneath them she wore nothing, as the ceremony demanded. This had at first seemed daring and grown up. But now, in the thick air of the chamber, Hysena felt sweat form on her slim body, sticky at her armpits and running in rivulets between her breasts, itching abominably as it ran over her stomach and gathered in her pubic hair. The heavy wool chafed her nipples and she longed to rub them, but the ceremony demanded that her hands be held unmoving in the position of supplication.

She was not to know that this was the least, the very, very least of the discomforts that she was to endure during the three years of her training. Nor could she know that the first lesson in the horrors and humiliations that would befall her was so close.

Hysena gradually became aware that the room was silent. Tarrip had finished the rite and the candidates had fallen to their knees to receive the Prophet's blessing. All but Hysena. With a smothered gasp, she quickly knelt, unfortunately nudging the girl in front who in turn bumped the girl next to her. Like throwing a stone into a pond, the ripples ran through the kneeling group, disturbing one of the most solemn ceremonies on Qalle.

She remembered little of the rest of the ceremony, making her responses and vows to serve the Prophet automatically, and at last it was over. The girls stood in a bare anteroom, throwing back their hoods with relief. All eyes were on Hysena. She saw the tall, haughty Uplander sneering down her characteristically long nose, a huge sun-bronzed Kallinian, her warrior eyes blazing at the way this skinny Argon had humiliated her and by implication her people. Even the tiny, doll-like figure of the candidate from the fertile plains of Sis Narash, the most peaceful people on the planet, was looking at her with scorn.

As far as she was capable of coherent thought, Hysena Macarydias wished she were dead.

The door to the anteroom opened with a crash. High Priest Tarrip walked in, flanked by two women wearing the robes of Sister Elders.

Tarrip stared at them in silence, his normally pleasant if ugly face black as thunder. The steel heels of his high boots tapped on the stone floor as he walked around the subdued group of girls.

'Well?' Tarrip suddenly barked, making them all jump. 'Thirty years I have presided over the Novice Initiation ceremony. Thirty years. Longer than any of you have been alive. You vow to uphold the faith, the tradition and most of all the.....' he drew a huge breath and bellowed loud enough to be heard in Calith, 'THE HOLY DIGNITY OF THE TRUE PROPHET!' He glared at them, face suffused, spittle on his mouth. Behind him, the two Sisters stood impassive, one a big, beefy woman of around forty, shapeless of figure and evil eyed. The other was younger, smaller, prettier. She wore a look of concern rather than of anger.

Tarrip continued his slow way around the room. 'We expect lapses,' he continued in a more kindly voice, 'you are but youngsters. Part of what you are here to learn is how to avoid mistakes. It is just misfortune that a mistake of such magnitude was made before the gathered gentility of the civilised lands of Qalle.' He turned to face the girls. 'From your mistakes, from each error, you shall glean a lesson, a thing to remember so that you may not err again in that way.' His voice was soothing now, paternal almost. The frightened girls had begun to relax, thinking that Hysena's lapse would be regarded as a clumsy accident that caused no harm. So the shock was all the greater when Tarrip stood directly in front of Hysena and said, almost whispering, 'Remove your robe. You shall be whipped.'

She stared at him in wide-eyed silence, more shocked than she had ever been in her life. Whipping was for criminals! For vagrants and drunks! Did he not know she was a Lady?

'My Lady Hysena, I am waiting.'

She managed to work some saliva into her mouth. 'S-sir, Father, I-I cannot. I wear n-nothing underneath,' she stammered. Even the men she had seen being whipped before the church at home when she had been able to sneak away from her guardians had worn loin cloths to preserve at least a little of their dignity. And she had never even heard of a woman being so punished! Her frightened eyes darted about the room as if seeking a place to run. She felt the need to vomit and worse, to urinate. She whimpered when she saw the beefy Sister carrying a whipping horse towards the centre of the room. The woman set it down with a grunt and began to adjust the legs.

Hysena stood on the verge of a faint. She saw the eyes of her fellow initiates. The Uplander girl still sneering, the Kallinian almost smiling at her terror.

'Lady Hysena, if you have not removed the robe by the time Sister Colya has made the horse ready to receive you, it shall be torn from your body and thus returned to your Father that he may know the shame you bring on his proud house.' Tarrip's voice was icy.

Eyes blinded by tears and with fingers made clumsy with fear and shame, Hysena fumbled at the buttons on the heavy robe. There were twelve of them, solid silver, running the full length of the garment, but she only had to undo the first six before the heavy cloth with its rich embroidery slithered quietly from her slim shoulders and revealed her body.

Tarrip had long learned to conceal his lust when he saw a young girl disrobe, and the Prophet knew he had seen many! He had hoped to make the fiery Kallinian the first; always break the potential troublemakers as soon as possible was his rule, but this one was a little beauty. He drank in the sight of her small, brown-nippled breasts and flat stomach with its tight navel. The robe caught on her hips and with a despairing sob, Hysena let the garment pool about her ankles. His eyes gleamed as he drank in the sight of her *mons* with its covering of silky black hairs, hairs that were not so thick as to conceal her lips and the cleft of her cunt.

She stood in the middle of the room and he walked around her to admire as pretty a pair of buttocks as he had seen for many a year. Her face, though distorted by her tears, was also pretty, he noted, with high cheekbones and cat-like, wide-set eyes of a blue so deep as to appear almost purple. Her jet black hair was cropped short in the fashion of her country, showing the fine shape of her skull.

'Ready, Holy Father.' Sister Colya's accent was that of a Calith peasant, which was all she had been until 'called' to the Prophet. Tarrip found it useful to have a few of her type around the seminary; stupid, sadistic women who would carry out his bidding without question, knowing he could reward them in ways that delighted even their dull sensibilities.

With an impatient gesture, the holy man motioned the nude girl towards the horse. It consisted of a cylinder of wood about which had been fitted a layer of padding and a covering of soft leather. It was supported by four sturdy legs that could be adjusted to fit the height of the victim. A strap was attached to each leg to secure her.

As if in a trance, beyond tears, Hysena approached the apparatus. Sister Colya stepped behind her and with a thrust of her powerful arm, caused the hapless girl to fall across the horse. Hysena felt the leather warm against her belly and was aware of the rasp of her pubic hair against the thick padding as Colya, with the skill of long practice, shoved her further forward so that her buttocks pointed to the ceiling. Tarrip had positioned himself such that he could savour the moment when Colya pushed the long, shapely thighs apart and began to attach them just below the knee to the legs of the horse. The blackness of the hair between her spread legs was in stark contrast to the pure whiteness of her skin. Her thighs were held painfully wide and even as he watched, Tarrip saw the lips of her sex peel open, exposing the pearly pink inner membranes. Her buttocks were now covered in tiny goose pimples and between them he could see the inviting dot of her virgin anus.

Colya had now secured the girl to the horse, and stepped back to admire her work. She knew Tarrip would not allow her to have this one, or any of the new group, until he had worked his way through them all, but if she was good, he might let her beat one or two of them.

Tarrip drew the well-worn tokan from his jewelled belt and circled the helpless novice, savouring the last few moments before he beat her. He made his own tokans, selecting leather that was supple enough to bend, hard enough to hurt but not so hard that it would cut. The striking ends he varied, sometimes fashioning a single, wide tongue of leather, sometimes splitting it into a dozen tines of differing lengths that could cover a wide area of skin with a single blow. He might add beaded thongs to the ends, beads that would lash into his victim an instant after the leather struck, beads that would assault the secret crevices that the main body of the cruel device would not reach. The handles were all similar; stiff cylinders of smooth leather or wood, designed to penetrate his victims if he so chose, varying from less than an inch thick, ideal for novices, up to formidable devices the thickness and length of his forearm. These had to be used with skill lest the recipient be damaged. Tarrip was very skilled.

The one he held now, a simple design with a single split in the beating end and a handle of ceremonial rather than practical design, was drilled through with a series of holes that caused it to whistle as it curved down onto the trembling flesh of the girl being punished. These holes left a pattern on the skin. 'I have sinned,' the pattern read, 'I have sinned.'

He leaned down, ostensibly to speak into the ear of the terrified girl, in reality to gain a closer view of her breasts. They really were lovely, he thought, hanging ripely from her chest, moving enticingly with her sobs. 'Forgive me, daughter,' he whispered before standing and moving behind her.

He lifted his arm high, then brought it down. The tokan sang and then bit into the firm young flesh of her left cheek with a fine crack. Hysena screamed and bucked, hopelessly trying to twist away, her buttocks clenching and parting, briefly hiding and then revealing her anus. The lips of her sex seemed to gulp at Tarrip as they moved, squeezing together as her muscles contracted in pain. He laid another blow on the other buttock, garnering another, shriller scream and another delightful display from her writhing cheeks, a third, below the first, the message 'I have sinned' standing out lividly on the flawless skin. He paused to admire his handiwork and Hysena's trembling cunt as it moved against the leather of the horse.

With a barely hidden gasp of excitement, he noticed the sudden gleam of juices on the lips of her sex, and his nostrils flared at the unmistakable scent of arousal. Beneath his robe, his prick, already stiff, threatened to break free from the tight pantaloons he wore on these occasions, lest a rampant erection become visible. The rare ones who became aroused, even subconsciously, could be something special, and he revised his plan to beat her until his arm grew tired. He could mould this one in such a way that she would become his personal property, become as slavish to him as a dog. Tarrip decided to be merciful.

But not too merciful.

He adjusted his aim, and, striking with considerable strength brought the tokan down directly between the straining legs.

The Initiate tokan was designed not to cause maximum pain — that would come later — but for an innocent like Hysena, a pampered Lady, who had never in her life been so much as slapped on the wrist, the pain as the whistling leather lashed into her most secret and sensitive place was beyond endurance. Hysena Macarydias fainted.

Tarrip kissed his tokan and thrust it into his belt, then turned away from the delightful spectacle of the nude young girl to address the others. They wore expressions that ranged from fear to, in the eyes of the haughty Uplander, lust.

'This girl has offended the eye of the Prophet,' he intoned sonorously. 'She, all of you, are now the property of the Prophet, as you stated in your recent vow. It is my humble task to ensure that His will and His dignity be maintained. This is only the first lesson. Learn from it that you too do not share her fate.' Turning back to Sister Colya, he again passed his eyes over Hysena, taking in the knobs of her spine, the now livid buttocks and the folds of her exposed sex, visibly damp. 'Take her and prepare her. She shall stand as example until midnight.'

When Hysena awoke, she found herself, still naked, lying face down on a bed in a small but well-lit cell. She wiped the tears from her cheeks with her fists and looked around her. Apart from the bed, which had no bed linen, the only features were an icon of the Prophet on one wall, a heavy door and, in one corner, a sunken bath from which tendrils of steam rose. The thought of soothing water on her abused body was overwhelming, but already Hysena was learning. She could not risk anything, even bathing, without permission.

She was startled when the door suddenly opened, and Sister Maria, the younger of Tarrip's assistants, the one with the kind eyes, entered the room, carrying a towel and a covered basket. She smiled down at Hysena, still on the bed.

'How now, child?' Her voice was as gentle as her eyes.

'It was a terrible thing, sister,' whispered the girl, struggling to hold back her tears. 'How could such cruelty exist, and here, in the Citadel?'

Sister Maria gently but firmly helped her from the bed and led her to the pool. 'Do not say "cruel", child. It is not possible for the Prophet to be cruel, but He demands obedience from all, especially from those chosen to serve Him. Here. Come into the bath. It will soothe.'

Gratefully, Hysena stepped down into the blood-warm water. Sister Maria reached into her basket and withdrew a piece of soap-root and handed it to her. She watched meditatively as Hysena began to cleanse herself. Surreptitiously, she withdrew one arm up the sleeve of her robe and down her body until she could stroke her vulva with long, sensitive fingers, parting the moist outer lips and squeezing her clitoris between finger and thumb. She smiled inwardly as she remembered the shock of her own initiation some ten years earlier; the horror of being stripped naked and tied with her back to a bench by the two Sisters who had, at Tarrip's instruction, seized her struggling legs and hauled them high and wide, pulling them back until her feet were above her shoulders, her sex open and vulnerable to the Priest's ministrations.

Beneath her robe, her fingers moved more quickly, one sliding easily now into her slick vagina as she watched Hysena who was soaping her small breasts. That first pain! The tokan had slashed into her time and time again, bearable when Tarrip had struck from the side and beaten her buttocks and thighs, but when he stood between her wide-spread legs and, staring intently at her exposed sex, lashed directly onto her secret lips, she, like Hysena had shrilled her screams before thankfully fainting.

'Do not turn away, girl. I need to be able to report that you are thoroughly clean.' Hysena, working the soap down her body, had risen from the water and turned her back to wash between her legs. Sister Maria wanted to watch; mingling the delightful spectacle of the young virgin's naked body with her own reminiscences.

Hysena whimpered at this new humiliation, but dared not disobey.

Covering herself with her hands as much as possible, she worked up a thick lather in her pubic hair. The sensation was pleasant after the abuses she had suffered. She could feel that her labia were swollen from the effects of the leather tokan, but the slippery feel of the soap as she worked it in was soothing.

Watching her, Sister Maria felt her own juices begin to flow more freely, and reaching more deeply between her legs, she slipped the tip of one finger into her anus. How far she had come in ten years! To be able to do such a thing to herself (and to others, of course!) whilst gaining pleasure from watching this young snippet rubbing soap into herself.

She let her mind drift back, remembering how she had awoken from her faint, paying no attention to whatever Tarrip was saying as her pain and humiliation were so great. She had paid attention when the Priest had stopped talking and had moved in between her legs, still held wide by the two Sisters. At a signal from him, each of them had slid a hand down her thigh until they touched the lips of her sex. At another signal, each of them had pressed two fingers into her, and then pulled her vagina wide. Tarrip had leaned forward eagerly, staring into her. He reversed his grip on the tokan, holding it by the leather blade, and then rubbed a musky-scented ointment along the length of the phallus-shaped handle, working his hand up and down as if masturbating it. His smile was a terrible thing as he moved the instrument towards her, and Sister Maria shuddered at the memory. She remembered the combination of fear and excitement she had experienced at the first touch of the thing on the lips of her sex, the burning sensation induced by the ointment, a burning that became an itch that made her moan and wriggle against her bonds. Even then she was unsure as to whether she was trying to wriggle away from the tokan and the hot fingers of the two Sisters who held her open, or whether she wanted them to press into her. She had no option either way. With a slow, inexorable thrust, Tarrip had fed the leather phallus into her. The two women pulled her legs even wider and she could feel the great tendons of her thighs straining. Inch after inch slid into her, drawing a scream as it met and then split her maidenhead. But the ointment as well as increasing some sensations reduced others, and she felt hardly any pain, just a growing feeling of fullness, as if she would split like a log as the tokan slid further and further into her. Each time she felt that surely no more could enter her, the priest pushed the terrible thing even deeper.

'Secure her legs,' the priest had said, his voice thick with lust. The two holy women had each taken one of the silk ropes that hung from the ceiling and secured them about her thighs. The ropes ran through pulleys and Maria found that her legs could be opened wider than she would have believed possible. Utterly helpless, she looked down the length of her body, seeing that, despite herself, her nipples were hard, that her hips were working with Tarrip as he slid the tokan in and out of her vagina. One of the Sisters reached for her breast and Maria screamed again as her nipple was cruelly twisted. The other sister had moved beside Tarrip and, at a nod from the priest, lifted his robe to his waist, tucking it into his belt and revealing to Maria's disbelieving eyes his huge prick. Sinking to her knees, the woman took the swollen glans between her lips. With a thrust of his hips, Tarrip forced his length fully into her eager mouth, clapping one hand to the back of her head to force himself even deeper.

His other hand was working the tokan faster and faster in Maria's cunt, and she had seen that the Sister who was abusing her breasts had raised her own robe and was working three fingers deeply into her cunt.

She shuddered as she remembered that first, shattering orgasm, the sensation that had run through her body, wringing a scream from her lips as her hips writhed and bucked, her abundant juices making her thighs slick and her pubic hair matted. She hardly noticed, at first, that the priest had withdrawn the tokan and had positioned himself between her wide-held thighs. Her eyes had flown open though when she felt the hot tip of his penis being rubbed up and down the lips of her vagina by the sister who still held it.

Tarrip's smile had been a combination of lust and triumph as he leered down at his hapless victim. He leaned into her slowly, drawing out the pleasure as he forced his huge prick into her helpless cunt, his hands sliding over her sweated hips and up to her breasts. With a grunt, he thrust himself fully home, the passage made possible by a combination of the ointment and Maria's own secretions.

The difference between the tokan and Tarrip's prick was immediate to Maria. The first had been cold and unyielding whereas the flesh of the priest pulsed and throbbed within her and felt hot as Hades. She felt his considerable weight pressing her cruelly down against the bench, the ropes cutting deeper into her wide-held thighs and yet more sensations as he began to grind his pelvis against the bulge of her pubic bone, crushing her clitoris between their bodies. Another orgasm hit her, and then a third as the priest grunted and his prick pumped powerful jets of seemingly red-hot sperm into her...

Standing with the warm water of the bathing pool lapping against her naked thighs, the Lady Hysena Macarydias watched in amazement as the Holy Sister seemed to go into some sort of fit. Her eyes were glazed and unseeing, her breath was fast and a low keening was coming from her. Beneath her shift, Hysena could see, one of her hands was working convulsively between her legs, the other rhythmically squeezing her breast.

Unconsciously, Hysena's fingers, buried in the soapsuds between her legs, began to move in sympathy. She felt the heat rising within her as first one and then another finger slid into her own vagina, the way made easy by a combination of the fragrant soap and her own growing arousal. Deep in her mind, a small voice was telling her that this must be wrong, this was one of those forbidden things that her tutors had warned her about without ever going into detail. But oh, it felt so nice! With one hand, she rubbed some of the soap over her small breasts, their nipples hard as buttons, the other exploring the mysteries of her sex, a thing she had never dared before today. But today was not a normal day.

Sister Maria dreamily allowed her memories to fade as the last ripples of her orgasm shuddered delightfully through her. With a guilty start, she realised what she had been doing and quickly pulled her hand from her vagina. She looked over to the girl in the pool and, fighting to hide a smile, took in what she was doing. Hysena's eyes were screwed shut, one hand moving over her soapy breasts, two fingers of the other darting in and out of her cunt. Her movements were sending little ripples across the pool and she had straddled her legs for better balance, allowing the Holy Sister a fine view of the lithe young body in all its beauty.

The girl opened her eyes and realised she was being watched. With a gasp, she snatched her fingers away from her vagina, then flung herself backwards into the pool with a huge splash, wanting the water to cover her. She surfaced, coughing, and began to cry.

'Sister, forgive me, I couldn't help myself...' The older woman regarded her with a steady gaze, weighing alternatives. A spanking for the girl was justified and she might even report this to the High Priest, but could she risk seducing her at this early stage? The child had a rare beauty, and once she began to punish that succulent flesh, she might not be able to contain herself and if the girl talked and word got back to Tarrip that someone had enjoyed her before him...

On the other hand, Hysena had already, to a degree, alienated herself from the other initiates and would need a friend. And for Sister Maria, having the girl dependent on her could be valuable. These girls were the elite of Qalle and, assuming they survived the next few years, would become powerful. And the Lady Hysena's family were among the most powerful of them all. Having such a potentially powerful ally could help Sister Maria with her own, deeply secret ambitions.

Arranging her features into an expression of sternness, she reached down into the pool to take the hand of the sobbing girl and used the action to rinse the evidence of her recent arousal from her fingers.

'Step up, child.' She helped Hysena from the pool. 'Your body is forbidden to you until you have passed successfully through the first stages of the rite. It is a possession of the Prophet and any pleasure it may experience is at His bequest. As Holy Father Tarrip explained, all transgression must be met with a lesson, and you must now receive another lesson.'

'Please, no, sister. I cannot face more!' The girl's wail was a pitiful thing. She fell to the ground and curled into a weeping ball. Sister Maria took a moment to admire her damp curves.

'My Lady Hysena, you will learn to face much, much more in your time here. If, that is, you are seen fit to complete your time here. This will strengthen you. That is a part of what you and your sister-candidates are to learn; strength. Already the Prophet has clearly taken an interest in you; why else would you be here now? All things are His bidding. And who knows,' here her voice became conspiratorial, 'if you bear your lesson well, He may reward you.'

The last statement gained Hysena's interest, as Maria had intended. 'Reward me, Sister?' she said in a tiny voice. 'Can I be deserving of reward when the Holy Prophet is so displeased with me?'

'He is not displeased with you. He wishes only that you learn, and it is His decree, spoken through the Living Prophet on Qalle, that Initiates, and even Sisters when necessary, be taught in a manner that shall be remembered. Now, stand.'

The girl complied, struggling awkwardly to her feet. She had begun to shiver now, both at the cold of her still-damp body and in anticipation of what was about to happen.

'Spread your legs and place your hands on the ground in front of you.'

The position was not difficult for one as young and supple as Hysena. Sister Maria stood behind her, feeling arousal bubble up inside her as she drank in the sight of the nude girl so helplessly exposed to her eyes. She laid her hand gently on one of the up-turned buttocks, revelling in its rubbery firmness and allowing the tips of her fingers to touch just a few of the wiry hairs that curled up from the junction of her thighs.

'I am not so strong as the high priest, and shall use just my hand.'

With her last words, Sister Maria lifted her hand high and brought it down with a sharp CRACK! on the girl's bottom.

Hysena jerked and squealed, but more in reflex than in true pain. She had braced herself for the searing agony that she had experienced through Tarrip's ministrations, but this was nothing in comparison. A second smack landed, and this time the sister's hand wasn't immediately raised. Instead, she briefly stroked the globe of Hysena's buttock, almost as if she was soothing her, not punishing her. The third was directed at the soft flesh high up the column of the girl's inner thigh. This stung quite painfully, but again the hand seemed to linger and now when it was slowly withdrawn, Sister Maria's thumb brushed against the soft outer lip of her sex. Hysena caught her breath and without conscious thought allowed her knees to bend a little and her back to arch downwards, an action that exposed her even more fully to

Maria's lustful eyes.

The next dozen slaps were administered skilfully, designed more to arouse than to punish; some sharp slaps with the ends of stiffened fingers, some mere tokens delivered full onto her bottom with cupped palm. A final spank was delivered up between the widespread thighs, directly onto the now-swelling lips of her vagina. The hand again lingered, the long middle finger lying along the slit of Hysena's sex, its tip moving almost imperceptibly against her clitoris.

Hysena could not contain the groan that came from deep in her throat, no more could she help herself falling to her knees. Her hips began to move in rhythm to Sister Maria's quickening finger, and as the holy woman felt this she ran her finger into the slippery depths. She was a little surprised that her finger encountered no resistance; surely this one must be virgin? Still, there was more than one way to broach a maidenhead. And by the Prophet, her arousal was swift! The priestess had slid a second finger into Hysena's sex, both now buried to the knuckle, the pad of her thumb stimulating the girl's anus in small, circular movements.

'How now, my lady?' she asked softly, knowing the answer as the Initiate pushed her hips back, trying to force Sister Maria's fingers deeper into herself.

'Oh, Sister, it is like, uhh, nothing I have felt before.' Hysena's voice was growing ragged.

The priestess withdrew her fingers, drawing a moan of disappointment from the girl.

'The Prophet has chosen to reward you. And through me, you shall receive His kiss. Now, go to the bed and lie on your back.'

Hysena got to her feet and walked a little unsteadily to the bed. The flush of arousal had reddened her small breasts, the nipples were stiff and gave them a delightful upward tilt. She lay down on the bed, her thighs spreading instinctively.

Sister Maria watched in delight as she saw the lips of the girl's vagina part, exposing the inner delights to her eyes. She knelt at the side of the bed, almost as if she were praying. Leaning forward, she placed a kiss on Hysena's breast, feeling the nipple stiffen even further as she gently sucked it into her mouth. The girl moaned and writhed as the Holy Sister's hand slid over her flesh, across the taut muscles of her belly to the downy softness of her pubic hair.

Feeling her way with an experienced touch, Sister Maria found Hysena's clitoris and stimulated it gently with the tips of her fingers, then ran them along the lips of her vagina before dipping them into the hot and eager opening.

Hysena's groans were now virtually sobs. Her hips were twisting and heaving as her passion grew. With eyes screwed shut, she did not see Maria raise her head from her breast, but felt the succession of soft kisses that traced the progress of her mouth as it moved over her body, licking briefly at her navel, biting softly on her pubic hairs, taking some of them between her teeth and tugging at them like a puppy worrying a blanket. The questing tongue touched the very tip of her clitoris with the most gentle of motions, and Hysena screamed as her first ever orgasm arrived like a lightning strike.

Even the experienced Sister Maria was a little alarmed at the intensity of the youngster's reaction. Her back arched like a bow, supported by just her head and her heels as she lifted her hips to an impossible height, grinding her pubis against the Holy Sister's mouth with a strength that forced her head and shoulders up and lifted her knees from the floor. Maria thrust her tongue deep into Hysena's cunt and wondered at the strength of the internal muscles that gripped it almost painfully. The rhythmic contractions went on and on, each one accompanied by a screaming moan from the Initiate, who now wrapped her hands behind Sister Maria's head, pulling her hard against her pelvis with a grip that threatened to suffocate her.

Eventually, the sensations faded and Hysena sank back onto the bed, soaked with sweat and saliva and the secretions from her vagina glistened between her thighs, still flung wide in careless abandon. Maria looked down at her in some wonder. She could see that small shivers were still causing ripples across the girl's belly and that the lips of her vagina still pulsed, opening and closing like the gills of a fish. Then these too ceased, and the girl lay quiescent on the bed.

'Truly the Prophet has blessed you,' said Sister Maria, stroking Hysena's breast. The girl shivered in ecstasy at the touch, using her hand to clasp the Sister's hand to her.

'I begin to understand, Holy Sister.'

'That is good. However,' she paused and licked her lips, selecting her words with care. 'However, some things should remain between the Prophet and yourself. It is probably wise to be discreet, little one. Perhaps it would be best not to talk of this with your sister candidates — or at least not until you have discovered which of them are to be trusted.'

Sister Maria stood and moved briskly to the pool where she knelt to wash her hands. 'Now, my Lady Hysena, there is one more thing for you to endure before the day ends. Wash yourself and prepare your mind'

The girl fought to conceal the sudden despair that sent shivers through her, shivers that were so different from those that she had so recently experienced. Was there no end to the punishment? Was every day going to be like this? For three years?

As she washed, she became aware that Sister Maria was speaking.

'...you must stand as example until midnight. Are you listening to me, girl'?'

'Yes, Holy Sister. But I do not know what it means.'

'I have just said. Learn to pay attention, Hysena, and your time will go much easier. You will stand in the Initiates' Hall until midnight, and have only bread to eat and water to drink.'

That didn't sound to hard, and Hysena was mildly surprised at the tameness of the sentence.

The older woman continued, 'You will be an example

to your peers who may not talk to you or you to them. And you shall be naked and restrained.'

This time Hysena could not contain her anguished cry. To have been beaten by strangers in front of strangers had been a terrible thing, but was over quite quickly. But to have to stand naked before any and all passing eyes for a period of hours...

'You have had much to endure today. I will give you something to help, but you must swear to me that you will say nothing to anyone, ever.'

By now Hysena was ready to swear anything if it would only get her through this next ordeal. She nodded her head dumbly.

For Sister Maria, this was a calculated risk. She hunted through her basket and withdrew a fist-sized box of obsidian that had been worked will curious designs. The box had been presented to her in a ceremony that, were Tarrip or any of his people to learn of it, would see her dragged from the Citadel at the end of a rope and then made to suffer agonies beyond belief before her head was finally struck from her body.

The box appeared to have no opening, but as she gave it a curious twist and pressed a certain sigil, a lid popped open. She withdrew a small cloth bag and allowed a small pill to roll from it into the palm of her hand.

Delving again into the box, she produced a bottle of clear liquid. 'Now, take this pill with some of the drink. When you get to the hall, High Priest Tarrip will cause you to stand as he makes one of his interminable speeches. You will then be given bread and water. You will be stripped and secured, but this drug will make the punishment easy to endure.'

Silently, the girl did as she was bid, choking down the pill with a mouthful of the bitter liquid. She had tasted nothing like it and gasped as she felt a curious warmth flow through her.

As Sister Maria helped her into the simple white shift of the Initiate and led her along the long corridors of the Citadel to the hall, Hysena felt that her senses were growing until every crack and scratch in the ancient corridor was magnified to her sight, she could see more clearly than she had ever done, her hearing was as acute as the owl's. She could catch the lingering scent of her recent excitement, and that of Sister Maria, too.

She felt quite calm when the Holy Sister presented her to the high priest. Without moving her eyes, she could see the other girls that she had met at the ceremony that morning. How young they looked! Even though they were all of an age, Hysena felt herself to be old and wise in comparison to these. They regarded her with expressions that ranged from fear to pity, from contempt to what might have been desire.

When the old priest finished his speech, not a word of which she had paid attention to, and ordered her to strip, she did so with simple dignity, slipping the garment over her shoulders and allowing it to puddle at her feet. Instead of the shame she had felt before, Hysena was now proud of her nudity. Her heightened perceptions made her aware of her body in a way that she had never previously been. She felt her nipples crinkle in the coolness of the room, was aware of the unusual feeling, not unpleasant, of the slight draught that played around the private area between her legs, always before covered. She made no resistance when Colya, the peasant-faced sister, led her to a frame at one end of the room and strapped her to it at ankles and waist, leaving her hands free so that she could eat her meagre meal. The frame was designed in such a way that her hips were thrust forward, bringing her mons into prominence and she actually enjoyed the moment when the coarse woman, under the cover of adjusting the straps, pushed her rough finger between Hysena's legs and into her vagina. Hysena was amused at the look on the woman's face when she found the passage to be slick with the juices of arousal.

The hours passed. Hysena remained strapped naked to the frame, aware of the eyes of her peers that glanced up at her from time to time, the eyes of the high priest that seldom strayed from her form. She was feeling as if she had a power over them all, as if her ability to make them look at her placed them in thrall to her. Even when the effects of Sister Maria's potion began to wear off, when she began to feel cold and her feet began to ache from the effort of standing for many hours, some of that feeling of power remained.

This was the end of just her first day, she reflected, and so much had happened. Alone now in the hall, the others having left hours before, she gently caressed herself, careless of the fact that at any time a servant might enter or even Tarrip himself. Her fingers ran over her nipples and down across her belly to tease her pubic hair before gently caressing the sensitive outer lips of her sex, and she wondered what the next three years would bring.

2.

Hysena awoke in the same cell in which Sister Maria had done those strange and wonderful things to her. Her mouth was dry and she was aware of the dull ache from her abused buttocks and thighs.

Throwing aside the blanket that covered her, she looked at her naked body with new eyes. She examined her breasts, now able to touch them without the feeling of guilt she had experienced whenever she had dared to do so before her arrival at the Citadel. The traditions of her people meant that the more intimate functions of her body were taboo and such knowledge that she had had been gleaned from one of the maids in her father's palace.

But now, today, she was in the mysterious Citadel, centre of all power on Qalle, the neutral zone of the planet, the place where warring factions would come to negotiate in the hope of avoiding war with its resultant death and rapine and seizing of slaves.

Here was where Hysena and her peers from the other great families would learn something of history and custom, would come to know each other on a personal basis in the hope that this would lessen the likelihood of them wishing to fight in the future.

And they would of course learn discipline.

She had progressed with the examination of her body to the area that had caused such feelings when manipulated by Sister Maria. Her elbows were hooked into the hollows of her knees, which were drawn high to her chest, and her fingers were holding open the lips of her sex. Craning her neck, Hysena was trying to look into herself, fascinated to see the shiny dew that began to form inside the opening and to feel an inkling of her previous sensations as her fingers explored.

There was a knock at the door and she just had time to arrange herself demurely under the blanket and compose her face in an expression that she hoped concealed her disappointment at being interrupted. The incomer was an

Ercli slave girl, one of a race that were prevalent throughout Qalle; simple but loyal people who did much of the drudgery. This one was a year or two older than Hysena and brought her a twinge of home-sickness, looking as she did so much like the slave who had been presented to her back in Argo on the occasion of her sixteenth birthday.

The slave said nothing, not unusually for her kind, but held out a white Initiate's shift. Hysena quickly slipped into the simple garment and felt her mood change to one of apprehension. In the room with its closed door, she had felt safe, but now as she followed the slave along strange passages, the stone floor cold under her bare feet and conscious, without the bolster of the potion the Sister Maria had fed her, that under the shift she was naked.

The cloth was of cheap, poorly woven cotton that chafed her nipples, making them erect and when she glanced down she was alarmed to see that the dark shadow of her pubic hair was mistily visible through the thin material.

She was led into a roughly decorated room that was bright with the light of the morning sun that shone through a strikingly big window. The scant furniture was dominated by a table that took up much of the available space. At its head was the peasant-faced Sister Colya and five of the other six places were filled by the young women who were to be Hysena's companions from now on. As one, they turned to look at her.

'Ha,' the Sister called in her harsh voice. 'So, we have famous Macarydias to eat with us. My lady can stand for breakfast if her bum is still sore, eh?' She roared with laughter at her witty sally. Hysena, blushing, took the remaining seat at the end of the table.

Colya clapped her hands and two Ercli slaves scuttled into the room with cups and plates. The food was simple but of good quality; oat cakes with syrup, fresh fruit, cheese, good white bread with bowls of oil to dip it in and there was milk, water or a thin beer to drink. Colya was tearing great mouthfuls of meat from a joint of cold mutton and swigging beer between bites. She spoke around her meal, spraying the table and the nearest Initiates with gobbets of both. 'Now, here in Citadel, you do what you're told when you're told, or will be wriggling like Lady Hysena. Respect at all times is the rule. To each other as well as us Sister Elders and the like. Yes?'

Some of the girls exchanged glances but none spoke.

'Yes?!' Colya's voice was a frighteningly loud roar.

A few of the apprehensive Initiates muttered 'Yes, Holy Sister,' but Maris Ap Stuvin, daughter of the richest man on Qalle, was more concerned with the partially chewed lump of meat that had flown from Sister Colya's mouth to lodge on her cheek. With an expression of disgust, she took the slimy morsel between finger and thumb and flicked it into a corner of the room.

Maris, whose mother had died in the act of giving birth to her, had been spoiled from her earliest days. Tall, with blonde hair that reached her waist, she was blessed with slim hips and breasts that seemed too large for her narrow shoulders to support. Her beauty was marred only by the petulant thrust of her lower lip and the look of disdain that was her normal expression.

Her father had made his fortune from the levy of tolls on the trade caravans that used the Upland roads. He knew his only legitimate child to be somewhat wayward, but his servants kept her worst excesses from him. He did not know, for instance, that she had taken her first lover at the age of fourteen. The groom she had seduced had been so terrified that the Baron Stuvin would learn of the act that he had hanged himself. The Baron had been apprehensive about allowing her to travel to the Citadel, but, as always, Maris had her way, thinking her status would allow her to bully and boss her way through her time there. She was about to find out otherwise.

Observing both her expression and her action, Sister Colya rounded on the girl.

'So,' she roared. 'Table manners of Holy Sister don't meet with approval of House Stuvin, eh? Please to stand on chair. Now!'

The girl's first, automatic reaction was to refuse, to shout back at this ugly harridan who dared to shout at her. Then she remembered what had happened to Hysena. She had found the sight of that punishment enormously exciting, the vision of Hysena with legs wide, her cunt and breasts on show and being belaboured by the fat priest had almost made her climax there and then. It had been three frustrating hours before she had been able to sneak into an empty cell where she had thrown up her gown and rubbed herself to a frantic climax. It did not for a moment occur to her that such a thing could possibly happen to her.

She had dithered for too long. Sister Colya came suddenly to her feet, sending her chair backwards with a loud crash. With surprising speed for one who looked so clumsy, she grabbed Maris by one arm and swept the end of the table clear of plates and cups, throwing an avalanche of food and drink over the nearest Initiates, sending them squealing from the table. Maris was hurled onto the cleared space with a force that bruised her shoulders and knocked the breath from her body. Unable to even scream, she was helpless to resist as Sister Colya wrapped her huge arm under her knees, elevating them to expose her bottom. The assault briefly paused when the sister saw that the girl was wearing white silk underwear.

'So,' she hissed, 'not only are manners of Holy Sister to be criticised, but rules of Citadel are not for likes of House Stuvin, eh?' With frightening strength, Colya pressed down on the girl's thighs, bending her double and forcing her long legs against her breasts. The silk of her underwear rode up, sliding into the crack of her bottom. With a spatulate finger, the Sister pushed the slippery material into her, bringing the lips of her vagina into view. Her pubic hair was as fine and blonde as the hair on her head, the sister noted with relish. Holding her down with one powerful arm, Colya began to beat the girl with her hard, callused hand.

Maris at last was able to drag some breath into her

lungs, and then let it out in a shrill scream. The sound only served to inflame Colya, and her arm rose and fell faster. Her ugly face was flushed with lust and she pressed her upper thighs against the table, bringing the rounded corner of it into contact with her own sex. By flexing her knees slightly, she was able to rub her clitoris against the hard wood as she beat the girl, enjoying the sight of her cunt, now exposed almost entirely, and the fine, big breasts that bounced and trembled under her shift as she struggled.

She reached her climax with an animal grunt and gave the girl one final slap before sitting back in her chair, panting.

From her end of the table, Hysena felt her heart go out to the Uplander, knowing just how she must be feeling. But she could not deny that her burgeoning sexuality had been stirred. She had not been able to see much from where she sat, just occasional glimpses of thrashing thigh and once a view of the blond-haired lips of her sex, divided by the material of the contentious undergarment. She had felt herself growing moist and this feeling was growing as Sister Colya ordered the now unresisting girl to stand on her chair.

'Not so haughty now, eh?' Colya was in an excellent mood. Tarrip had given her permission to beat one of the Initiates ('...and one only, sister. I know your appetites!') late the previous night when, after the punishment of Hysena with both of them in a state of high arousal, he had ordered her to his sumptuously appointed quarters and used her as only he could, bringing her to orgasm after orgasm with his tokans, his tongue and his prick, squirting thick gouts of sperm into her mouth, her cunt and finally, gloriously, into her anus.

Standing forlorn on her chair, Maris was resigned to the command to strip, expecting it after having witnessed Hysena's humiliation. She looked across to the other girl, expecting to see her enjoying the spectacle, but was surprised and not a little touched to see the Southern Roader give a sympathetic moue and a little shake of her head as if to say, 'I'm on your side, I know how you are feeling.' For such a selfish person as Maris, this was both a shock and an encouragement.

When the order to remove her shift came, she in turn gave Hysena a quick, tight smile, and reached for the hem of her garment.

Sister Colya did not see the silent exchange between the girls. She was still enjoying the after-glow of her orgasm and was watching intently as the tall, blonde girl on the chair began to reveal her body. First her knees and then the long, slim thighs came into view. A slight hesitation and then the bulge of her mons was revealed, the fat lips of her sex made prominent by the white silk of her undergarment that was still dividing them. Colya drank in the sight of her flat stomach and held her breath as the cotton shift rose slowly over the swell of alabaster white breasts.

'Ha! Fine big tits they grow in Uplands. Must be good mountain air!' She slapped the one nearest to her, enjoying both the squeal from the girl and the way her breast jiggled. 'Now,' she continued, 'I show you best use for heretical knickers.' Taking the hem of the expensive silk in both hands, Colya tugged downwards, exposing Maris' cunt to the room. For a moment, she paused to stare at the blonde pubic hair and the pretty lips that peeped shyly through before ripping the garment from the cringing girl. 'Turn and hold back of chair,' she instructed.

Maris carried out her bidding, glad that her front was hidden from the hungry eyes of the Sister, and braced herself for the first blow.

But Sister Colya had not yet finished humiliating her. She turned to the other girls.

'You and you,' she snapped, indicating two of the cowed and aghast initiates. 'Come here. Stand either side of this wicked girl.'

Silent and apprehensive, the two stood and moved slowly to flank Maris.

One was Silka who came from Sis Narash, the low

plains where most of the food on Qalle was produced. She was, of course, the same age as the other initiates but looked much younger and stood a head shorter than the next shortest. The other was Leel; a plump, red-headed princess of Calith whose normal demeanour was one of fun and friendliness.

But she wasn't smiling now as she took her station at the flank of the unfortunate Maris and exchanged scared glances with little Silka. Surely, no fault had been found with either of them? She was intelligent enough to realise that her turn would surely come, but, please the Prophet, not yet.

Colya was standing behind Maris, hands on hips, the torn silk underwear dangling from her fingers and still admiring the girl's nakedness. This was a new idea for punishment and she knew that Tarrip would forgive her the presumption because of the novelty.

The room was silent but for the heavy breathing of the Holy Sister and the faint sobs that Maris was unable to prevent.

'You girls, pull buttocks apart.' Colya gave the instruction in a voice thick with lust. The two girls exchanged horrified glances, knowing, despite the short time they had been in the Citadel, what even the suggestion of a refusal would bring. Gingerly, Leel placed the palm of her hand on Maris' buttock. It was the first time she had touched another girl in this way. The flesh was warm and taut to her touch and she could feel a deep, constant trembling under her hand.

Following the lead of the bigger girl, Silka placed her own hand on the other buttock. Reluctantly, they eased the globes of Maris' bottom apart.

Sister Colya's eyes were wide and her breath was quickening as she watched. The blonde pubic hair hid little of the charms of the initiate and as well as the smooth outer lips, the pink inner folds of her sex were now clearly visible. There was, Colya noted with disappointment, no sign of moistness, as there had been with Hysena when she had been similarly exposed the previous day.

Without taking her eyes from the girl, Colya fumbled on the table for one of the dishes of oil intended for the dipping of bread. She swirled her index finger in this, and slowly, savouring the sensation, sank it to the knuckle into Maris' anus.

Maris cried out at this new assault. She had not been able to see what had been happening behind her, but knew what she was displaying to the others. The feel of the hands of the other Initiates on her skin was not unpleasant — she had expected the Holy Sister to instruct them to beat her — but when they pulled her buttocks apart she felt even more nude than she already was. She had sensed the approach of Colya's questing finger and had expected to feel it violate her vagina, not knowing that Tarrip had expressly forbidden this. She had had fingers inside her before, not least her own, and had experimented with various objects to find new pleasures, but the thought of putting anything into the other entrance to her body had never crossed her mind. Now she bit her lip in an effort to stifle her cries as the Holy Sister worked a second oily finger into the tight passage, stretching the tight ring of rubbery muscle in a way that nature had never intended.

Colya enjoyed the sensation as the muscles tightened spasmodically about her fingers, almost tight enough to cut off the blood supply, and revelled at the sight of them buried deeply inside the wriggling girl. Despite the warning of the Holy Father, she could not resist the temptation to slip her thumb into Maris' vulva and, with a pinching motion, she was able to feel her fingers through the thin membrane that separated the two passages. For a few moments she worked them within the girl before withdrawing them. She watched as the two openings contracted then with one hand she arranged the wisp of torn silk over Maris' bottom and, using her oiled index finger, began to push the material into her anus.

There was a collective gasp from the watching Initiates, and Maris could not prevent a whimper as she felt the garment being worked into her.

Sister Colya did not cease in her work until just a tiny of shred of silk was visible. She stepped back to admire the effect, feeling pleased with herself at inventing a new perversion.

'Now, get off chair. You spend rest of mealtime running around room. You others, sit down and finish breakfast.'

The silence in the room was broken only by the slap of bare feet as Maris ran around the table, tears streaming down her cheeks, aware that her big breasts were bouncing and swinging for all to see, conscious of the bloated feeling inside her bottom.

Colya ate with relish, enjoying the sight of those fine, big tits, their small nipples erect from the motion and, each time she passed, the scrap of white silk protruding almost jauntily from her anus and accentuating the rolling motion of her buttocks.

Eventually, the meal ended. Maris was allowed to stop, but had one final thing to endure.

'Get on table and touch toes,' the Sister instructed. Maris complied, knowing what was going to happen and gritting her teeth in anticipation.

Colya took a firm grip on the small piece of silk and with one firm, steady tug, drew the material out of her.

'You will remember lesson, eh?'

'Yes, Holy Sister.' Her voice was tiny and held only a hint of the arrogance that had been prominent before.

'You Initiates, all stand over there in line. You, Maris Ap Stavin, put on shift and stand with others.'

Silently, the young women did as they were bid. Sister Colya, hands on hips, stood before them. 'Now I make check that no other girls have been naughty like Uplander. All of you, raise clothes.'

Reluctantly the six Initiates bent and took the hems of their shifts and raised them over their thighs.

Eyes aglow, the Holy Sister drank in the sight of the six young cunts simultaneously revealed to her. That the girls were reluctant only increased Colya's titilation, the slow passage of the rough cloth rising over knees and thighs before revealing the junctions of their legs started the wetness between her own legs once more. She ran her eye along the line. Hysena she had seen, a neat growth of jet-black curls. Next to her the tiny Silka seemed to be quite bald, but a closer examination revealed an almost invisible down. Jagdig, the Kallinian, was in stark contrast. Bigger even than Colya, the girl from the warrior race seemed gigantic next to the little Sis Narashan. Her thighs were as big as many a man's, but shapely for all that. Her skin was darker than the others as her people had no nudity taboo and often roamed naked across their sun-baked lands. Her opulent pubic hair completely obscured any view of her vulva. Leel was plump but not fat, the coppery-red hair on her head a perfect match for that between her legs. Nephraan, from the Dersis Sea, was tall and willowy with long light-brown hair. Her legs, thought Colya, were the best; slim and elegantly curving, topped with a scanty covering of almost straight hair that allowed the lips of her sex to be seen. The Holy Sister was excited to see that this girl had a clitoris the size of the top joint of her little finger, clearly visible even though she had her legs together. Colya allowed herself a brief fantasy of sucking on such a delightful morsel. She took a final look at the line of young sexes, committing them to memory for later contemplation before clapping for the Ercli women.

'You go now to dormitory where you will sleep during time at Citadel. In one hour, instruction of duties to Holy Prophet begins. You will be called.'

They left the room, a subdued group, each making mental adjustments to what they had expected in this place.

When the girls had left the room, Colya threw the bolt on the heavy door and sank back onto her chair. Holding the recent vision of their exposed parts in her mind, she hauled up her robe and spread her knees.

She looked down at the slit between her legs and stroked and tugged her abundant pubic hair. The remains of the mutton joint that she had enjoyed for her breakfast was lying on the table. Spontaneously, she grabbed it and with a single motion, thrust the greasy bone into her cunt, at the same time crushing a nipple between the finger and thumb of her other hand.

She conjured a vision of the tiny Silka, the Sis Narashan, standing before her, raising her shift to expose her little cunt, its lips hardly obscured by the fine moss of her pubic hair. In her mind, she saw the youngster part those lips with the fingers of one hand and with the other tug her shift higher to expose her tiny breasts to Colya's view. The Holy Sister thrust the mutton bone faster and faster into herself as she imagined the red-headed Leel lowering her head and pressing her tongue into Silka's sex, licking along the divide between her legs and up to her clitoris. In her mind she heard the girl whimper and moan as Leel's tongue delved deeper into her, imagined Leel pulling up her garment, bringing her red-haired sex into view, spreading her legs and turning her body to allow the Holy Sister access to her moist parts...

A series of animal grunts escaped from her drooling lips as she climaxed. She wriggled the mutton-bone deep inside herself one more time and then withdrew it and tossed it carelessly onto the table for the slaves to clear. Smoothing her skirt down over her thighs, Sister Colya stood, reflecting that the day had started well. She wondered what other pleasures it might bring.

In the dormitory Hysena was busy with her own thoughts. The room that would be home for much of the next three years was austere, situated on the top storey of the Citadel. It contained six rude beds and six small cupboards in which the candidates could keep the meagre belongings they had been permitted to bring with them. The small, barred window overlooked an enclosed courtyard, and by craning it was just possible to see the tip of the tower of the Seminary where the Initiates' male equivalents were housed. Segregation was, of course, the very strictest of the constraints under which the candidates laboured.

Having placed her possessions in the small cupboard, Hysena took stock of her surroundings. She knew some of the others; Princess Leel had attended one of the great balls given at Argo the previous year and Silka had been present during the last Tariff conference, held every five years and attended by all the great houses of Qalle to determine the level of tolls to be charged for travel through the land.

On the bed next to hers, Hysena saw that Maris was lying face down on her bed, crying quietly. She had not met the girl, but rumour had carried something of her wild reputation. Timidly, Hysena touched the sobbing girl on the shoulder.

'The pain soon passes,' she said softly. Maris's shift had ridden up above her knees and Hysena could see the red weals on the backs of her thighs, imprints of Sister Colya's hard hand.

Maris twisted her head and looked up at Hysena. Her normally pretty face was reddened and stained with tears. She sniffed. 'It is not the pain of my body, it is the shame.'

Hysena shrugged, feeling the rough cotton of her shift rub against her own weals, not yet healed.

'I felt shame when it was my turn.' She looked at the other candidates, all of whom were listening to the exchange. 'I think we will all be shamed. It is the way of the Citadel, it seems. Our fathers must know something of what the training entails, and some of our mothers have certainly undergone this ordeal. It is our strength, our forbearance that they test, as well as our piety. We must not let them break us.' The silence that followed this speech was broken by the sound of hands clapping slowly. It was Jagdig, the giant from the warrior tribe of Kallinia.

'So,' she said, advancing towards Hysena, 'it is the council of House Macarydias that we submit like timid kittens to these indignities? That we allow our bodies to be abused and lewdly displayed for the amusement of others?'

'Are you scared of the pain or ashamed of your great body?' Maris snapped from her place on the bed, showing a flash of her impetuous nature.

Jagdig's brown eyes narrowed, her voice was a hiss. 'Do you call me coward, Uplander?' She rose to her full height, hair almost brushing the ceiling. Beneath her shift her firm breasts hardly moved as she advanced on the supine Maris, nipples like shield-bosses showing clearly. Her pubic hair was so thick and wiry that a few strands had pushed through the thin cotton, showing in stark contrast against the white cloth.

From her place behind Jagdig, Nephraan studied the magnificent buttocks, round as cannon balls, swaying with an unconscious sinuousness as the warrior girl moved across the room. She caught her breath and bit her lips to prevent a groan escaping. In her way, she was as wanton as Maris, though more subtle, more intelligent in her adventures, and her inclination was towards women. Jagdig was the most striking example of her sex that Nephraan had even seen. She felt warmth in her belly and the prickle of moisture between her tightly clenched thighs.

Silka held up a placatory hand, a hand that seemed absurdly tiny compared to the huge fists that were moving menacingly towards Maris.

'Jagdig, she is hurt and upset. I am sure no harm or insult was intended.' Her voice was quiet but clear throughout the dormitory. There was no hint of admonishment or censure in her tone, simply a statement of fact and sense. Her people were renowned throughout Qalle as mediators and her own training in such skills had begun at her mother's knee almost before she could walk.

But it would take more than softly spoken words to placate the Kallinian. Something had happened to Jagdig, something she would never had believed possible, something she would die rather than admit. For the first time in her life, she was experiencing fear.

Her people had only recently been admitted into the Council of Trade, the group who represented the richest and most powerful peoples of Qalle and who effectively divided the wealth of a world between them. Before their entry, the Kallinians had amassed their wealth by plundering those who passed through or even close to their lands. Only after years of delicate negotiation had they agreed to be bound by the Council treaty and abandon their predacious ways. In exchange, they would receive a share of the tolls collected, a share that would allow them to live to the standard to which they had become accustomed. There were other incentives; they were given seats on the Council, invited to the major social occasions. And they were allowed, for the first time, to submit candidates as Novice Initiates.

Jagdig's mental approach to her Initiatehood was the same as her mental approach to life; when something opposed you, you attacked. If you won, good. If you lost, you plotted your revenge as you bathed your wounds and in the meantime, trod soft about your enemy and studied his weaknesses. But in this accursed place there could be only one winner. Were she to fight the Holy Sisters or the Priests she would be punished and probably sent home to face utter disgrace. If she failed to fight, the time would inevitably come when she must submit to exposure and humiliation (she cared nothing for pain, which was why Maris's jibe had cut so deeply). She could not run away. She could do... nothing. She did not know how to cope with such a thing and so, in an instant, decided that she would force events by beating these mewling milksops to whimpering heaps and then take her punishment as a warrior should, laughing in their faces and crying defiance. Were she then sent from the Citadel at least it would be with her head held high.

With a careless sweep of her powerful arm Jagdig brushed the tiny figure of Silka from her path, sending the girl tumbling across the room to land half senseless on the opposite bed. Only Nephraan noticed that slight form had fallen with her shift above her waist, her lower body and the almost hairless slit of her vagina exposed. Hysena and Leel, galvanized by Maris's shrill scream and

Jagdig's roar moved to grab the warrior woman as she reached for her terrified victim. A backhanded blow caught Leel across her plump breasts, sending her crashing back into Hysena. As the two fell, Jagdig took Maris under the armpits and hoisted her effortlessly.

'Now, Uplander, you said something to me. I did not quite hear it, so perhaps you would care to repeat?' Her voice was a hiss and Maris, kicking feebly in the painful grip could do nothing. Jagdig flexed her shoulders, bringing just a little of her strength to bear and felt Maris's ribs bend beneath her hands. The breath came out of Maris in an agonised wheeze and her face began to turn purple.

Hysena, having scrambled to her feet, lunged again at the warrior girl, grabbing her from behind. It was as if a fly were attacking. Not deigning even to use her hands Jagdig arched her pelvis forwards and then with a contemptuous display of strength, crashed her buttocks back into Hysena's stomach. The force of the blow lifted her from her feet and sent her flying through the air. She was saved from the serious injury she would certainly have sustained by being cudgelled against the wall of the dormitory only because she had taken a grip on Jagdig's shift in a futile attempt to pull the bigger girl away from Maris.

The thin cotton was ripped from neck to hem, and Jagdig was left standing naked, her victim squirming feebly in her grip.

When the fight had started, Nephraan instead of moving to help Maris had backed into a corner, snatching a blanket from the nearest bed to cover herself, reverting to a childish belief that hiding under it might protect her from The Monster. When after a few seconds she realised that she was in no immediate danger, she peeped out from the blanket and her response to what she was seeing changed from those of a child to those of a young wanton. She saw Silka tossed away, her shift fluttering about her hips to settle above her waist as she fell. The doll-like form was left half stunned, one leg on the bed, the other draped over the edge offering Nephraan an unobstructed view of her sex. Hidden by the blanket, the girl was able to slip a hand between her legs. She was already moist and her finger slid easily into her cunt as she concentrated on the unfortunate Silka's slim body. Glancing across the room, she saw the moment when Hysena was sent flying and the body of Jagdig was exposed. A soft moan escaped her as she saw those firm buttocks in all their glory and her hand began to move faster.

The door to the dormitory crashed open, and there stood Tarrip.

It took him a moment to assimilate the sight; Jagdig, naked, holding the hapless Maris at arms' length; Silka sprawled on the bed, starting to move now but with her shift still about her hips displaying the cleft between her legs; Hysena about to launch herself again at Jagdig.

The roar from the Holy Father seemed to shake the very fabric of the building.

Instantly, the girls froze. Looking guiltily over her shoulder, Jagdig let Maris drop to the floor where she lay groaning.

'And this is how you feel that those selected to serve the True Prophet should reward the honour offered to you?' Tarrip's voice was now ominously quiet. Jagdig felt the berserker rage drain from her, and the adrenaline high was replaced with the knowledge that she had been denying in her rage, that to be returned to her people after such a shameful event would not incite them to fall upon the Citadel and raze it to the ground to avenge her; more likely she would be used like a captured slave by the men of the tribe before being flung into the forest, her legs broken with clubs, to be eaten alive by the wild animals.

There was a clatter of footsteps in the passage as Colya and Maria arrived, also drawn by the commotion. Tarrip turned to face them.

'Well Sisters, see what a bunch of savages we have to tame.' As he had done after Hysena's indiscretion at the ceremony of the previous day, Tarrip began to pace menacingly around the room, eyeing each of the girls in turn. He had found that this technique could reduce the most strong willed to a state of terror, a state he found agreeable in his charges. He reached the end of the dormitory where Jagdig, still stark naked, stood. To his slight apprehension, the Holy Father found that he had to look up to meet her eyes. It was the first occasion he had had to study a Kallinian, and he shivered inwardly as he ran his eye over her naked form, a shiver part fear, part anticipation of what he wanted to do to that incredible body with its huge breasts and swelling hips and buttocks.

Despite her feeling of contriteness, Jagdig's pride made it necessary to hold the Holy Father's eyes as they stared into hers. Eventually she had to look away, seeing there a cruelty that transcended anything she had before experienced.

Seeing her gaze drop, Tarrip gave a brief nod of satisfaction and turned again to look at the others.

'Who is responsible for this outrage?' he asked calmly.

Glances were exchanged between the girls, none of them willing to speak.

From where she lay on the bed onto which she had been thrown, Silka had regained her senses and, hastily covering her naked lower body, she struggled to her feet.

'Holy Father, forgive us, but it was nothing more than high spirits. We are aware of the honour that has been bestowed upon us, and...' her voice petered out as she saw the priest's glare. The last thing that Tarrip wanted was a credible explanation. Without speaking, he crooked a finger at the slight figure and beckoned her to him. Slowly, twisting a fold of her garment in her fingers, Silka approached the forbidding presence of Tarrip.

Hysena looked up at Jagdig, willing her to speak, to admit that she was responsible for the altercation, but to her angry amazement she saw that the warrior girl, hidden from Tarrip's view, had a small, malicious smile on her lips. Catching her eye, Hysena flashed the bigger girl a look of contempt before stepping up next to Silka who was now facing the Holy Father.

'Sir, it is as Silka says,' she said with simple dignity.

Despite himself, Tarrip was impressed. Above all others, this girl must know what would happen if she drew attention to herself. He was not the only one to be startled. Maris, Leel and Nephraan were all trying to make themselves as invisible as possible and all would have had to admit to a feeling of relief when Silka had been singled out. But they were all the products of their proud families with a sense of honour and tradition.

Maris, still hugging her bruised ribs was the first to move, taking her place next to Hysena, looking nervously at the Argon, knowing that she had earlier revelled openly as she watched her punishment. To her relief she saw Hysena return her look with nothing more than warmth. Soon, five girls, all nervous but all determined to follow the example set by Hysena Macarydias, stood before the high priest. Only Jagdig stood apart.

Tarrip tapped his lips with a finger. The situation was unusual, unique even. During the early part of their training, he would try to set the candidates against each other, so as to foment argument between them, thus allowing him the excuse to punish them. Only as they passed to the higher stages of their initiation did they normally begin to bond. But here, it seemed that the Southern Roader had already brought them together. Except the Kallinian, of course. A rare specimen, this Hysena!

He addressed himself to the warrior girl. 'You do not stand with these?'

'I was... insulted.'

'By which?'

Jagdig pointed at Maris.

'But as they all stand with her, by implication they must all have wronged you?'

The Kallinian frowned, not knowing where this was leading, but gave a small nod.

'And you wish to avenge the insult?' The priest

continued in a silken voice that Colya and Maria recognised as the tone he used when he was anticipating a particularly exciting punishment. He drew the tokan from his belt. A violent shudder ran through Hysena at the sight of this instrument of torture, and there was a general gasp of dismay from the others. And then there was another gasp as the high priest reversed his grip on the implement and handed it to a stunned Jagdig.

'Vengeance is only in the gift of the Prophet,' Tarrip said, 'and through Him may you mend the slight you have suffered.' He looked at the others, enjoying the expressions of shock on their young faces.

A slow, triumphant smile began to grow on Jagdig's face. She swished the tokan experimentally, the motion causing her magnificent breasts to swing as she hefted the leather. She cracked it against her open palm, gaining in excitement at the flare of pain, imagining how it would be to use this thing on the flesh of those who had insulted her.

Tarrip caused the Initiates to kneel at the ends of their beds, their heads pressed to the thin mattresses, their posteriors raised. Their buttocks were still covered, but this would soon change.

'You may start when you wish, Initiate Jagdig,' Tarrip said, 'giving each the punishment you think they deserve.' He studied her body as he spoke, seeing her quiver in anticipation, her quick breathing making her breasts rise and fall, the huge nipples now fully engorged and the size of the top joint of the Priest's thumb. His eyes were drawn to the shock of jet-black hair between her muscular legs and he imagined those legs being forcibly pulled wide to allow him access to the hidden inner delights. He knew, as Jagdig did not, that that time was close.

The girl turned, displaying her firm buttocks to Tarrip's eyes as she stalked between the beds, selecting the first victim.

Silka, she decided would be first. The girl from Sis Narash had annoyed her with her reasonableness, going against the warrior ethos. Jagdig stood next to the slim form, the boyish buttocks outlined through the white cotton shift. She flipped the shift up, exposing her small bottom. Jagdig again swished the tokan, making it hiss through the air then she brought the leather around in a vicious swing, landing it with a loud crack across the centre of her target. Silka had hardly time to scream before the next blow landed, lower down on her thighs. She twisted away from her tormentor, now lying sideways on the narrow bed, her garment rucked up around her waist. Jagdig's next blow landed on the outer part of her thigh and in her agony Silka rolled onto her back, perhaps desperately thinking that if her buttocks were hidden, this torment would stop.

Above her, Jagdig merely smiled a cruel smile as she was offered a new target, a far more intimate target. Concentrating on her aim, she brought the tokan down between the girl's navel and the bulge of her pubis, landing it accurately on the soft, sensitive skin of her belly. Silka's scream was shrill and loud and her legs scissored wildly at the pain, first crossing in a frantic effort to hide herself but finding that this was merely torturing her abused flesh further she unconsciously flung her legs wide, fully exposing her short slit. Jagdig was not going to miss such an opportunity. She struck with the speed of a snake, lashing the tokan down onto the vulnerable lips.

Panting slightly, Jagdig looked down at her hapless victim and felt the rush of pleasure that the bully feels at the sight of a totally helpless victim. She hooked a thumb into the neck of Silka's shift and ripped it from her, exposing breasts that were hardly discernible, their nipples like little pink apple pips. The final stroke of the tokan was across these, but a much softer stroke, a mere gesture as there was little pleasure to be had from a victim who was unconscious, but still a blow sufficient to leave a vivid red stripe across the little apples of her breasts.

The warrior girl looked over to where Tarrip stood.

He blinked his hooded eyes at her.

'Very good, Jagdig. Pray continue. Sister Colya will keep the count.' The priest smiled at the Holy Sister. She smiled back, knowing that each blow Jagdig landed would be repeated on her own body, and that she, Colya, would be allowed to strike them, reducing this proud warrior to a snivelling heap before she and the Holy Father slaked their every lust on her helpless body.

Jagdig was in a state of high excitement after the punishment. Too excited to take in the lush furnishings of Tarrip's quarters to which she had been led, she enjoyed the way her blood sang at the memory, her arm aching pleasantly from the beatings she had administered to those mewling whelps in the dormitory. How glad she was now that she had agreed to become an Initiate!

At home, she had witnessed the punishments meted out to those who had offended the more fundamental rules of her people. The most common of these occurred when a warrior who had shown particular bravery returned from battle and was rewarded by being granted his choice of the women who were of age in the tribe. Should the chosen woman refuse, or even show a lack of enthusiasm at his attentions, that woman would be taken forcibly to the Great Hall and tied by ropes slung over the cross-beams of the high ceiling. Stretched until her toes hardly touched the huge table, the unfortunate would be left to dangle, naked, before the eyes of the people as they feasted. When the warriors had sated one appetite, they were allowed to sate another.

One by one the men of the tribe would take the woman as they wished, sometimes conventionally, standing belly to belly as they thrust into her. Others could have the victim lowered to her knees and take her from behind, choosing whichever passage they favoured, and sometimes a warrior impatient for his turn would choose to take the woman's mouth as the other worked to his climax behind the plunging hips.

Jagdig was not, of course, a virgin, having taken the traditional three lovers at the feast held to celebrate her elevation. She had been careful to select as her first, one of the tribal elders, a venerable old man of some seventy years, one arm off below the elbow from a battle that he never tired of recounting. He had been surprisingly, then quite delightfully, lusty and Jagdig had nearly achieved orgasm with him.

'Sit, sit, Initiate Jagdig.' The voice of the high priest was friendly. 'You have done well, very well. Here. Take some of this wine. Not the poor stuff you drink at your meal, but the finest from Sis Narash.'

Glowing from pride and not a little from lust at the recent memories, Jagdig failed to see the sly slide of Tarrip's eyes as he looked over at Sister Colya. The large woman came forward to offer the girl a fine glass brimming with wine. 'I have put herbs in, to restore warrior strength,' she said.

'It is a kind thought, Holy Sister, but my strength is not dented by such a small exercise.' Jagdig spoke in the manner of an equal, thinking naively that these two had now, seeing her strength and ability to cow her contemporaries, accepted that she was not to receive the sort of treatment that had been foisted upon the other initiates.

She felt the spiced wine coursing through her blood, a feeling of relaxation flowing into her muscles. She did not suspect that she had been drugged, thinking that the emotions that she was experiencing were due only to the arousal from the beatings that she had administered to those weaklings in the dormitory.

As the drugged wine took effect, the priest saw a sheen of sweat grow across her sun-darkened brow, saw her fists clench and the magnificent breasts heave, their nipples full and dark. He glanced over at Colya who seemed almost unable to contain her desire. Positioned out of the sightline of Jagdig, the Holy Sister had already pulled up her skirt and was stroking her cunt with her rough fingers.

'Patience, Sister,' Tarrip cautioned quietly, 'This one must be fully subdued before we commence.' As he spoke, there was a tap at the door. Startled, Tarrip rose from his seat, re-arranging his erection more comfortably beneath his robe as he did. He opened the door.

'Sister Maria. This is a pleasant surprise. Sister Colya and myself were about to, ah, reward the Initiate Jagdig for the task that she carried out on behalf of the Prophet.'

The woman made a perfunctory bow towards the Holy Father. 'I have just now finished ministering to the hurts of her peers, and on this occasion found that the Prophet has urged me to witness her reward.'

'All praise to the Prophet,' intoned Tarrip piously. He was delighted at her rare appearance at such an event. He not unnaturally found her to be more attractive than the earthy Colya, but now that she had some position of power within the Citadel, a power that to his frustration he did not fully understand, he had only occasionally been able to induce her into the more private manifestations of the Will of the Prophet.

For herself, Sister Maria found Tarrip's excesses somewhat distasteful. She was a very highly sexed woman, but utilised a more cerebral approach to satisfy her desires, preferring the gentle seduction, the application of pain to stimulate rather that to terrify — although she would admit in intimate moments that terror, both given and received, could represent the greatest of stimulants. She found it, however, politic to join Tarrip on occasion.

This time, she had decided to join Tarrip in his rooms for more than just political reasons. Prime among these was the Initiate Jagdig. Never before has she seen such raw sexuality, such inherent cruelty in one so young. The thought of being allowed to indulge herself with such a one had roused her hot blood the moment she had seen the girl.

Sister Maria's lusts tended to be split quite evenly between female and male. She was often drawn to seduce one of the young lads from the adjoining Seminary, her favoured scenario being to arrange herself and her young lover before the large mirror that decorated the wall in her cell, revelling in the view of hard young buttocks and rubbery muscles working above her eager body, seeing in the reflection the column of a hard prick and tight bulging balls as her choice eagerly thrust away between her spread thighs. It was rare for her to reach a climax in this manner — they tended to be too quick — but when they had finished, she would have them lick her, coaching them on an intimate tour of her erogenous zones, culminating with her clitoris. The risks in tasting such forbidden fruit were, she felt, ameliorated by the added spice of fear that the very risk brought to the experience.

Her decision to join in with the 'reward' owing to Jagdig was also promulgated by anger.

She fully accepted that the girls who arrived at the Citadel needed to be tamed — some more than others — and she knew that the methods employed gave her an outlet for her sexuality that she would be unable to find elsewhere. She had been awed by the raw power demonstrated by Jagdig in the dormitory, but also sickened by the sadistic nature of her attack on the helpless girls.

Before coming to Tarrip's rooms, she had ministered to the injured flesh of the sobbing youngsters. Commonly, she would have taken advantage of the opportunity to indulge herself with one or more of them, using her skilled fingers to rub her soothing unguents into the striped and bruised buttocks and breasts as she had done with Hysena. But these girls were almost hysterical and in too much pain to be capable of arousal. She had done what she could, reassuring and soothing, her anger growing as she spread cool ointment between Leel's legs. Beneath the coppery curls, the lips of her vagina were swollen and Maria found little pleasure as she gently rubbed cream over them. Little Silka's breasts were a livid red, and she had winced in pain as the Holy Sister touched her nipples.

Now she stood in Tarrip's apartment, looking at Jagdig who sprawled comatose on the couch. Her nipples had shrunk and now lay almost flat in the centres of her wonderful breasts. Even lying sideways as she was, their shape had hardly changed, standing proudly from the broad chest beneath her muscular shoulders. As she studied them, Maria felt herself grow moist.

Tarrip felt his own lust growing ever stronger. His vastly experienced eyes had caught the moment when Maria's anger had changed to another far more agreeable emotion and he rubbed his massive prick through the cloth of his robe. Sister Colya's emotions were of a base nature that admitted little subtlety. She was terrified of Tarrip but this terror added a piquancy to her arousal and the times when he allowed her to assist him in the discipline of the girls could bring her to a state of arousal that sometimes threatened to overwhelm her. She had not bothered to cover herself when Maria had entered the room and now she had four of her thick fingers pressed deeply into her body as she stared with hungry eyes at the naked form of the warrior girl.

'Very well Sisters, we shall commence,' he said. Rubbing his hands together, Tarrip walked across to where Jagdig lay.

He contemplated the still form of the girl as he considered the range of delicious options. Over the years he had built up a formidable array of implements for use on his charges, implements that could inflict mild pain to extreme agony. Jagdig, he decided, was deserving of a punishment beyond that which he would normally mete out to a girl so recently arrived at the Citadel. He swung open the door of the large cupboard that contained row upon row of whips, tokans, simple birch canes as well as the more esoteric clamps and restraints. As he considered his choice, the two Sisters were, with considerable effort, dragging the still insensible form of Jagdig to the Punishment Frame.

The Frame was a device of Tarrip's own invention. It consisted of a series of rods and bars that could be bolted together in a variety of ways, and by use of ropes with leather and metal fetters a victim could be restrained in various positions that allowed Tarrip access to whichever part of the unfortunate's anatomy his whim drew him.

Following Tarrip's directions, Colya and Maria manoeuvred Jagdig so that she was bent forward, her buttocks higher than her head and supported by a wide bar beneath her hips. They pulled her arms forward, securing them at full stretch with leather cuffs about her wrists. This position allowed her heavy breasts to dangle and Colya could not resist the temptation to fondle them, wondering at their weight and firmness as she ran her hands, open palmed, over the warm flesh.

The two women moved behind the girl and secured her ankles, buckling two more leather cuffs about them before threading rope through metal rings sewn to the leather. They each tugged on a rope, pulling the long, muscular legs wide until the muscles of her thighs were straining to their utmost. With her feet secured to the floor and her legs pulled wide, Jagdig was now totally exposed. The double bulge of her buttocks divided to display the lips of her sex set in a growth of pubic hair almost as abundant as that of Colya. Maria ran her finger from the girl's coccyx and along the split of her bottom, rubbing gently the whorl of her anus and then feeling the fleshy softness of her labia. There was no hint of moistness there, but that would soon change.

Sister Maria turned to Tarrip, who was still picking over his choice of implements, for all the world like a child choosing which toy to play with, she thought.

'Shall I awaken the Initiate, Holy Father?'

'She is secure, sister?'

'The Holy Father may wish to inspect her restraints.'

Tarrip did so. The construction of the Punishment Frame allowed him to walk right around the Kallinian, and he admired her naked from all angles, ostensibly checking her bonds but in reality stoking his lust even higher, running his hand over her skin, squeezing a nipple here, a buttock there. With his spare hand he absently swished the tokan he had selected through the air. 'Wake her,' he abruptly instructed Sister Maria.

Jagdig became aware of the smell of bitter smoke.

She opened her eyes and sneezed, then tried to pull away from the shallow dish in which a pungent powder was smouldering and which Sister Maria was holding beneath her face. Still drowsy from the drugged wine, it was several moments before she realised that she was unable to move. With a roar, she tried to rip herself free. Tarrip, Maria and Colya each took an involuntary step back as Jagdig's anger was unleashed. They watched apprehensively as the Punishment Frame shook and twisted. It even seemed that she might succeed until Tarrip stepped behind her and brought the tokan down in a hissing curve that ended with the hard leather blade of the implement lashing onto the exposed flesh of her upturned buttocks. The priest's arm rose and fell faster and faster as he sought to subdue the girl with sheer pain. Her yells turned to screams as Tarrip worked. The tokan he had selected was one of his heaviest, a formidable instrument nearly three feet long, the blade consisting of three tines of leather that had been steeped in brine to harden them. The handle was of wood that had been bound with leather in a manner that left the surface ridged along its length.

He beat her mercilessly, the leather leaving vivid weals over her bottom from the tops of her thighs to the small of her back. Eventually, the priest paused, his chest heaving as he sought to recover his breath.

Tarrip walked around the bound girl until he could look fully into her eyes. They still held defiance.

'When my people hear of this, you will suffer,' Jagdig snarled at him, still struggling but now with less strength. For her, the humiliation was unbearable.

'As the Prophet wills,' Tarrip murmured with maddening calm. He was tapping the tokan against his thigh as he looked down at her. 'However, unless you show yourself able to appreciate the lessons your people sent you here to learn, it is possible that you will not see them again. Your very father agreed that you would remain here until I judged you fit to be returned. The process may take many years.'

Jagdig was silenced. Her struggles stopped at the thought that her ordeal might be prolonged indefinitely, that her father would agree to such a thing. But in her heart, she knew it to be true. Her warrior people were a proud race and now they had joined with the other races of Qalle her father was determined that his people would become an accepted part of society. To that end, she had been dispatched to the Citadel to learn the ways of the other races. She wondered if her father knew what this education entailed, and decided he probably did.

But the indignity! Here she was strapped naked to this frame for the amusement of these, these peasants...

She gasped out loud as another blow landed on her abused bottom, a different sort of blow. Turning her head as far as her restraints allowed, she saw that the priest had been replaced by Sister Colya who was using a thin, whippy cane to beat her.

Colya took her time, savouring the sensation of having this girl in her power. Between strokes, she was running her hand over Jagdig's behind, revelling in the warm, firm flesh that was now ribbed with an overlapping series of weals, already turning purple on the tanned skin.

'She grows wet, Holy Father,' she remarked, pressing the palm of her hand to the Initiate's pudenda.

'Perhaps her shouts were of pleasure, Sister Colya,' Tarrip replied, putting a note of amazement into his voice. 'The tickles she has received clearly do not pain such a powerful young woman.'

'Perhaps she is more sensitive in other places.'

'An interesting thought, sister. Perhaps Sister Maria will assist you in re-arranging her in a position to allow us access to those other areas.'

With the skill of long practice, Maria and Colya manoeuvred the bars and ropes of the Punishment Frame, pulling the girl upright and then hauling her arms back bringing her proud breasts into greater prominence. Tarrip flicked one of the big nipples with the nail of his first finger, eliciting a snarl from Jagdig. The priest repeated the experiment and watched with interest as the nipple engorged until it stood out from the centre the breast like a ripe mulberry.

Jagdig twisted hopelessly in her fetters. The two sisters had fixed a bar behind her at the level of her waist and now were adjusting it to force her hips forward.

Tarrip stood before the helpless girl with his thumbs tucked into his belt. He ran his eyes over her naked form. Having made final checks on her bonds, the two Sisters took their places either side of him.

Jagdig glared at them. She had all but given up trying to get free, knowing it to be hopeless, but she was determined not to give them the satisfaction of seeing her cowed like those other weaklings. She paid little attention as Tarrip in his sonorous voice explained that it was the will of the Prophet that, having punished those who had offended her, she must receive an equal punishment. She concentrated on her anger, picturing and planning the terrible revenge she would exact on Tarrip, vowing silently that she would have him chained naked and helpless to this very frame.

She was jerked rudely from her reverie as a sharp pain took her.

'This one will take much instruction, I think,' Tarrip was saying, finger and thumb cruelly pinching one of her nipples. 'But in the end she shall bend to our will.'

His face moved until it was inches from Jagdig's and she could smell the wine on his breath as he stared directly into her eyes.

'In the end they all bend to the will of the Prophet' His eyes held the glitter of the fanatic. 'All.'

Jagdig squealed as he suddenly took a pinch of her pubic hair and ripped it from her body.

She cursed as she felt the sting of tears, angry at her body's betrayal.

Tarrip stepped back from his victim and looked in turn at the two Holy Sisters. Colya, not unexpectedly, could hardly contain her eagerness to get her hands on the Kallinian and Tarrip with characteristic sadism decided that Sister Maria should be the one to continue the punishment. He gestured the older woman to sit on one of the hard chairs against the wall of the room and took his own place next to her.

Colya whimpered in her frustration but did not hesitate to do his bidding. She knew full well that it would amuse him to send her from the room if she dared to disobey.

'Sister Maria, oblige me and continue with the Prophet's work.'

Maria dropped him a brief curtsy.

When she spoke to the captive, her voice was soft and gentle and this disconcerted Jagdig almost as much as the evil thickness of Tarrip's voice.

'My child, you are brought here to learn. The methods chosen by the Prophet are not ours to question. He demands above all our absolute obedience. Until you are prepared to grant Him this, and until your actions show that the pledge is sincere, it is our unhappy duty to continue this instruction. Now, girl, do you give us your promise to obey. In all things?' She allowed Jagdig to see the small whip she held in one hand. It consisted of a multitude of fine threads, each strung with a series of tiny glittering beads. The whole thing was only a foot or so long.

To Jagdig it did not look dangerous, nothing like the formidable tokan the old priest had wielded with such effect shortly before. She snorted contemptuously, only just resisting the temptation to spit at Sister Maria.

Maria sighed. Her anger had lessened although she was still in a mild state of arousal at the sight of the naked girl and the foreknowledge of what was to come, but she regretted the impulse that had made her select the hair-whip to carry out her share of the lesson. The fine threads and small size of the implement were deceptive. Still, the girl was here to learn.

'Am I to take your silence as refusal?' she asked in her soft voice.

Behind her she could hear Tarrip shifting impatiently

but she knew that the delay would serve to inflame the priest and in this small way she could add another thread in her attempt to bind the Holy Father, to bind him slowly and without his knowledge until such time as she could report her readiness to act.

Jagdig was once again fully in control of herself. 'When I am free, I shall tear down this foul building with my bare hands and with you ins...Ahhhh!'

She had hardly noticed that Sister Maria had stroked the hair-whip across the plump bulge of her breast beneath the nipple.

At first there was a tickle, as if a fly were crawling over her skin. But rather than fading, the tickle grew in intensity until within seconds it felt as if molten lead had been poured over her. The sun-darkened skin of her breast glowed an angry red as the incredibly fine hairs of the whip did their work, the tiny beads that were of sharp-edged crystal attacking the nerve endings beneath the soft, sensitive flesh.

Maria repeated the apparently gently stroke on the other breast. There was fear now in Jagdig's eyes. What was so frightening was the softness of the contact and the certain knowledge of the pain that would surely come. The hair-whip hissed like a snake as it descended, the only sound in the room. Jagdig could not contain her cry of agony as the pain hit her. And the pain had hardly begun to fade before the next lash landed, and the next. Taking care not to let the stokes overlap, Maria worked carefully over Jagdig's heaving breasts, avoiding the nipples, then, her arm moving in a steady rhythm, down her ribs and across her taut belly.

Jagdig was all but paralysed with the agony of it. Her powerful muscles were rigid, straining hopelessly against her bonds. Perspiration sprang out on her forehead. She could scarcely draw breath but, oh, how she needed to scream!

Sister Maria stepped back and looked at the naked girl. Her skin was red from neck to navel and she was writhing in pain, her breath a whimper.

Maria looked over to Tarrip and Colya. She could see the bulge of the Holy Father's erection under his gown and from the look in his eye she knew he would not be able to contain himself for much longer. For her part, Colya was squirming on her hard chair, one hand pressing her robe tightly to her crotch, the other rubbing her breast, not caring who saw. Maria felt little arousal as yet and she waited patiently until Jagdig's spasmed muscles began to relax and her eyes opened.

'I ask you again, Initiate Jagdig. Will you comply to the rules of the Citadel?'

Not for nothing was Jagdig a warrior. Every element of her being wanted to scream that she would do anything if only this torture would cease, but deep inside her still burned the flame of her pride. Setting her jaw, she did her best to look defiant though she did not dare to speak.

'It seems she still has not learned, Holy Sister,' observed Tarrip.

'As ever you are correct, Father Tarrip,' Maria replied, the sadness in her voice genuine as she felt the girl had already endured more than her share. But duty was duty. She looked into Jagdig's eyes.

'I ask you one last time. Do you submit?'

'Never!' The girl's voice was cracked and held little of the defiance she intended.

And Sister Maria spoke the most terrifying words she had ever heard.

'In that case daughter, now I must really hurt you.'

It took a few moments for the words to sink in, and in those moments Maria struck three times, once on each nipple and then upwards onto her exposed vagina.

As Jagdig felt the feathery touches of the hair-whip, the last motes of her self control were shattered and she was screaming before the pain came. Her screams were high and shrill, her powerful body was twisting and shaking with such force that once again her tormentors feared that the Punishment Frame might not be strong enough to contain her agony.

Jagdig certainly did not think she could contain it. She

existed in a universe of pain, concentrated in her nipples, her vulva and her anus.

Tarrip enjoyed the sight of the great warrior girl thrashing in her torment. As her strength grew weaker and the danger of her escaping from the Punishment Frame faded, the priest was able to settle back in his chair and watch the sweat-soaked form as it twisted in its bonds. The big breasts heaved and shook, their nipples fully engorged now as a result of Maria's assault on them and the rosy hue that the whipping had given them added to the attraction.

The priest allowed his gaze to drop to her waist. Jagdig's hips were working almost as if she were experiencing orgasm rather than agony, and her cries, now sunk to whimpers, added to this thought. Tarrip fixed his eyes on her sex. Jagdig's sweat had dampened her pubic hair, slicking it to the skin of her vulva. He licked his lips and thought of how, soon, he would penetrate her.

Seeing the priest pull up his robe and start to masturbate, Sister Maria crossed to him and knelt between his spread thighs.

After that first time, all those years ago when Tarrip had so painfully taken her virginity, she had begun to seek ways in which she could protect herself from his advances. She had learned his desires (many), his fears (few) and his vulnerabilities (hidden). Patiently, persistently, she wormed her way through his defences with the priest scarcely realising. She discovered a little about the power and politics within the Citadel that operated at a level high above that of the Priesthood over which Tarrip ruled, the secret factions that silently waged war against each other for control of Qalle.

Her curiosity had been noted, an evaluation made; should this inquisitive youngster be encouraged or prevented? Could she be a spy? Was she a danger to them?

She was watched carefully for over a year. A decision was arrived at, an approach made and Sister Maria became a member of the Society of T'arn...

Her own mental strength and the teachings of the Society taught her to use her body as a tool. She felt neither desire nor revulsion as she knelt and contemplated Tarrip's swollen genitalia. The shaft of his prick was so long that she could wrap both her hands around it, one above the other, and still not cover its entire length. She felt the heat of it on her palms as she slowly massaged him and heard his breath quicken. She lowered her head towards the swollen plum of his glans, having to open her mouth to its full extent to encompass it.

The Holy Father shuddered at the touch of Maria's clever fingers and hot mouth. These days she could only occasionally be induced into using her delightful skills for his benefit, but those times were pearls almost beyond value. He groaned as his prick slipped down her throat and he wondered as he always did at how she had learned to take his full length without choking, the only one of the hundreds of women he had had able to do this. As her head began to move lusciously and her fingers caressed his heavy balls, he looked back to where Jagdig was hanging from the Punishment Frame.

She was almost quiet now, only the occasional whimper escaping from her exhausted and abused body. Her eyes were shut and tears were still leaking from the closed lids. The red bloom raised by the hair-whip had begun to fade and her nipples were no longer stiff.

Tarrip looked at Sister Colya who had raised her own robe and had three fingers sunk deeply into herself, her eyes flitting between the sight of the now subdued Kallinian girl and Tarrip's huge member buried deep in Maria's throat.

'Very well, Sister. You may take your turn with her. But perhaps she has taken sufficient pain for the time being. Perhaps the Prophet would be appeased were she to offer pleasure rather than receive punishment.' Colya contained her frustration. Her hands had been itching to beat Jagdig. She felt that the hair-whip was not a proper thing to use. Even though the pain it caused was entertaining, she enjoyed the sound of leather lashing into helpless flesh, enjoyed the physical feel of the tokan as it jolted her arm at the point of contact. She had already had a number of orgasms, their intensity increased at the thought that it would soon be her turn to beat the helpless Initiate.

But this game could be fun, and if she were very lucky, Sister Maria might grant her the rare treat of stimulating her when she had finished with the Holy Father.

As the sea of pain slowly ebbed, Jagdig became at least partially aware of her surroundings. Her every muscle ached from her struggles. Being naked had never before concerned her, but now she was ashamed at the spectacle she must be presenting to this evil priest and his two damnable termagants. Reluctantly she opened her eyes. The younger of the two women was praying before the priest.

It took her battered mind some while to realise what she was in fact seeing.

Jagdig felt oddly detached as she watched Sister Maria fellating the priest and to her surprise she felt the tingle in her loins alter subtly from pain to the first tug of lust. She did not resist as the older woman began to rearrange her restraints.

She found herself kneeling on the base of the Punishment Frame, a bar below her waist elevating her buttocks, her arms pulled high behind her, forcing her head lower than her hips.

Tarrip watched with unalloyed pleasure, grunting occasionally as Maria performed a particularly enjoyable caress. He saw that Jagdig had, at least for now, given up all thoughts of resistance. With an uncharacteristically gentle gesture, he stroked Maria's head as once again he felt himself sliding down her accommodating throat.

'Perhaps we may all relax a little, Sister Maria,' he said.

Maria took his meaning. She lifted her head from his lap, giving his prick a squeeze as she did, and rose to her feet. Giving him a smile that owed all to her training and little to desire, she undid the buttons of her robe, letting it drop from her body and stood nude and demure before Tarrip.

'I am willing to help the Holy Father to relax.' She allowed a husky tone into her voice and hooded her eyes as she looked down at him, rotating her hips wantonly.

His eyes were on a level with her hips and his hand went to his erection as he stared at her cunt, then raised them to her breasts. Although she was thirty years old, her body was still firm and trim, her breasts perhaps a little lower that when he had first taken her, her hips a touch wider, but now she was so much more experienced he found her the most desirable of all the women that were available to him, the fact that she so rarely made herself available only serving to increase his desire for her. Now she turned from him and walked to where Colya was securing Jagdig, giving her buttocks an exaggerated sway.

The older woman saw her nakedness and twisted her cruel face into a smile.

'Ah. So, now is our turn to play, eh?'

Maria frowned. 'Play, Sister? Forget not that this is the Prophet's work that we do.'

Colya looked guiltily over to Tarrip who rubbed a hand over his mouth to conceal a smile. 'I think Sister Colya meant 'pray,''

'I see,' said Maria, entering into the game, 'I pray your forgiveness, Sister. Perhaps you would lead us in the prayer?'

Colya looked from Maria to Father Tarrip, both of whom were wearing expressions of piety. These moments confused her. Although ostensibly of equal standing with Maria — both were adepts — she knew that her colleague had powers and privileges well beyond her comprehension or aspiration.

She had never known why she had, at the age of seventeen, been plucked from her job as a meat skinner in the city of Calith to become a Server to the Prophet, only that the work was far more pleasant and although her power was, in terms of the Citadel, minuscule, it was far greater than she could ever have achieved outside. Her feelings towards the Prophet were mixed. Naturally, her childhood in the orphanage had been laced with lessons, often humiliatingly physical, about how all were born to serve Him and to do His bidding, she became confused at times such as this which seemed to contradict the teachings about Carnal Sin. As a youngster, it had been her relentless quest for Carnal Sin that had so often bought her trouble but she would never know that it was those very appetites combined with her lack of intelligence that had drawn Tarrip's attention and it was he who had ensured that she was promoted far above her abilities simply to provide him with a useful foil.

Eyes glittering, she struggled out of her robe. Some five years older than Maria, her body was beginning to blur. Her breasts, once as proud as those of the girl she stood before, had begun to droop, but the nipples were huge and stiff in anticipation. Her belly was swollen and the mass of her pubic hair grew over it almost to her navel. With one hand she seized Jagdig's hair and raised her head. The girl was still half-unconscious and Colya used her other hand to slap her awake.

Reluctantly, Jagdig swam up from the dark, comfortable place into which she had sunk. Her eyes opened and blinked as she tried to assimilate what she was seeing. Her vision was filled with the sight of Sister Colya's crotch and the thick columns of her thighs. From somewhere behind her she could hear Tarrip's voice.

'Initiate Jagdig. In His mercy, the Prophet offers you a choice. You were permitted to avenge your hurts upon those who slighted you. To balance their pain, you yourself have received pain. This is the True Justice of the True Prophet. Now He offers you the chance to show your obedience to Him by offering pleasure to others. Do you accept this task?'

As he talked, Colya was twisting her hair, making her eyes water and she barely understood the words.

'Or,' the priest continued, 'shall the lesson of pain continue? Choose, warrior woman.'

Maria was studying Jagdig, noting that her eyes were not focusing and that she was hardly reacting to the pain she must be feeling from Colya's grip on her hair.

'I think she hears you not, Holy Father.'

'Mm. probably you are correct, Sister.' Tarrip bowed down next to Jagdig until his eyes were on a level with hers. He reached under her chest and suddenly crushed one of her nipples between his powerful finger and thumb.

Her eyes flew open at the sudden flare of agony, and Jagdig came fully awake. She saw Tarrip's evil eyes staring into her own, the un-lovely form of Colya's pudenda just inches from her face. To her relief, she felt a little of the inner strength upon which she had always been able to rely seeping bock into her bones.

'Well? What is it to be?' Tarrip's voice grew harsh as he saw the light of anger flash in the Kallinian's eyes. He had truly believed her broken.

Jagdig ran her mind back over what the priest had said, and discerned his meaning. She had had adventures with women as well as men, and enjoyed them. But this foul creature? With her mind now once again under her control, she considered options. If she withheld, they would beat her again and her very being quailed at the thought of the terrifying hair-whip. The alternative, unpleasant though it might be, would be little more than that; unpleasant. She swung her eyes to look at the Holy Father. Sister Maria was using her hand on the biggest prick she had ever seen. By now most of the pain of her beating had vanished, leaving a maddening itch between her legs, an itch that such an organ might assuage. And should she acquiesce, it might lead them to believe that she was cowed and if their vigilance relaxed for just a few moments...

Her thoughts took only seconds, but it was too long for Tarrip.

'This one is determined not to learn. Endeavour to

teach her, Sister Colya.' He stood, wiping his hands on his robe.

'No! I shall do as you ask! Please...' part of Jagdig despised herself for such a cowardly outburst, but the memory of her recent pain was too close and the reaction was pure reflex.

Tarrip narrowed his eyes. The fear seemed real but he had not missed the defiance that the girl had demonstrated. This one must be watched for a long time before he could be sure she was truly in his control.

Sister Colya felt a sudden spurt of arousal when the Holy Father gave her permission to beat the Kallinian. She scurried eagerly to the cupboard and quickly selected a long tokan with a single heavy blade and a handle as thick as her wrist.

She was out of Jagdig's sight and the Initiate, although she had her voice under control, was again on the verge of descending into a state of quivering, screaming hopelessness. When the blow landed across her exposed and spread buttocks, the scream that she was unable to contain was as much one of relief as of pain. Instead of the mild tickling that foreshadowed the unendurable agony of the hair-whip, there was a dull blow that shook her whole body, causing her prodigious breasts to swing with such force that for a moment her open mouth was covered by their soft skin. Tarrip, standing to one side, drew in his breath at the sight. He shared with Colya the view that punishment should be overt rather than subtle, and the sight of Jagdig's proud tits swinging like ripe fruits in a storm aroused him far more than seeing her twisting and screaming without her body being touched.

Ever alert to his moods, Sister Maria began to move her hand fasten on his prick, feeling it grow even harder as he watched both Jagdig's and Colya's bodies. Colya's breasts were swinging even more than the Kallinian's as she went to her work with a will, laying the tokan on with all her strength. Maria squeezed Tarrip hard to get his attention. He glanced at her and saw the look in her eye.

She ran the tip of her tongue along her upper lip and then slowly, sinuously, turned her back on him, releasing his hard, hot flesh and then bending from the waist, she took her ankles in her hands and presented herself to him.

Tarrip took his prick in his own hand and rubbed it frantically, his eyes darting from the Punishment Frame where Colya continued to belabour Jagdig, down to what Sister Maria was displaying for him. With his free hand, he felt between her legs, encountering the soft lips of her cunt and the wetness between them. He fingered her for a few seconds, enjoying the sensation as she pushed back at him. She released her ankles and moved her hands onto her buttocks, spreading them for him, showing him the pink inner lips and the tight whorl of her anus. Unable to contain himself any longer, Tarrip positioned the tip of his penis at the inviting entrance and with a single, groaning thrust, sank himself to the balls into Holy Sister Maria. He felt her inner muscles tighten about him almost as firmly as her hand had and it was with difficulty that he pulled back to begin another stroke.

Quickly, Holy Father and Holy Sister found a common rhythm and the sound of their flesh slapping together joined the louder noise of Colya's tokan lashing into Jagdig's bottom and legs.

Tarrip took hold of Maria's hips for better purchase and she had to place her hands on the floor to save herself from being pushed over as his hips worked faster and faster. She gave up trying to match his strokes, but rotated her hips to constantly change the angle at which he entered her, bringing different frictions to his desperate prick.

He climaxed with the roar of an angry bull. Maria was only just able to contain the strength of his final thrust and she felt the hot pulses of his sperm as he vented himself deep into her vagina, his fingers cutting painfully into her hips as he sought to bury himself even deeper in her body.

Maria felt the sweat from Tarrip's brow dripping onto the skin of her back. Still bent forward and supporting herself upon her hands, she raised her head to look at Colya. The older woman had stopped beating Jagdig when she had heard the Holy Father reach his noisy climax and smiled conspiratorially at her colleague. Even Jagdig, concerned with her own problems, had twisted in her restraints to enable her to see the sight of her prime tormentor as he fucked the demure looking Sister.

The warrior girl had found this latest indignity almost easy to bear. Yes, it had been painful, but lacked the terror of the assault from Maria. It was the sort of pain that a warrior was expected to be able to cope with, if not administered in the way a warrior might expect. But she felt that now she had resisted the worst these people could offer. She knew what would now follow, but that would be nothing in comparison. The sight of the old priest sweating and snorting over his submissive lackey had increased the stirrings of her own body, abused though it had been. Sister Maria, seen in her modest robe and with her quiet, pretty face and figure had seemed the epitome of holiness. To see her now, naked, her shapely breasts curving from her body, the pink nipples standing out like raspberries, was almost shocking. As she watched, Tarrip, red faced and panting, withdrew, and Sister Maria stood upright. The hair on her sex was the same light brown as that on her head and was of the same fine texture. Her inner lips were distended from the priest's ministrations and glistened from his efforts. She wore the same slight smile that was her normal expression, as if she had just led them in prayer rather than having slaked the lusts of the high priest and this too was deliciously shocking.

Having finished a most satisfactory beating, Colya was now ready for a different form of entertainment.

'Now, girl,' she said to Jagdig, moving to where the Initiate could see her. She placed her fists on her broad hips and stood with her feet parted. Looking up, Jagdig saw that her sex too was wet, but it engendered in her only revulsion. With an effort, she repressed a shudder as the woman spoke.

'I ask same question as Holy Father. Are you ready to do will of Prophet?'

Jagdig was able to keep the hatred from her voice, 'If I can, sister. Instruct me.'

'So! Even brave warrior can learn power of Holy One, eh, Father Tarrip!' Her voice was triumphant, believing the girl to be beaten.

'Early days, Sister, early days,' murmured the priest. 'I will admit she does seem to have learned her first lesson.' He was not taken in by the seemingly subdued Kallinian, knowing too much about her race to trust even one who had been through what he had witnessed. 'Still, she shall have her chance to demonstrate this new-found compliance. Perhaps she would be more comfortable lying down rather than kneeling in that awkward position?'

Once again Jagdig had to submit to the indignity of being arranged for the convenience of her tormentors. It was an effort not to struggle, to maintain her new role of defeat.

Tarrip was by now in the best of moods as he rang for refreshments. Not for a moment did he trust Jagdig, but he was confident that she would try to convince him that she was truly beaten and whilst she was playing this part he could expect her to do even more to convince the three of them. He had seen it all before.

The two Ercli slaves, one male, one female, who came into the room bearing trays of food and drink expressed no surprise at the sight of the High Priest of Qalle and the two Holy Sisters naked together, nor at the sight of the big Initiate girl being expertly manipulated on the Punishment Frame. They never did. Tarrip toyed briefly with the idea of adding them to the entertainment, but although they would be as compliant in that as in everything else that they did, he tended to find their type unsatisfying. It hardly seemed to matter what you did to them or had them do to each other, they seemed almost totally lacking in emotion of any sort.

Tarrip totally failed to see the look that was

66

exchanged between Sister Maria and the two diminutive figures. But then, he was not meant to.

'Come, eat and drink Sisters, before we recommence.' His voice was expansive as he waved a cold chicken-leg on which he was he munching. He took a long and satisfying draught of wine from the jug he held in his other hand. By all that was holy, doing the Prophet's work could give a man an appetite!

Nothing loath, Colya joined him, leaving Maria to check the last of Jagdig's restraints.

Jagdig was surprised to fine herself in an almost comfortable position. She was on her back, a soft cushion under her hips for reasons that were all too clear. The cords that held her at ankles, knees and wrists were of cloth now rather than leather and although her legs were parted they were not stretched wide. She had no doubt that this would soon change as she could see where the ropes ran through sheaves that would allow her limbs to be hauled into whatever position would most amuse her three tormentors.

As she checked the last of the restraints, Sister Maria saw that the girl was looking at Tarrip and Colya, who were making ribald comments as they ate and drank. She saw Jagdig's throat contract.

'Are you thirsty, child?' she asked in a voice kept soft for only Jagdig to hear.

Despite herself, Jagdig nodded.

'Wait.' Maria rose and without looking at Tarrip or Colya, poured a measure of wine and returned to kneel next to the Initiate, holding up her head to help her swallow the refreshing liquid.

Tarrip noticed this and frowned, but said nothing. With a little wine in her, the girl would be even more biddable.

Maria was speaking softly to Jagdig. 'There is little more to endure this night. I know you are a warrior, but this requires strength of a nature alien to your proud race. You may refuse, the choice is yours always, but it will not be easy. That is the point.'

The voice of the Holy Sister was soft and hypnotic. Even the fierce warrior girl found the tone soothing, believable. Jagdig swallowed more of the wine as Maria continued to hold her head. She became aware that the woman was stroking the damp hair away from her temple with her thumb and was strangely moved at this small gesture. She looked into the eyes of the holy woman and saw nothing but compassion.

Tarrip was growing impatient. He was now well recovered from his bout with Maria and keen to sample the charms of the warrior.

'Well, Kallinian?' he called, 'what is your answer?'

'I submit to the will of the Prophet.' Jagdig's voice was low but, she was pleased to hear, steady.

Tarrip smiled at Colya. 'Assist me, woman,' he commanded, struggling to pull his robe over his head. Moments later he stood naked above the supine Jagdig. Already erect, his penis presented a frightening sight as she stared up at it, even bigger than it had appeared when she had seen Maria stimulating him.

Grunting ponderously, Tarrip lowered himself until he was squatting astride Jagdig, his buttocks resting on the tense muscles of her belly, the tip of his prick twitching just below the level of her breasts. Without needing instruction, Maria and Colya took station either side of her and pressed the immense breasts together. Tarrip slid his hips forward, sliding easily over her sweating skin and his prick eased between the mountains of soft, hot flesh.

Despite her inner resolution to take this assault without resisting, Jagdig felt her nipples engorging and an involuntary contraction of the inner muscles of her vagina. She saw the massive plum of Tarrip's glans as it emerged from between her compressed breasts, just inches from her face.

As he pushed ever forward, she perceived his intention and twisted her head away.

With an angry snarl, Tarrip pinched her stiff nipples, twisting them until she felt the tears start from her eyes.

'Submit to the will of the Prophet, girl!' He grabbed for her hair and dragged her head forward.

Giving in to the inevitable, Jagdig allowed her mouth to fall open and felt the hot, bulbous end of the Tarrip's prick as it slid between her unwilling lips. Her jaw was forced ever wider as the priest forced more of himself into her. He rocked forward, now supporting himself on out-thrust arms, his hips directly above her face as he sought to discover how much of himself he could cram into her.

Jagdig could no longer breathe. She started to choke and struggle under his weight. Her eyes opened to the frightening sight of his face, the nostrils flaring, the eyes glittering with lust, the lips an unnatural red and dripping with spittle. Inch after impossible inch forced itself down her throat.

Tarrip felt her struggles and chortled with delight. 'See, Sisters. Now she enjoys herself!' He withdrew enough to allow her to snatch a desperate breath before once more forcing himself down her throat. 'But,' he added, panting a little now, 'she still shows signs of resistance.' With a suddenness that left Jagdig gasping he withdrew completely and sat back on his haunches, crushing her breasts beneath his buttocks. 'Perhaps she is not yet worthy to receive the full blessing of the Prophet.' He struggled to his feet and once more stood over her, meditatively working a fist along the length of his member.

'Spread her legs.'

Using the ropes binding her ankles, the two Holy Sisters drew Jagdig's legs wide as the priest knelt between them. He probed at her sex as it became exposed, parting the outer lips with his thumbs.

Again Jagdig felt her body betray her as she was touched so intimately. Her juices began to flow freely as Tarrip pressed a finger into her and rubbed her clitoris with his thumb. Her legs were widespread now, but not painfully so. The cushion under her buttocks lifted her so that her sex was presented with utter vulnerability for whatever the Holy Father intended. Perhaps the worst thing was that now, as he worked away at her, she was lifting her hips towards him, wanting more than just his fingers inside her, wanting — no, needing — him to assuage her.

As if reading her thoughts, Tarrip lowered himself until she felt the tip of his prick nudging at the entrance to her vagina. With a whimper of desire, the warrior girl thrust frantically with her hips, desperate now to have him deep inside her.

Maria watched as she saw Tarrip slide fully into Jagdig, her own lust now building. She crossed to Colya and ran a hand over the other woman's plump buttocks. Her colleague needed no furthen encouragement but turned and took Maria in her arms, kissing her fully on the mouth. Maria squirmed a hand between their bodies, wriggling it down until she encountered the wiry bush of Colya's pubic hair and began to move her fingers over the oily nub of her clitoris. For her part, Sister Colya slid her hand between Maria's legs from behind and, knowing what her younger colleague liked, worked one, then two fingers into her anus.

The two Holy Sisters broke from their kiss but continued to pleasure each other with ever more slippery fingers as they looked to where Tarrip was grunting and heaving over Jagdig.

She was moaning with pleasure as the priest hammered into her. His prick seemed to reach up to her heart and his pelvis was grinding delightfully into her clitoris at every stroke. Her breath grew ragged and her cries ever more shrill as her climax approached... and suddenly the weight was lifted from her, the massive prick that was filling her in a way she had never before experienced withdrawn, leaving her empty and unfulfilled. She cried out in her anguish.

Kneeling back from her Tarrip wore a sardonic smile as he watched the proud warrior woman as she twisted in frustration. He had lost none of his skill, he reflected, able to judge to a hair just when the girl was at the very brink. Her struggles seemed almost as frantic as when they had been beating her, but now she was desperate for their touch, any touch. She worked her pelvis and legs, trying to get any form of friction on her vulva.

The priest went to the table and poured himself another cup of wine. He watched the spectacle before him as he drank. Jagdig was still writhing with frustration, her bonds preventing her from touching herself in the way she so desperately needed. With amusement Tarrip saw that her eyes were fixed on the two Holy Sisters who were locked in oblivious embrace. Maria had her back to him and he could see Colya's fingers moving in and out of her anus. Maria had lowered her head and was kissing Colya's big, soft breast and had managed to work nearly her whole hand into the older woman's cunt. His prick twitched.

'Sisters. We neglect out guest.' They broke with some reluctance. Tarrip heard the sloppy noise as their fingers slid from each other's bodies. 'Sister Maria, I think the Initiate would show you how skilled is her tongue. And perhaps Sister Colya would enjoy your own revered attentions.'

Knowing from experience what was required of them, the two quickly moved to position themselves.

Maria knelt astride Jagdig's head and carefully lowered herself until she felt the Kallinian's breath on the damp folds of her sex. In case the girl failed to understand, she rubbed her clitoris gently against the tip of her nose and reached beneath herself to part her lips.

Desperate for any bodily contact and praying that her turn would come, Jagdig began to lap at Sister Maria, flattening her tongue and running it along the full length of her slit before pressing it as deeply as she could into her vagina. She felt a weight on her own hips and shuddered in anticipation; prick, tongue, anything would serve to satisfy her, but, Holy Prophet, make it now!

But the weight on her felt wrong. There was pressure, but none of it where she so desperately needed it. She felt Maria shift above her and was able to see between the spread legs. Once again she moaned her frustration.

Colya arranged herself comfortably, using the girl's body as a cushion. Lying face up, she wriggled forward until she could feel the soft double bulge of Jagdig's breasts beneath her ample bottom, her head on one of the muscular thighs. Then she spread her legs as Sister Maria bent forward to press her mouth to her cunt.

Tarrip watched, moving around the three women, enjoying the different sights that were available to him. Colya's big breasts had sagged either side of her and she was kneading them as Sister Maria buried her face between her legs and was using the fingers of both hands on her. Bent forward as she was, Maria was exposing her charms when Tarrip moved behind her. He enjoyed the sight of Jagdig's tongue as it moved over her, now on her clitoris, now delving into the pink opening of her cunt. Maria had reached behind herself and was wriggling a finger in her smaller opening.

Jagdig, her frustration growing by the moment as she heard the moans and gasps of the two older women, as she felt the heavy body rolling on hers but not touching her in any way that could satisfy her, as she caught the maddening scent of arousal, hers and theirs, sensed another presence near her head. Rolling back her eyes, she again saw the formidable silhouette of Tarrip's penis approaching. Only inches from her eyes, it seemed even more massive and she longed for him to once more bury it deep inside her. Instead, she had to suffer the agony of seeing it sink slowly and voluptuously into Sister Maria, see and hear as he worked in and out of her as she moved her hips back and forth to meet his thrusts. She unconsciously moaned in sympathy with Maria as the high priest withdrew before she reached her climax, and then gasped in disbelief when she saw what he was about to attempt.

Maria felt her orgasm building when Father Tarrip withdrew. For a moment she thought that he intended do to her what he had done to Jagdig and her anger flared. But then she felt the pressure of him against the alternative entrance that she was offering, and felt her heart jolt in sudden anticipation.

His penis already slick and lubricated from her cunt, Tarrip found it easy to sink himself into the Holy Sister's anus. A single slow, firm thrust and he was buried in her to the balls.

Maria screamed in a mixture of pain and ecstasy, her bottom lifting to meet him. She buried her face in Colya's sex, and Colya came on that instant, her bucking body forcing the air from Jagdig, whose head rose and whose attempt to suck breath into her body resulted in her drawing Maria's inner lips deep into her mouth, her teeth catching inadvertently on the sensitive folds. Maria screamed again as orgasm took her. Tarrip's own roar joined those of the women. He pulled his prick from Maria's bottom as it began to pulse and, holding it in his hand, directed the gouts of hot sperm over Jagdig's upturned face.

The high priest of Qalle and his two Holy Sisters lay sated. Beneath their tumbled bodies, Jagdig wept.

3.

The Warrior Prince Xarrith aged 18 — son of Xarrith, King of all the Tribes of Kallinia, and Jagdath, first Concubine of the King — watched with interest as the two Ercli slaves fucked on the floor of his room. He grinned over at his companion.

'Just as well he's as small as you, Tasnar. If I tried, I'd burst her like an old wine skin.'

The Sis Narashan flashed him the brief smile that represented just about the greatest show of emotion he ever allowed himself. His eyes too were on the two small forms, the female straddling the male, their bodies moving together in the age old way.

'It's you who will end up an old wine skin, Xari.'

Xarrith slapped his knee and roared with delight. 'Tasnar! A joke! You made a joke! Just wait until they hear of this in the refectory. They will compose a new saga for you.' He dropped his voice to a stage whisper and pretended to look about the room for spies. 'But make sure they do not hear of this in Sis Narash. They will sit in a circle about you and frown for a full year... but then, that's all they do anyway. That and take the hard earned gold of honest thieves such as my father. Hey you!' He turned his attention again to the copulating Erclis. 'Take his cock in your mouth and lie so I may see your cunt.'

The slaves, without comment or apparent resentment, re-arranged themselves as directed, the woman wrapping her arms about her companion's hips for purchase and then opening her legs in the direction of Xarrith. Enrapt, he watched them in silence, his hand busy with a massive erection that he displayed with no embarrassment.

They made incongruous friends, Xarrith and Tasnar. The Kallinian youth had reached his full height now and stood a full six and a half feet although it would be some years before his already formidable bulk reached its full potential. He was more pale skinned than most of his type, a result of having spent a year and a half as an Acolyte of the Prophet.

Now half way through his second year, he had lost most of the sullen resentment that had accompanied him to the Citadel. In that first year he had learned that the regime was nothing like as difficult to cope with as he had been led to believe. Not for the first time he thanked the Prophet that he had not been born female. If only half the tales he had heard of what they were made to go through were true...

He grinned again at Tasnar. 'Hey, little warrior. Get out your weapon and enjoy yourself.'

'Little Warrior' was not wholly a joke. In his first days at the seminary, Xarrith had sought to impose himself on his group in the only way he knew. One after another, he had pounded his peers into bloody heaps, ignoring the Sis Narashan as beneath his contempt. The day had come when, after a contest in the refectory with the candidate from Dersis who had actually lasted beyond the first minute and who had had the temerity to blacken one of his eyes and whom he was about to stamp into the ground, he had felt a gentle touch on his arm.

'That one is beaten, Warrior Xarrith. I am ready to take my chance although,' the tiny figure, a full foot shorter than Xarrith, had paused as if in thought, 'perhaps you need a day to recover from such a close bout?'

For a moment, Xarrith had been stunned with disbelief. Then he roared as he assimilated the insult.

'What!? You miserable little manikin!' He shook a hand the size of a ham at Tasnar. 'Go! Run before I take your baby's balls as a bracelet.' Tasnar had not flinched, not even raised his hands, simply stood with an irritating, insulting half-smile on his face.

'What would a Kallinian know of balls? I hear only their women have them.' Tasnar turned his head to address the other frightened boys who were witnessing the event. One of them giggled.

Xarrith's jaw actually dropped. Then, in a greater rage than he had ever known, almost bursting with the need to swat this fly who dared to say such things to him, he spread his arms to crush the very life from Tasnar.

Even now he did not wholly understand what had happened next. Somehow, impossibly, he was flying through the air to fall with a crash that knocked the wind from his lungs. From when he lay, half dazed, he saw his tormentor standing completely at ease, his face serene, hands clasped loosely in front of him.

Xarrith scrambled to his feet. They were ten feet apart and in that distance the warrior was able to accelerate to a speed that would have brought down a horse. Tasnar waited until the last moment and then, with exquisite timing, simply seemed to melt away before Xarrith. This time, with nothing to check his attack, the Kallinian collided with the closed door of the refectory with such force as to start it from its frame, winding himself a second time and adding a bloody nose to his hurts.

The deeper hurt, the unbearable one, was inside his head and it was this that served to steady him. This time he approached as carefully as if stalking a snake, nerves alert to the sudden strike. He circled the Sis Narashan well outside the reach of those skinny arms. The lad did nothing. Just turned to remain facing Xarrith, that infuriating half-smile never leaving his face, his arms loose at his sides. In his mind's eye Xarrith could hear his brother warriors laughing at the time he was taking to blot out the tiny man before him. He lunged, and the world exploded.

He awoke flat on his back, the diminutive figure of the Sis Narashan leaning over him and wiping his brow with a cool, damp cloth. He struggled to rise, but fell back with a groan. It felt as if every bone in his body was broken. He glared at Tasnar who looked back without expression.

'Soon, I shall kill you.' Xarrith tried to snarl but his voice was weak.

Unmoved, Tasnar continued to minister to his hurts. 'When you meet a powerful adversary, you must vanquish him or become allies. I would prefer alliance.'

He suddenly grinned. 'Besides, I have no wish to crack my foot on your thick skull again!' And despite himself, Xarrith found himself smiling back.

Now, as he looked fondly at his companion, Xarrith reflected that he had no firmer friend on the whole of Qalle — no, not even among his own people.

He looked back at the Ercli couple on the floor. The woman's mouth was still busy on her companion's small penis and her spread legs gave Xarrith a fine view of her neat vagina, its scant pubic hair hiding nothing.

Looking again at Tasnar, Xarrith saw that he had now raised his own robe and was rubbing himself. The smaller youth spoke:

'I think I shall put that empty cunt to some use,' he said, stripping off the brown robe of the second year Acolyte that was all he wore. Despite Xarrith's earlier comment, his prick was of a respectable size, made to look bigger by his lack of height. His body was finely muscled and it had not taken long for word to spread among the bullies and pederasts of the seminary that the Acolyte from Sis Narash was far more than he appeared.

Tasnar touched the Ercli man on the shoulder and he immediately wriggled back from the woman. 'Up,' he instructed her. Quickly, she presented herself on all fours, elevating her slim bottom for him. He stroked between her legs, wondering not for the first time at how these odd little people failed to show any feelings. She was wet enough for him to enter her easily, so presumably gained something from the act. Shrugging mentally, he pressed the head of his penis to her and felt her pushing back at him as he slid home. He reached around the slim body to take a breast in each hand. As with most of her type, her breasts were as diminutive as the rest of her, but her nipples were huge in proportion and grew harder than any others he had known.

He saw that Xarrith was still rubbing himself. 'Her mouth is not being used. Why waste your scant strength when she could suck you?'

Xarrith grunted. 'As she will not moan for me anyway

I suppose some use should be made of her mouth.' He knelt at her head. The Ercli woman's mouth hardly seemed big enough to even encompass Xarrith's glans, but she was able to get nearly half of his length past her lips.

Together, the two friends used the woman. Xarrith reached his climax first; she was skilled with her mouth and tongue. When he arched his back he was surprised at how much of himself she was able to take. He enjoyed the sensation as she sucked the sperm from him, swallowing every drop.

Behind her, Tasnar's buttocks were a blur and he sighed with satisfaction when the exquisite sensation arrived.

They had the woman bathe them in the sunken pool filled with warm water that was the privilege of Xarrith as the Leading Acolyte, a position he had won more by his ability to menace his tutors than his piety and knowledge of scripture and lore. The young warrior amused himself in the pool by fingering her, tweaking her nipples and poking a finger into her behind when she was rubbing soap-root over Tasnar's genitals. He grew half an erection when she, not having reacted to his gropings, washed that area of his anatomy, and he toyed with the idea of taking her again. But for all that she and her ilk provided an outlet for his sexual needs, he found it a joyless act and longed for a real woman, one of the lusty girls of his own people for preference.

Only once during his time at the Citadel had he enjoyed the comforts of a woman who responded with enthusiasm to his efforts, and even that event had an unreal, dream-like quality to it. Tasnar certainly thought it was a figment of Xarrith's frustrated libido.

One night, Xarrith had been woken from a deep, dreamless sleep by the figure of a woman. She carried a hooded lantern that produced just enough light for him to be able to see the finger on her lips and the soft beauty of her eyes. She had given him a small cup containing a bitter but not unpleasant liquid which he drank without thinking, being as he was more asleep than awake. He remembered the warmth that had suffused him as he followed the ghostly figure of the woman, a woman dressed in the robe of a Sister elder as she led him through the familiar passages of the Seminary. And then the passages were no longer familiar. To his befuddled mind, it seemed that the woman had caused a section of the solid stone wall to vanish and then Xarrith had found himself walking along narrow, dusty passages with no windows.

There were gaps in his memory, but he remembered standing in a small but comfortably appointed cell. It had seemed quite natural when the woman had helped him to take off his robe and then she had undone the buttons of her own robe and, letting it slither from her slim form, stood naked before him.

As soon as she had dropped her garment, Xarrith had begun to engorge at the sight of her shapely breasts and the fine pubic hair that formed a neat triangle at the junction of her thighs. Still without speaking, she had knelt before him and taken his member into her mouth. She had not moved her mouth on him in the manner of other women he had known, simply allowed him to swell into her. He had felt himself growing, felt the gentle pulses as his blood stretched him, lengthened him. He felt the pressure growing on his prick as it filled her still mouth and grew down her throat until he was fully hard and her lips were stretched to encompass the very root of him. For the first time a woman had shown herself able to take his full length into her mouth.

Then she had begun to move her mouth on him, gently tickling his balls with the tips of her fingers as she did. To Xarrith it seemed that every nerve ending had somehow become twice as sensitive and he gasped at the exquisite sensations as the fingers of her other hand caressed his taut buttocks and then slid over his skin to tweak his nipples. Xarrith was able to do nothing but stand with fists clenched at his sides as the rapturous feelings grew and grew until he felt himself dissolve in an almost unbearable explosion of ecstasy as his seed erupted into her throat.

It was as if the strength had been sucked from him along with his semen, his knees threatened to give way and the woman wrapped a surprisingly powerful arm beneath his shoulders and helped him to the bed.

'The Holy Father himself could not best such a weapon.'

He did not remember her lips moving as she spoke in a gentle voice that was on the threshold of hearing. 'I think it will need little rest before entering into the lists once more.'

His prick had softened but lost little length. He lay, head propped on a large bolster, trying to make sense of the odd feeling that he was watching himself as he lay naked on the bed. But Xarrith's people had little use for mirrors and he had never before seen one of the size that covered almost the entire wall opposite the bed. The drugs that had dulled his perceptions while accentuating his sensitivities left him in a dream-like state and so it came as no surprise when the nude woman began to dance.

She sang quietly as she moved, a song with a plaintive tune that dug into his brain and it seemed the meaning of the song was only fractionally beyond his understanding even though the words were in a language he had never before heard.

She moved lightly about the room, her eyes never leaving his. At first, her arms were held wide from her body and she used her hands and fingers expressively; now they depicted flowers swaying in a breeze, now an animal running from the hunt. With a subtlety that almost evaded Xarrith's confused mind, her dance gradually became lascivious. Her fingers would brush her nipples, bringing them erect in the centre of her moving breasts. She touched herself delicately between the legs and he saw the shine of her juices in the light of the many candles that burned in the room. He became aware of the scent of her and his erection grew again, as hard as iron, so hard he ached but he was unable to move however much he willed his hands to do so.

Her dance now brought her close to where he lay and her fingers were busy between her legs, parting the lips of her sex to display the nacreous inner folds. She turned from him and bent, moving her buttocks in enticing circles and then pulling them wide for his eyes to see her from behind, to see the chiselled bud of her anus. Sweat broke out on his brow as he watched her dip a finger into the tight opening, sliding it in to its full length before slowly withdrawing it.

He was whimpering with his need when she, in a movement so sudden as to startle him, threw a long, shapely leg across his straining body and impaled herself upon him. In that moment, whatever spell had paralysed his body was broken and he began to move his hips in a desperate effort to bury himself in her, wanting to drown himself in the heat of her body. Her need seemed as great as his and she thrust back at him, their flesh meeting with a slapping noise as she ground her pelvis against his.

Her orgasm was powerful, her back arching like a bow, her inner muscles almost painfully tight about him as they contracted.

She fell forward upon him and they lay for a while in silence.

Eventually, she stirred. Xarrith's hands were resting on her mature buttocks. He stroked them gently, revelling in the feel of their firmness and shape.

'Beat me,' she had whispered, her breath hot in his ear. He looked into her eyes, wondering if had heard what he had heard and she nodded.

Tentatively, he lifted one hand and brought it down on her, a gentle slap no harder than might be used to chastise a child.

'Harder. Beat me harder.' He did as he was bid, using both hands on her now, increasing both the speed and the strength of the blows.

His prick had not left her and now once again it began to harden and grow into the depths of her cunt.

'Yes. Oh yes, warrior. Now you begin to have the measure of it. Harder!'

He was using a considerable part of his strength on her and she was panting and bright eyed, her body rubbing against his. The palms of his hands were tingling as he continued to spank her, but the harder he did so the more delighted grew her cries, her climaxes coming almost constantly...

Although he had gone over the events of that night time and time again, Xarrith had no recollection of how he had returned to his bed. There were snippets of memory; pictures of her body above him, below him, kneeling in front of him as he took her again and again.

He stood in the pool, erection once more rampant at the thought of that night.

'You appear ready for another battle, warrior,' remarked Tasnar, noting his condition.

'I prefer something that battles back, even though she eventually hopes to lose the war,' he replied, stepping from the pool and drying himself vigorously on a blanket taken from his bed. He pulled his robe over his still damp body and crossed to the window. The sky was grey and a thin, miserable rain of the sort that could persist for days was falling.

'And now what, Xarrith?' Tasnar asked, belting his robe. The day was one free from instruction and, with the exception of morning and sunset prayers, the Acolytes were free, although they were expected to spend their time in contemplation and learning.

'Brother John will be sleeping off his wine, Brother Keem will busy and Father Lisnan will be with Father Tarrip, no doubt teaching an Initiate. Let us explore.'

Tasnar raise his eyes to the ceiling and sighed in exasperation. 'A dream, Xari. You drank too much wine at dinner and dreamed of the fat tits and dribbling cunts of your countrywomen.'

'If I were dreaming, who drained my balls and wore my prick down to the size of yours?' replied Xarrith. 'Well, not quite so small.'

For weeks after the event, he had lain awake at night, waiting for her to return to him but it was now nearly a year since it had happened. He had spent many hours prowling about the corridors, often at night when she haunted his mind and stole his sleep, tapping on the walls to hear if there was space behind them, looking for cracks between the stones or concealed niches that might contain hidden devices to open the secret way.

The main reason that Tasnar wanted to convince his friend that he had been dreaming was that he knew with certainty that there were indeed passages hidden in the walls of the Citadel.

Tasnar took his studies far more seriously than did Xarrith. In the future he would be required to act as mediator on behalf of his own people or to solve disputes between opposing peoples. For this it was necessary that he have a firm grasp of the history of all the tribes of Qalle and in his studies he had learned that, during the times when war raged across the land, no raider had ever succeeded in taking the Citadel. The stories told of how apparently successful attacks had been thwarted by the sudden appearance of defenders where no defender had been moments before. This led to a wide-held belief that the Holy Prophet intervened at such times of dire need, sending His own invincible warriors to defend the most holy place of Qalle. The priesthood did little to discourage this notion.

Tasnar, who had been taught to be sceptical of all things, had drawn his own conclusions. Although he was most careful to make obeisance to the Prophet, he held his own silent belief that the Holy One mostly helped those prepared to help themselves. He had, soon after Xarrith had first told of his mysterious night visitor, examined more closely his surroundings and had seen that there were places where the walls seemed unnecessarily thick...

It was very early one dark, cold morning when a surfeit of beer from the previous evening had forced Tasnar to make a trip to the gaderobe. Although half asleep and somewhat hungover, he had instinctively ducked behind a pillar when he saw a light coming towards him. It was not that he had no right to relieve himself at that time of night, simply his instinct to remain out of sight, to avoid doing anything that might draw attention to himself. That and the fact that Father Lisnan seemed to be making some effort to walk quietly; he held his sandals in one hand and had his lantern turned down to a mere glimmer. Tasnar's heart had jumped when Lisnan, who was the senior priest in charge of the Acolytes, stopped just a few feet from where he was hiding. But the priest had not seen him. He stooped down and seemed to fiddle with the wall and Tasnar's eyes had widened when a section, just wide enough to admit a body, had silently slid aside. The priest slipped through the opening and a few seconds later the gap in the wall vanished.

Tasnar had waited to see if the priest would reappear and then stepped cautiously from his hiding place to examine the wall. To all appearances it was no different from any other area of the passage. The cracks between the blocks of heavy stone from which it was constructed appeared just as did those surrounding the mysterious section that he now knew to be false. He crouched down as Father Lisnan had done and ran his fingers along the mortared sections between the blocks. There was a tiny metal catch. It would be invisible to anyone walking along the passage and who would feel the need to bend down and examine that section of wall?

He had not risked opening the secret door; the priest might have been just behind it. He hurried back to his dormitory, wondering when the safest time to explore would be. He did think of taking his friend along on the adventure, but whilst there was none better to have at your back in battle, the big Kallinian was hardly suited to the quite, subtle approach that would be necessary. Tasnar would go alone.

He chose the night of the celebration of the Second Battle of Ystar when the hoards of raiding Kallinians had finally been vanquished and forced to sue for peace. At the celebration, tradition insisted that a toast be drunk to each of the twelve generals who had fallen during the war and two more to the young soldier who had stood alone at a breach in the city wall, defying the last desperate thrust of the invaders until the city guard had been able to rally to him.

It had not been difficult for him to conceal the fact that he drank hardly a thing and he waited until the last of the priesthood had been carried to his cell, robe smeared with vomit and still singing, and then another hour until he could be sure all of them were snoring in their beds.

The door to the passage had opened easily. The trigger to close it from the inside was not concealed and Tasnar made sure he would not be trapping himself by operating the mechanism a time or two before proceeding.

The passage was narrow and the light from his lantern showed it to be bare of decoration. There was much dust but this was disturbed, suggesting than it was used not infrequently. It twisted through the building and at times he had to negotiate steep, worn steps. He totally lost his sense of direction as the minutes passed and was beginning to wonder if the passage led anywhere when he saw light ahead and for a moment nearly panicked at the thought of discovery. He looked wildly around for somewhere to hide, but there was nowhere. Then Tasnar realised that the light was not moving. Cautiously he moved forward, turning down his lantern as he did. There was a small gap in the wall, allowing a beam of light into the gloomy passage. When he reached it, he found that the aperture was small enough to be covered by his thumb. He put his eye to it and barely managed to suppress a gasp of amazement.

In the revealed room he could see his cousin Silka and another girl, a rather plump red-head whom he thought he had seen before. With them was Father Tarrip. The girls were standing with heads down and the high priest was swinging a tokan and pacing up and down before them.

The passage had led him all the way to the Initiates' quarters.

Through the narrow gap, Tasnar could hear the angry rumble of Tarrip's voice although he could not quite tell what he was saying. But it was clear from his tone that he was berating the girls.

It was the first time in a year and a half that Tasnar had seen a woman other than an Ercli slave and he feasted his eyes on the form of Silka. The white robe of the Initiate was loose on her body but the belt at her waist showed her slimness and he thought he could see the protuberances of her nipples. Her companion, much larger, was lush of body and there was no doubt about her nipples. They showed clearly, forced against a robe that was tight on her, displaying breasts that were a world away from the tiny offerings of the Ercli.

As he watched, Tasnar saw the priest gesture to a wooden bar that he had not previously noticed. It ran at waist height the full width of the small room, crossing his line of vision.

With obvious reluctance, the red-head draped herself over this, bending almost double. Tasnar felt his excitement growing as her plump buttocks were outlined as the cloth of her robe tightened.

In the seminary, the Acolytes held endless discussions as to what went on in the part of the Citadel that was forbidden to them. There were many rumours of how their female counterparts were subjected to terrible punishments and during his first year, when he had shared a dormitory with five others, the imaginative description of the vicissitudes of the girls they knew to be a short but unattainable distance from them was counterpointed by the creak of the beds as they did the only thing they could to assuage their frustrations, the six of them masturbating frantically as the descriptions became more and more lurid.

Tasnar had believed little of it, but now it seemed he was to learn the truth.

He watched as Silka, at another gesture from the high

priest, moved behind the bending girl and raised her robe. It was as if she knew Tasnar was watching and wanted to titillate him by carrying out her task as slowly as possible. The white cotton was inched up the legs of the red-head, revealing well-shaped if fleshy calves and the dimpled backs of her knees. Tasnar's hand stole up his own robe to grasp a now rampant erection as a pair of thighs the size of Silka's waist were revealed. The creases at the base of her buttocks came into view and finally the full glory of her behind was revealed. Tasnar had never seen a woman of her size naked before. He had previously considered the slim figures of his own people to be the most attractive on Qalle and had thought the larger women he had met to be rather ugly. His appreciation of the larger form was intensified when Tarrip took station beside the girl and ordered her to move her feet apart. She did so and now Tasnar was treated to an unobstructed view of her sex. The red hair at the junction of the now spread thighs was a match for that on her head and grew in tight curls over the wedge shape of her pudendum. The opening into her body was slightly parted by her position and the ragged edges of her inner lips were protruding slightly. It was the most erotic thing Tasnar had seen in his short life and he had to make a conscious effort to still his fist, not wanting to come too soon. He forgot any fear he might have had at being caught in such a forbidden place looking upon such forbidden sights.

The crack of the tokan as it bit into flesh came clearly through the stone wall as did the shrill scream of the girl. With a sudden surge of excitement he remembered who she was. Princess Leel of Calith! One of the highest noblewomen of the whole of Qalle was standing naked just feet from him! He had met her at the trade talks and had been too tongue tied to respond to her friendly approach but had taken furtive glances at her when he thought she was not looking in his direction. They had been some years younger then, she much less plump and with none of the womanly curves she was now displaying which was why he had not at first recognised her. His hand moved faster on his hard flesh at the realisation that he was watching the woman who would one day be among the most powerful of all women kick and scream as the Holy Father beat her deliciously trembling flesh with slow, deliberate strokes of the tokan.

Eventually, when her bottom was glowing a uniform red, she was allowed to stand and Tasnar groaned in frustration as her intimate delights were hidden as her robe once again covered her. He managed to hold back from orgasm only by looking away and staring with fierce concentration at the floor.

When he looked back he nearly came at once at the changed sight in the room. Far from having finished with the princess, she now stood with her hands on her head and was stark naked.

Her large breasts bulged whitely towards Tasnar's hiding place, shaking with her sobs. Her nipples were tiny in comparison with the size of her breasts, little pink dots the size of apple pips. He looked down to her cunt. Again her legs were parted and now he was able to see the full length of her slit. From that distance it was hard to be sure, but Tasnar thought he could see the gleam of arousal on her lips. Her scream came to him again as Tarrip swung the tokan in a hissing arc that landed full across the luscious breasts, making them swing and quiver even more.

Tarrip finished beating the Princess Leel in his normal manner, bringing the leather blade of the tokan up between her spread legs to impact on the most sensitive part of her body. She was allowed to take her hands from her head and, as the priest intended, they went straight between her legs in an attempt to rub away the wicked stinging.

Seeing the noble Leel rubbing her cunt, her tits reddened and those tiny nipples hard from their beating was more than Tasnar could stand and he had to bite his lip to prevent himself crying out as he came. He used the hem of his robe to mop up the copious outflowing, not wanting to leave stains that might be discovered on the floor of the passage.

He knew he should not risk his luck too far by remaining for much longer but could not resist another look.

He wished that he could hear as well as see what was happening in the room. It appeared that Tarrip was offering Silka a choice. He had pointed to the bar over which Leel, who was still stroking herself, had been so excitingly beaten, and then gesturing towards himself.

Silka wore an anguished expression and then seemed to come to a decision, kneeling before the forbidding figure of the Holy Father. He said something and gestured to the girl, this time impatiently. She stood slowly and then to the hidden Tasnar's delight, took off her robe.

He had never really thought of her in a sexual way. They had more or less grown up together, but she, being a year younger had seemed more of a nuisance than anything. She was an only child and kept wanting to join in the games Tasnar played with his fellows.

Now, as he saw her tiny form revealed, he once again felt his prick hardening. Even by the standards of her race she was small, and in the forbidding presence of Tarrip and compared with the generous curves of Princess Leel she looked doll-like and extraordinarily vulnerable. Tasnar felt his heart go out to her, his essential decency wanting to find a way to rush into the room and rescue her from her fate. But that was impossible. So he might as well enjoy what he was seeing and think of retribution on behalf of his kinswoman when the opportunity arose.

Silka was again on her knees and now Tarrip was raising his own robe to reveal his spectacular erection.

Tasnar felt his eyebrows crawling up his forehead at the sight; Xarrith himself would be impressed by such a weapon.

Leel certainly seemed impressed as Silka opened her mouth wide to receive the priest. In her corner of the room, for the moment forgotten, it seemed to Tasnar that her eyes were about to pop from her head. Her fingers were busy between her legs and she looked as if it was only with great effort she was holding back from joining in.

Tasnar was impressed at how much of Tarrip's length Silka was able to take. At least half of his length was crammed into her mouth and he could see her jaw working as she sucked on him.

After a few minutes of this, the Holy Father withdrew his member, now made even longer from her efforts, took the girl beneath her arms and effortlessly lifted her until she was held with her face on a level with his own.

For a moment it seemed to Tasnar that he was going to kiss Silka and his stomach shrank in sympathy at the thought. But the priest had other ideas. Tasnar heard him bark a gruff command and instantly Silka, still suspended, opened her legs. She was being held with her back to the Acolyte and at her action he was able to see the almost hairless slit of her cunt. Another order and Leel came eagerly forward. From a table she picked up what Tasnar recognised as one of the bowls that commonly held oil for the dipping of bread at meals. There was no show of reluctance as the princess of Calith coated her fingers with the slippery stuff before anointing Silka between her spread legs. She spread the oil generously, working it over the contours of the vulva, her fingers even slipping into the opening of her sex before continuing over the slim backside, leaving it gleaming. Even her anus was coated and again Leel was unable to resist the temptation to push a finger into her, although Tasnar doubted that she would be capable of accommodating the Holy Father in that place.

Pouring more oil into her cupped hand, Leel now began to rub it into Tarrip's penis, moving her hand up and down its considerable length for what seemed longer than necessary. She was still holding the member when Tarrip began to lower Silka.

He lowered her slowly and Tasnar clearly heard her gasp as the tip of his engorged prick touched the oiled skin at the entrance to her vagina. Leel held Tarrip's shaft in one hand and used the fingers of the other to open Silka to accommodate him, and guided the priest into her.

Tasnar wished he could see Silka's face as she was lowered further and inch after inch of the priest slid into her body. He saw her lift her knees until they were resting Tarrip's hips and her heels moved around behind him, as if to pull him more deeply into her cunt. Leel was kneeling to one side of the couple, rubbing and squeezing the Holy Father's heavy balls with one hand and using the other on herself, pressing her fingers as deeply as she could reach into her own cunt. Out of sight of them, Tasnar's hand was a blur as he frantically rubbed himself.

Still deeply impaled on him, Tarrip carried Silka across the room until the girl was resting her behind on the table. He laid her back and began to pound into her with a force that threatened to split her asunder but she gave every sign of enjoying his attentions as her hands began to knead her small breasts and pinch her erect nipples. Refusing to be left out, Leel bent over the straining body of the little Initiate and to the delight of Tasnar, used her tongue to stimulate her clitoris.

The sight was enough. The young acolyte reached his second orgasm and again using his now sticky robe to cleanse himself and resolutely resisting the temptation to take a final look, he turned up the wick of his lamp and made his way back to his quarters.

Leel watched with impatient frustration as the Holy Father continued his efforts with Silka. Half way through her first year as an Initiate, she was growing used to the ways of the Citadel. Although she hardly enjoyed the beatings that she and her fellows had come to expect, they all learned that what usually followed meant that the beating became exciting in itself and most of the initiates now became aroused as soon as sentence was passed.

She still shuddered with distaste as the sight of the ugly form of Father Tarrip, but the feeling of that massive prick invading her body had brought her to peaks of sensation she could never have dreamed of in the formal environs of Court

And that was another aspect of life in the Citadel. At home, most of the young noblewomen were expected to behave in a manner befitting their station and Leel had been chaperoned to the point of screaming. But here, the most outrageous acts were sanctioned by edict of the Holy Prophet.

The thought of standing naked, rubbing her cunt (a word she had hardly dared think until she got here!) and waiting for one of the most holy men of all Qalle to... fuck her when he had finished with little Silka would have been unthinkable, but cloistered here with no outsiders a very different set of rules applied.

She looked bock at Silka. The doll-like body was straining as she neared her climax. Her legs were wrapped as far around the priest as she could reach. Leel ran her hand over the slim, sweated body, tugging on an erect nipple and then down to stimulate the distended clitoris that protruded from the lips of her sex that were spread wide by Tarrip's plunging organ. She took Silka's hand and guided it to her own cunt. The nimble fingers slid over the red curls and into the opening of her sex. Leel felt them stiffen inside her and Silka gasped and shuddered in orgasm.

'Prin ...cess, ah, Leel,' Tarrip's voice was ragged as he neared his own climax, 'I would... finish in... your, uhh, mouth.'

Leel cursed silently (another skill she had learned here!). It seemed that she would not get what she so desperately desired and now her jaw would ache for the rest of the night. Of all the lessons she had learned, the main one was instant, unquestioning obedience and so she did not hesitate to remove Silka's hand from between her legs, kneel at the feet of the Holy Father and open her mouth.

He withdrew from Silka and Leel took his length and stretched her lips over the huge girth. The taste of Silka filled her mouth along with the hard, hot flesh of Tarrip. She could feel it pulsing and tried not to gag as he invaded her throat.

He came with his characteristic bull-like roar and the Princess Leel felt the hot, salty inundation flood her mouth. She could not swallow fast enough and felt streams of the stuff trickling down her chin to drip on her naked breasts.

Later the two girls, now respectable in their robes, walked together back to their dormitory. They were damp from the bathing pool and Silka moved a little awkwardly, her sex sore and chafed from the ministrations of the Holy Father, her hips aching from the strain of having her thighs being held so wide apart.

The two youngsters reached the dormitory. The others were in their beds, but lay awake wanting to hear about their punishment. In the short time they had been together, a tradition had developed that victims related their adventures in as salacious and inventive a manner as possible, titillating their audience until the dormitory seethed with sexuality.

'..and Father Tarrip then placed me on a table and forced my legs ever wider and forced his mighty prick into my body until it seemed I must burst,' Silka was saying. 'And not only did I pleasure the Holy Father to his greatest satisfaction, at the same time did I thrust my arm to the elbow into the sodden vagina of Leel, Princess of Calith, giving her a pleasure so great that she made over to me all her fortune that I may do so again!' There was a shout of appreciative laughter. Silka was a skilled storyteller.

'And then?' demanded Hysena, her deep blue eyes sparkling, her fingers beneath the covers moving gently over her moistening sex, allowing her pleasure to grow slowly, knowing that her enjoyment of what soon would follow would be all the greater for the wait. She knew that all the others would be doing the same and looked about the room, deciding with whom she would share herself that night. For a moment, Jagdig entered her thoughts and her enjoyment slipped as she thought of the warrior woman alone in her cell, naked and restrained.

Silka finished her tale amid much laughter and applause, bringing Hysena's thoughts back to the moment.

'And now,' Silka was saying, 'which of you will play the physician and minister to our fearsome hurts?'

'We know not that your hurts are so bad,' teased the willowy Nephraan. They had all played this game on many occasions and even Maris, all but cured of her haughty aloofness by the friendly nature of the others and the need for comfort when she had been selected for punishment, joined in eagerly.

Princess Leel pretended anger. 'We each were beaten in such a manner that we feared for our very lives, you miserable Sea dweller. Look!' She stood on her bed and raised the back of her robe to expose her plump buttocks to the hungry eyes of the girl from the Dersis Sea. The flesh was crisscrossed with a profusion of red weals that extended down her thighs almost to her knees.

'It would seem you have received a spank or two on your fat bum. Turn about that I may inspect for other afflictions.'

A small smile played about Leel's lips as she saw the four sets of eyes on her as she raised the front of her garment to her waist, bringing her red curls into view.

'Ah, yes, she has had a little tickling. But see here, ladies,' said Nephraan, pointing. 'This is a fearsome wound. Her body is deeply gashed. See this deep red wound! I shall kiss it well.'

Matching her actions to her words, Nephraan leaned forward and kissed Leel gently on the lips of her sex.

'She will not thank you if your kiss heals that wound, Neph,' said Maris. She had removed her own robe and sat up in her bed, playing with the small nipples of her large, shapely breasts.

'Ohh. That is good, Sister,' groaned Leel. She had her hand on the back of Nephraan's head and was pressing her pubis hard to the busy mouth. 'She may not heal my wound but she is indeed healing me of thoughts of the servant of the Holy Prophet. Ah. Yes, use your fingers on me.' Nephraan pushed both of her thumbs into Leel's vagina and parted the soft flesh, applying her tongue to the exposed clitoris, bringing further groans from the princess.

Enjoying the sight but not wishing to have anyone touch her own sex as it was still sore, little Silka slipped out of her robe and, lithe and naked, moved behind Nephraan. She lifted the hem of her shift over the long, perfect legs and applied soft kisses to her buttocks. Nephraan, mouth still busy, moaned her appreciation and parted her legs. She paused briefly in her work and rid herself of the shift that was hindering Silka.

The tiny girl from Sis Narash rubbed her little breasts against the smooth back and hugged Nephraan from behind, not failing to caress her petite breasts, smoothing her thumbs over the stiffening nipples and drawing another stifled moan from her.

Maris looked from the three girls to Hysena who was sitting on her own bed, contemplating the delightful tableau formed by Leel, Silka and Nephraan.

'It seems, Macarydias, our companions have no use for us at present,' she smiled at her.

Hysena smiled back. 'Perhaps I may visit your palace, Uplander?'

'That is a kind thought, but I shall refuse to receive you should you not dress in a manner appropriate to these noble surroundings.'

Hysena stood and dropped her shift to the floor. She twirled on the spot, displaying her trim figure. 'Does this fine gown reach your high standards?'

'It does indeed!' breathed Maris, 'it does indeed.' She lifted her arms to welcome Hysena into her bed.

For a moment, the two young Initiates simply held each other, smiling in friendship. Hysena stroked away a strand of fine, blonde hair from the face of her companion and then kissed her full on the lips. Their tongues met and squirmed against each other and as they embraced their breasts rubbed and their hips began to move as they sought each other.

Breaking from the passionate kiss, Hysena dropped her head to take a nipple between her lips. She bit on it gently and felt Maris grasp her more tightly. She forced a thigh between Hysena's legs and at the touch she spread them to allow the blonde girl to press hard against her hungry sex. She worked her hips faster now, bringing her clitoris into contact with the smoothly muscled thigh.

Maris released Hysena's slim body and changed her position on the bed until the two girls lay on their sides with heads opposed, each facing the sex of the other. Hysena parted the fine, blonde hairs that covered the sweet opening before her and pushed her tongue deeply into it, at the same time experiencing the glorious sensation as Maris did the same to her.

Glancing between the spread thighs that cradled her head, Maris could enjoy the sight of Leel, Silka and Nephraan. Leel was still standing on the bed with Nephraan using her fingers and mouth on her. Nephraan had now spread her own legs wide and between them knelt Silka. Maris saw that the Sis Narashan had blown out one of the candles and was pushing it into the other girl.

The room was filled with the moans and sighs of the five girls. Hysena gasped as she felt a finger insinuate its self into her anus and she sucked the inner lips of Maris into her mouth, making Maris gasp in her turn.

On the bed, Leel felt her orgasm approach and her legs could no longer support her. Silka and Nephraan helped her to the mattress. Silka withdrew the candle from Nephraan as they laid Leel on her back. Leel raised her legs, pulling her thighs wide and back until her knees touched her breasts. Nephraan squatted down over her face, lowering herself until the junction of her own wide spread legs came against Leel's mouth. She immediately felt the wonderful sensation of a hot tongue wriggling into her saturated vagina and contracted her inner muscles around it, trying to draw it more deeply into herself.

Silka felt Leel shudder in orgasm and heard her cries,

muffled in Nephraan's sex. Nephraan gave her own cry as she too came. Silka worked the candle as fast as she was able, at the same time rubbing the stiff finger of her clitoris and was rewarded by another cry and Leel came again and again. Silka suddenly withdrew the candle from the sopping cunt and thrust it accurately into the tight opening of Leel's anus, pushing it in until it was nearly engulfed but taking care not to lose her grip on the slippery wax.

Leel screamed again, her body rigid and trembling as the waves of pleasure took her.

Eventually the cries and moans from the five Initiates lessened and they lay in each others' arms, exhausted and content.

In a distant pant of the Citadel, in a cell so deep and dark that it could almost be termed a dungeon, the atmosphere was far removed from the happy games of the Initiates' dormitory.

Jagdig now was hardly recognisable as the proud Kallinian warrior. She had lost weight almost to the point of gauntness although she was still formidably powerful. Her sun-browned skin had faded at the lack of light and was now alabaster white save for the profusion of welts and bruises that crisscrossed her entire body. Her head had been shaved, making her appearance all the more startling.

There was no hair between her legs either, but that part of her body had not been shaved and she still shuddered at the thought of the humiliation the she had endured for its removal.

It had been some weeks after the savage beating she had received at the hands of Tarrip and the two Holy Sisters and during those weeks it seemed that not a day passed without her suffering at the hands of one or more of them as they tried to break her, beatings followed by caresses that left her aroused almost to the point of screaming in her need to be allowed to climax, but the skill of the high priest was such that she was left crying her frustration as the attention stopped in those critical moments just before the ecstasy would envelop her, leaving her body dripping with sweat, her cunt running with arousal.

Even at night there was no solace. She was left alone in the crude cell with her arms secured in such a way that she might touch herself no lower than her breasts, and even this was a refinement of Tarrip's cruelty. He knew full well what she must be suffering and knew that she would not be able to resist the small comfort of playing with her breasts and how this would build the frustration of not being able to bring herself relief. Her thighs were kept parted by an iron bar that was secured between them by two straps that went about her legs just above her knees, so that she could not rub her legs together to attempt to assuage her yearnings in that manner.

The removal of her pubic hair had been one more page in the litany of her degradation. For nearly a full day she had been held chained to the hateful Punishment Frame, naked, arms outstretched and lashed to a horizontal pole, another pole pressing against her buttocks and thrusting her hips forward so that her sex was prominent. The weight of her body was supported by her knees resting on a hard wooden base, further restraints about her ankles prevented her from being able to do more than shuffle to try and ease her growing discomfort.

For hour upon hour, a relay of her fellow Initiates at the direction of the Holy Father had plucked the thick, wiry pubic hairs from her skin, tugging them out with small tweezers. It was not particularly painful except when a fold of skin was caught, by accident or design, or when one of the girls took a bunch of hairs rather than single ones. When this happened, she could not always prevent a small squeal escaping her lips, despite her resolve to endure in silence.

They had started where her thick growth of jet-black hair began to sprout just below the level of her navel and, throughout that long day, worked steadily lower.

Father Tarrip had maintained an almost constant

presence, his eyes hardly moving from her sex as the hair was steadily stripped away. First the bulge of her pubic bone was cleared and then the very top of her slit and the softer skin of her lips and the hood of sensitive skin that covered her clitoris was exposed. Now there was a subtle change in her torture. Not only did she have to endure the indignity of being exposed so before her peers and the priest, but her body was beginning to respond to the light touch and the constant tiny flares of pain as another hair was plucked. The girls who were taking it in turns to work on her could hardly fail to notice as her inner lips began to engorge and turn a darker shade, the tip of her clitoris emerging from its cover. Her nipples had stiffened and, restrained as she was with arms wide as if she were about to embrace a lover, she could do nothing to cover them.

Tarrip's eye had gone to her breasts and she saw the small, cruel smile cross his face as he saw the state of her nipples.

'So, Jagdig the Warrior, once more I see you begin to appreciate our little games. Would you have me ask one of your fellows grant you what you so plainly desire? Shall I have her use her clever mouth between those muscled limbs?'

As he spoke Jagdig could think only of the repeated pin-pricks of pain as the hairs were plucked from her sex. It was impossible to avoid contact between the working fingers and Jagdig's skin. Occasionally her distended clitoris was brushed and a jolt would run through her body each time. But relief would not come, was not allowed to come. When the priest saw that her moment was near, he would instantly order that the work cease and Jagdig would be left on her own until all sexual feeling had left her. And then the cycle would begin again.

The most terrible time had been when Hysena had been working on her. The slim Southern Roader was working over the most sensitive part of her vulva, a finger width from the opening of her vagina. Jagdig had been exercising the greatest control she could muster in an attempt to disguise the level of her arousal in the hope that the priest would allow the work to continue past the point when her orgasm could not be prevented, but the Holy Father was far too wily to fall for the trick. When he saw the tell-tale shiver of her belly and the hardening of her nipples, he gave the order to stop, but this time remained with the pretty Initiate in the cell.

'My lady Hysena, you work with such diligence in this unpleasant task that the Holy Prophet has spoken to me that you are to receive His reward. Do you choose to accept?'

'I am greatly honoured, Holy Father.' Hysena stood with alacrity. She was finding the task of tugging the wiry hairs from Jagdig's groin far from unpleasant. Hate was alien to her nature, but she came close to it in the presence of Jagdig. Although there had been no repeat of the night when the Kallinian had raged through the dormitory with such devastating effect, during the weeks when she had still slept and eaten with the other Initiates there had been constant small cruelties and acts of spite that rendered transparent the facade of conformity she maintained when in the presence of the Elders of the Citadel.

The chance of revenge, however small, was not to be passed over.

Hysena stood, head hanging demurely as she awaited the pleasure of the Holy Father. Carrying out her task in such close proximity to Jagdig's open legs, she had found it hand to resist the temptation to bend forward and kiss the enticing opening presented to her, but she knew that if she did it might be her restrained in the Punishment Frame. No matter her feeling towards the Kallinian, she presented such an erotic sight with those powerful legs pulled wide and her spectacular breasts occasionally brushing the top of Hysena's head as she worked to strip away the hair, slowly exposing more and more of the soft, tempting skin, the girl was in as high a state of arousal as was Jagdig.

'Remove your shift.'

Quickly, Hysena pulled off the simple garment and stood, hands at her sides, waiting for the next order.

Tarrip drank in the sight of her for some time, admiring the small, perfect breasts with their saucily upturned brown nipples, nipples already stiffened in anticipation, the slim waist above the flare of her hips and the neat triangle of jet-black hair at the junction of her thighs.

'Turn,' he told her.

She turned on the spot to present her perfect behind. He noticed that she was almost free of marks there, the skin beautifully pale and enticing. He noted that it was clearly past time to mark her skin as she completed the turn, once again presenting her front to his eyes.

'Open yourself.'

Immediately her hands went to her groin and she eased apart the lips of her sex, pushing her pelvis forwards as she did to allow him a perfect view of the shining inner lips.

From the Punishment Frame, Jagdig gave a throaty groan of helplessness at the sight. Tarrip smiled in cruel satisfaction at the sound.

'Lie on your back and lift your legs,' commanded the Holy Father, taking a tokan from the table. It was a whippy implement, longer than his arm. At one end his hand could just encompass its thickness and it tapered to a finger width. The leather was really too soft to hurt much, but it marked skin beautifully.

Hysena lay on her back on the rough rug, her legs doubled back on her body, feet beyond her head. She had wrapped her arms behind her knees to maintain the awkward position.

Tarrip ran his eye over the long expanse of limb. The girl was so limber that she was able to hold her legs straight. They were pressed together along their length although this did not prevent him from seeing the crease of her sex nestled in a surround of black pubic hair.

The tokan selected by the high priest allowed him to

sit comfortably on a stool as he flicked at the supine body of Hysena. He had pulled up his robe and held his prick in his spare hand, noting the look of longing in the eyes of the captive warrior woman. To his experienced eye it seemed that the spark of defiance was all but extinguished, but he would take no chances with this one.

The backs of Hysena's thighs were reddened from her knees to the base of her buttocks now, and she had parted her legs slightly, allowing him a fuller view of her upturned sex. He began to work the tokan over the double swell of her bottom, the hand on his prick moving faster.

Hysena had at first kept her legs pressed tightly together, expecting the pain from the tokan to be far greater than it had in fact turned out to be and wanting to protect her most sensitive parts. To her surprise and growing pleasure, the implement did little more than sting and stimulate as it was worked over the length of her thighs. By the time the Holy Father began to attend to her buttocks, she had eased her legs apart and pulled them even tighter to her body. By twisting her feet outwards, she was able to bring an agreeable pressure onto the lips of her sex and this had the secondary affect of causing her labia to bulge outwards so that the tokan was actually striking her there, causing her to wriggle in a mixture of pain and delight.

'Now, my lady, straighten your legs and lie flat.'

Hysena unbent, allowing Tarrip a full view of the front of her body. He began again at the level of her knees, seeing how she raised her hips as the tokan neared her cunt. He suddenly increased the power of the strokes, laying them hard on the prominence of her pubis, causing her to squeal, but the squeal was as much of growing excitement as of pain. He worked up the soft skin of her trembling belly and then, altering his angle slightly, brought the tokan against the undersides of her breasts before striking down full on her nipples. Hysena bucked and screamed at the blow and Tarrip could see from the way her pelvis was undulating that her arousal was now almost total.

The front of her body was a uniform pink and her breath was quickening. The Holy Father judged it almost time to possess her, but first he must add a little more to Jagdig's frustration.

He instructed Hysena to once more raise her legs, this time holding them wide with her hands behind her knees. He ensured that the captive could see the full length of the slit that divided her legs before kneeing astride the smaller girl, facing her feet. He took the thick end of the tokan and fed it into her cunt. The Initiate pulled her legs as far apart as she was able, the better to facilitate the invasion of the soft leather cylinder. Working the implement ever deeper into her, Tarrip used his other hand to bend the pliant tokan into a loop until the thinner end was stroking her anus. Hysena moaned in frustration at the touch, longing for him to penetrate her there at the same time as he continued to excite her conventional opening so delightfully.

As he began to ease the thin finger of leather into her tight nether-entrance, Tarrip looked up at Jagdig. She was all but weeping in frustration, her big breasts shaking like jellies as she twisted hopelessly in the Punishment Frame, moving her hips back and forth in a desperate imitation of Hysena's movements.

When he knew Hysena to be on the very edge of orgasm, Tarrip pulled the tokan from her body and lay on his back, his twitching erection standing improbably thick and high. The girl quickly straddled him and, reaching between her legs, took the penis of the Holy Father in her hand to guide it to its destination, slipping it up herself slowly, drawing out the gorgeous sensation. As she felt her clitoris settle on the hard bone of his pubis, she began to move her hips, rising and falling only slightly, wanting to hold the whole of the huge length inside herself. The friction on her clitoris and the feel of the hands that had caused her so much agony twisting her nipples and squeezing her breasts until the pain made the tears start from her eyes brought her to a sobbing climax within seconds.

The Holy Father held himself from climaxing with difficulty as he felt the pressure of her inner muscles contracting with such wonderful strength around his prick. When she was quiet and he had himself under control, he rolled the slim body from his and stood.

He crossed to the Punishment Frame, his undiminished erection bobbing before him. The Kallinian was quiet now, perhaps guessing what was to come.

'And now, warrior, you shall have your just reward.'

She quailed at his terrible smile and closed her eyes. She felt the hot tip of his penis nuzzling at her mouth and as he pressed through her reluctantly parting lips, she could taste Hysena's secretions. She endured stoically as he filled her throat, trying not to react when he seized her ears to pull her head back and forth as he rammed himself in and out of her throat. He withdrew fully just before he came and directed seemingly endless gouts of his semen into her face. She felt the stuff, cold and slimy, running over her chin to drip onto her breasts, some of it falling saltily into her open mouth and stinging her tearful eyes.

Without pausing to wipe her, Tarrip conducted Hysena from the room, leaving Jagdig alone with her despair.

4.

Eventually, Tasnar led Xarrith on an expedition through the hidden passages of the Citadel of the True Prophet of Qalle. He had spent weeks cautiously exploring them, finding the network of passages was far more extensive than he could possibly have imagined. He quickly discovered that the aperture that had allowed him to see Princess Leel and his cousin Silka was not a lucky accident. As far as he could tell, every room in the huge building had its spy-hole, some more than one, and Tasnar learned much to make him smile about the habits of those who populated the most holy building on Qalle.

Some of the gaps had been blocked, presumably by those who occupied the room into which they had offered a view, and from the number of these Tasnar was able to make a rough estimate of the numbers who knew of the hidden network of passages. It was a very small number. Upon learning this, the young Sis Narashan became bolder in his exploration, finding many hidden doors similar to the one through which he had first seen Father Lisnan disappear.

A number of the doors led directly to the outside, leading Tasnar to think longingly of the world he had left behind. As well as passages and doors, there were secret rooms, some filled with the weapons that presumable had been used during the times of war. Others held treasures and Tasnar grimly made note never to allow Xarrith to suspect such existed, knowing full well the way his eyes lit up when he talked of his father's wealth and the manner in which he had accumulated it.

Just once had Tasnar encountered another using the secret ways, but such was his knowledge of the myriad branching passages and concealed rooms by then that it had been no task to slip safely aside until the unsuspecting figure had passed. He had caught a glimpse of the face lit by the light of a lantern and had been startled to see a serenely beautiful woman in the robe of a

Sister elder.

'By the Holy Prophet, Xari spoke true,' he whispered to himself. That very night he shared his knowledge with his friend.

Tasnar was lying at ease upon Xarrith's bed, watching the giant Kallinian pace the room in frustration.

'By the holy, hairy balls of the Prophet, what I wouldn't give for a proper woman!' Xarrith grumbled.

'Name the price you would pay, pauper,' said Tasnar.

Xarrith turned to his friend. 'Now, to have a real woman, here in this room, I would make you king of all Kallinia and give you five women to yourself.'

'Just five?' Tasnar stretched and yawned on the bed. 'That is hardly generous given the way your people breed like dogs.'

'Just one woman of my people would be enough to kill you, little warrior, and besides, I would need five thousand for myself, and then five thousand more on the morrow.' Even the thought of it was enough for his robe to grow a tent at the level of his hips.

Tasnar swung himself upright. 'Then listen to me, Xarrith of Kallinia. Tonight I will show you a glimpse of that paradise we hear so much of.'

Quickly he told Xarrith of his discovery of the passages but did no more than hint at some of the things he had seen, wanting the reality to be as delightful a surprise as it had been for him. He had little doubt that at least one of the spy-holes would yield sufficient fruit to satisfy at least part of the part of his friend's appetite.

'You must give me your most binding oath that on this foray, I am general. There is little chance of discovery, I think, but if we are discovered the consequences would be such that I would doubt our survival.'

Xarrith shrugged, his eyes glittering in anticipation. 'In battle, the risk is what makes the blood sing. Come. Let us away!'

Tasnar had found shirts and breeches of dark cloth and buskins of soft hide that would make no noise on the stone floors on one of his explorations and dressed in these, the two Acolytes, not without trepidation, entered the secret ways of the Citadel.

Tasnar showed his friend how to operate the hidden catch that caused the door to swing open. As he led the way confidently along the narrow passage, he pointed out the other doors including the ones that led to the outside, little knowing the deadly danger that this would later bring.

The first two spy-holes proved barren and Xarrith was beginning to think that Tasnar was teasing him with the hints of what he claimed to have seen. Then Tasnar put his eye to a third hole and by the way his body stiffened and from the indrawn hiss of breath, Xarrith guessed they had found their objective.

He waited impatiently behind the smaller youth in the passage and in the flickering light of the lantern he saw Tasnar slip his hand into his breeches and begin to make movements that were unmistakable. They had agreed when planning the expedition that, should they find anything worth seeing they would each have sixty breaths at the aperture, turn and turn about.

Xarrith was all but dancing with frustration and anticipation when Tasnar eventually stood upright and moved to one side. His breeches were about his knees now and he sported an erection than impressed even Xarrith.

'Make no noise, warrior, and remember — sixty breaths only!' cautioned Tasnar.

His breath already coming quickly, Xarrith applied his eye to the small hole.

There were three figures in the room. One, a bulky, powerful looking woman in the robe of a Sister elder was seated on a stool, idly swinging a long-handled tokan from one hand. She held his attention only briefly as he could now see what had made Tasnar so rapt and so hard.

Not knowing she was being observed, Sister Colya was disciplining Maris and Nephraan for some imagined lapse. The memory of how she had thrust the silk knickers into Maris had stayed with her and so delightful had she found the spectacle that she decided it was past time to repeat the experience. She decided to begin the punishment quite conventionally, seating herself on the stool and causing Maris to drape herself over her knees.

'You, Nephraan, pull up her robe.' The tall girl from the Dersis Sea had silently obeyed. Colya enjoyed having the girls undress and even punish each other, but that dratted Hysena had somehow brought all the Initiates (with the exception of Jagdig, of course) together and they lacked the disaccord within their group that could make such games so attractive to the Holy Sister.

Maris lay with her buttocks exposed to Colya's greedy eyes. She laid her hand on the soft, warm flesh, noting that the white skin held the marks of previous beatings. She ran her fingers along the crack until she encountered the plumpness of her cunt. She felt the girl wriggle as she forced a calloused finger into her, experiencing some difficulty as she was quite dry there, but even as she continued her assault, Colya felt the telltale slipperiness begin to form as Maris inevitably reacted.

Still, that was for later, she thought, and began to spank the girl, working over the surface of her bottom until it glowed a uniform red. Maris was crying quite satisfactorily when Sister Colya ordered her to stand and then to bend and hold onto her ankles, her shift thrown over her back to allow Colya to see her reddened behind and her favourite view of her sex with its fine, blonde covering of hair.

Nephraan she had strip completely before arranging her with a leg either side of Colya's own hips, her body supported uncomfortably on outstretched arms, her position allowing Colya to use both hands to beat her. As with Maris, she first ran a finger into Nephraan, finding it much easier to do so as seeing her friend being spanked had clearly aroused her. As the up-turned bottom that rested in her lap shook and trembled as she struck at it time and time again, the Holy Sister felt her own arousal growing. Her eyes went from the spread legs before her to where Maris was maintaining her own uncomfortable position, bent almost in half and holding onto her ankles. Colya saw that now there was a distinct sheen on the slightly parted labia of the Uplander; she too was responding to the treatment and to the sounds coming from Nephraan as the slaps landed on her skin and she cried and moaned as the punishment progressed.

When her hand was tingling too much to continue, Colya had Maris remove her shift and she drank in the sight of the two nude girls standing side by side.

'Now, both naughty girls will jump up and down until I say to stop.'

Resignedly, the two Initiates began the familiar ritual. Maris tried to make her movements as small and as smooth as possible, but even so her big breasts bounced and swung like bells. In a way, this was worse than being beaten, she thought. It was degrading and did nothing for her sexually. As with the others, she had come to learn that being beaten led to sexual gratification of a sort that even she in her adventurous adolescence had not experienced. She saw the lustful eyes of Sister Colya following every gyration of her breasts, straying occasionally to her sex and then to the equally naked body of Nephraan. In the first days at the Citadel, those carrying out punishment on the Initiates would practice at least a semblance of discretion with their own evidence of arousal at the sight and sounds of the lithe young bodies revealed before them, but that time had passed and now Colya had quite openly pulled up her robe to expose the great mass of hair that covered her lower belly and had the end of her tokan, thick as her wrist, pushed deep inside herself, causing the thick lips of her cunt to bulge around it.

From the corner of her eye, Nephraan could see Maris's breasts as they bounced but unlike the other girl, she found the situation stimulated her. In part, it was the anticipation of what Colya would do next to them, or have them do to each other. When she was ordered to actually take part in the punishment of one of her peers, she found it hard not to be over enthusiastic as she wielded the tokan or whichever implement she had been given. It was not that she wanted to cause pain to the girls whom she now regarded as friends, but she found that inflicting pain on them, having them helpless before her, caused in her such a heady feeling of power that on more than one occasion she had come without even the need to touch herself. Now she could feel the delicious tendrils of fear running through her as she watched the bulky figure of Colya using the tokan on herself, her face growing red as she neared her climax.

The woman came with a series of grunts, her eyes squeezed shut. The two girls did not pause in their jumps, knowing that even though the Holy Sister seemed not to be paying attention, should the sound of feet slapping on the cold stone floor cease or even falter, the retribution would be all the greater. They both knew from past experience that this was one of Colya's favourite games and that she could keep them jumping until they fell to the ground in exhaustion, at which point she would mercilessly whip the faller until she dragged herself once more to her feet.

So it came as something of a surprise when the Sister elder told them to be still as soon as she had recovered from her orgasm. They saw the look of cruel excitement in her eyes and wondered what was to happen now.

When Colya produced the squares of bright red cloth, the two girls looked at each other in puzzlement. It was only when the Holy Sister gave one of her crude chuckles and they saw that she had wrapped one of the scarves about two fingers that it dawned on them how the cloth was to be employed.

'Oh no,' Maris breathed and blushed red at the memory.

'Oh yes, eh? You know rules of next game, Maris Ap Stuvin,' Colya cackled in delight at the distressed reaction. 'You, Nephraan, bend over with hands on stool.'

Moving reluctantly, the girl took her position, knowing without being told to place her legs wide apart.

'Now you, Maris, you know what to do with scarf.'

'Me? But, Sister Colya, I beg, Ahh!'

Colya did not wait to hear what the Initiate would beg. Moving with a swiftness that startled the horrified Maris she stepped forward and delivered an open-handed slap to her breast. 'Be quiet and do as told, eh?' she hissed.

Trying to stifle her sobs, Maris knelt behind Nephraan and took the proffered scarf. She looked between the wide-spread legs of her friend. She could not remember how many times she had admired, kissed and fondled that pretty cunt, she had even at times slid a finger on two into her anus, bringing pleasure to both of them, but she felt no pleasure at the task now set for her.

Tentatively, she managed to introduce a corner of the cloth into the tight opening. She remembered that Colya had used oil to ease the way, and that it had been the very finest silk that had been forced into her own bottom, but she had no such lubrication and this scarf was of rough cotton. She turned to look at the Holy Sister who was again pushing the handle of the tokan into herself.

'Forgive me, Holy Sister, but is there any oil?' She cringed, half expecting another blow, but Colya simple gave her evil chuckle again.

'Too dry, eh? Well, big girls like you know where best to get slippery stuff to help cloth up bum.' She smirked at Maris, sticking out her tongue and wriggled it crudely.

Maris pulled the corner of cloth from Nephraan, feeling the shudder that ran through her as she did and placed a hand on the small of her back, pushing down to make the tall girl push her behind out further. She bent forward and applied her fingers to the soft bulge of Nephraan's sex and almost at once felt the slippery juices begin to secrete as she stimulated her. She felt the other girl respond, pushing onto the probing fingers and soon she was wet enough for Maris to slide four fingers into

111

her. Taking up the piece of red cotton cloth, she pushed it into the now slick opening until just a scrap of the material protruded from Nephraan's vagina.

Despite the humiliating position she had been forced to adopt, Nephraan was growing excited at the attention she was getting from Maris. She felt the cloth being pushed into her and then shuddered as the experienced fingers moved to her clitoris. The rough texture of the cloth inside her felt strange, a new feeling for her that served to excite her even further. Soon she felt the familiar tingle deep within her as her climax approached and she could not help herself from groaning as Maris squeezed her clitoris. Momentarily she forgot that Colya was watching and instinctively pressed her own hand to that of Maris.

'Ahh, yes, Maris, that is, mmm, so good.' she panted, 'draw the cloth from me as I come... Yessss!'

Maris did as her friend asked, pulling the scarf out of her with a single, long tug. She was surprised that Nephraan had reached orgasm so fast and with such intensity and felt the first tremble of her own excitement as she thought of how it would soon be her bending over the stool...

The scrap of cloth was now soaked with Nephraan's juices and, having first used her fingers to lubricate and widen the way, Maris found it a far more simple task than it had been to force it into her smaller opening.

'Good,' said Sister Colya, standing and crossing to inspect Nephraan more closely. She took hold of the protruding piece of cloth and tugged at it. 'Now I have way of catching you when you run from Holy Sister, eh?' She roared with laughter at her wit and the two Initiates managed a dutiful chuckle. She slapped Nephraan on the bottom. 'Now, stand so big-tit Uplander can bend and show off pretty cunt.'

Trembling in a mixture of fear and anticipation, Maris swapped places with Nephraan. She bent well forward and pushed out her behind, wanting to make access as easy as possible, hoping that the sensation would be less unpleasant if she did. At once, she felt Nephraan's fingers on her flesh, stroking along the length of her exposed slit. She put from her mind the thought of the Holy Sister, whose eyes she could almost feel burning into her, and tried to relax to the pleasant caresses. She felt herself grow wet and her nipples hardened as Nephraan eased first one then another finger into her and began to pump them in and out. Maris began to rock in time to the motion, twisting her hips in a corkscrewing action, surprised that she was enjoying the attentions of her friend almost as if they were alone. She gasped with pleasure when she felt a hot tongue lick her clitoris and when the fingers were withdrawn from her vagina she opened her legs even wider, now actually impatient to feel the scarf push inside her.

Nephraan arranged the cloth over Maris's up-turned bottom and with her thumb, began to work it into her vagina. She felt the other girl jerk as the rough material rasped against her moist, sensitive skin and heard the gasp of excitement as she forced the scarf into her. She added to the already abundant lubrication by running her tongue along the slit between the widespread thighs, even using her tongue to push more of the red cloth into her. As the last of it disappeared into the depths of her cunt, Nephraan worked her little finger into the smaller orifice, both to add to Maris's clearly growing excitement and to ease the way for what was to follow.

With the fingers of one hand gently rubbing at her clitoris and now three from the other deep in Maris's anus, Nephraan gripped the protruding sliver of cloth between her teeth and, when she felt Maris begin to shudder in orgasm, drew her head back, pulling the soaked scarf from the depths of her vagina.

'Now stick it up arse.' Colya's crude voice was shaky with lust. She had the thick handle of the tokan as far up herself as she could force it and was rotating it between her palms, spinning and twisting it in her cunt.

Maris had her spread legs facing the Holy Sister who could see her abundant juices now coated her inner thighs and spread over the plump bulge of her open cunt, the fine blonde hairs now slicked to the curves making her appear nearly as bald as little Silka. Colya moved slightly to one side, allowing her to see the big, dangling breasts of the Uplander, watching them ripple and bounce as the shudders of orgasm took the Initiate.

Working quickly, Nephraan fed the scarf into Maris's anus, using her fingers to continue to caress her labia, keeping her at a high level of arousal. When nearly all the cloth was hidden, Nephraan took the chance of taking her swollen clitoris between her lips and nibbling on it.

'Ahh, wonderful, my darling, so good...' Maris wailed as the second climax shook her frame. As it had the first time, the cloth inside her bottom made her feel full and bloated, but perhaps because of all she had been through since, she was able to appreciate this as a new sexual adventure rather than as the humiliation it had been the first time.

When she had recovered, Maris stood next to Nephraan before Sister Colya who had taken her seat on the stool and was flicking the tokan, making it hiss through the air as she regarded the two naked Initiates before her...

Xarrith became aware of the impatient thumb that was digging into his kidney with increasing force and reluctantly took his eye from the spy-hole.

'I would have though even a Kallinian could number to sixty,' Tasnar grumbled.

'I am sorry, little man, but even the Living Prophet and all His mighty hoard could not have dragged me from such a sight. Have you ever seen such a thing?'

Without answering Tasnar pushed forward and glued his eye to the hole. In the room the two girls were running round Sister Colya who flicked at the quivering buttocks as they passed. The blonde girl's magnificent breasts bounced as she ran, and he found the sight of the flashes of red cloth that protruded from their behinds quite captivating. As he watched, hand automatically going to his stiffening prick, he wondered if a liaison could be arranged. During his explorations, he had discovered the Initiates' dormitory and one of the secret doors close by. The risk would be appalling but the reward......Xarrith was right, he reflected. Risk did make the blood sing, but what risk! He did not know what punishment would follow discovery on such an adventure, but had not been joking when he suggested to Xarrith that he feared for their very survival. His researches into the Citadel had offered hints of people entering the forbidding walls never to be seen or heard of again. Was a few hours of ecstasy worth possible death? As he watched the taller of the two naked girls, now lying on her back with her legs held high and wide by the one with the magnificent breasts and the Holy Sister bringing the tokan down directly on her spread vagina, he almost thought that it was.

As she plied the tokan between the open legs of Nephraan and heard her shrill scream as the whippy leather bit into her swollen labia, Sister Colya was wondering whether to order one (or both!) of the Initiates to lick her soaking cunt. With a grimace, she decided against this, knowing from experience that, while all of them would do this delightful service for each other, they hated to do it for their Sister elder. Or at least this Sister elder. She suspected that they showed no such reticence with Marja and felt a bitter pang of envy at the thought, bringing the tokan down with all her strength in her frustration.

Nephraan screamed even louder as the cruel device once again bit into her exposed sex.

The sound of the scream came clearly through the wall to the ears of the fascinated Tasnar. Unlike Xarrith who had seen punishments carried out on his people at home, in Sis Narash the thought of treating another person in such a barbaric manner was anathema. He found the sight deeply shocking but even more exciting. Once again he applied his eye to the small hole in the ancient wall.

The two young women were now on their knees, bottoms high, the beguiling scraps of red scarf that had been forced into their anuses drawing the eye like targets. As Tasnar watched, he saw the Sister elder take hold of the pieces of cloth that showed and slowly draw them from their unusual hiding places. Again, he could hear the high keening of the Initiates as they felt the long, slow drag of the scarves rasping against their most sensitive membranes. The youth was surprised to see that each of the girls had a hand between the legs of the other and from what he could see of the expression on their faces, it seemed that they were experiencing at least as much pleasure as pain at the sensation. His own orgasm hit him and he could not hold back the long groan of pleasure as the seed pulsed from him.

'It seems that the performance is ended,' he said to Xarrith as he watched the two young women gingerly pulling their white shifts over their abused bodies.

'Ah well, this was more entertainment than hearing Brother Keem discourse upon the duty of honour,' Xarrith said, disappointment in his voice. He was still hard and had hoped for a second view of the beautiful Initiates being so excitingly used. Even if he could not be there to take part, just watching had given him far more satisfaction that he had ever gained by using one of the Ercli women.

'So, my lord general, do we now return to our cell or is there more diversion to be had in these dusty passages?'

Tasnar considered. They had been away from their own part of the Citadel for perhaps an hour and the chance of them being missed during so short a time was slight. They were expected to be present at evening prayers and their absence could lead to some irritating punishment such as cleaning the kitchens, but such was the reputation Xarrith had gained, even this was unlikely.

'I think our expedition may press further into enemy territory.'

The diminutive youth led the towering Kallinian

along the passages he had memorised, being careful to skirt the rooms where treasures had been secreted against who knew what future need. They climbed a tight staircase that spiralled up into the darkness, Tasnar cautioning Xarrith against the treacherously narrow steps.

At the top they paused, both panting a little from the steepness of the climb.

Suddenly Tasnar held out a warning hand and put a finger urgently to his lips. Xarrith froze, breath held and eyes darting about the shadowed passage.

For endless moments Tasnar stood with his head cocked to one side, a look of intense concentration on his face.

He relaxed with a quiet sigh. 'It was nothing. My ears play tricks on us. Come, we are nearly there.'

Eagerly, Xarrith followed Tasnar along the passage. Had his mind been in less of a sexual daydream of nubile flesh being forced into all manner of exposing positions, being penetrated by a fascinating variety of implements, he might have been more alert to his surroundings. From the time he could walk, he had learned to hunt and track through the forests and mountains of his homeland and thus was far better equipped than his colleague to sense danger. But the combination of arousal and the mental stance that saw him treat Tasnar as leader of the expedition meant that he was less alert than he perhaps could have been.

'Ah. This is the place.' Tasnar had stopped and was bending to peer through another hole.

'Begging the pardon of the general, but his humble slave begs to remind him that it is my turn.'

'Go just beyond me. There is another place from which to observe.'

Xarrith looked and saw that there was a narrow shaft of light crossing the passage a few yards from the first.

'What is this place?'

'It is where the Initiates sleep.'

'I hope that is not what they are doing.' Xarrith peered through the chink and waited for his eye to adjust to the sudden brightness.

The Initiates were not sleeping. There were three of them in the room, all dressed, to the intense disappointment of Xarrith, in the white shifts of their calling. Two of them Tasnar recognised as his cousin Silka and the fully-figured Princess Leel. The third he did not know, but he was at once taken by her poise and the way her short-cropped black hair allowed her almost black eyes to be seen to perfection. This girl was combing the red hair of the princess, hair that fell almost to the level of her buttocks.

At his own spy-hole, Xarrith too was enjoying the sight of the three Initiates. Even though they were robed, simply the sight of pretty young girls was a delight after the emotionless Ercli women. For him, the Sis Narashan held little appeal — not enough meat on her — and among his people any excess weight was seen as a sign that that person was neglecting the duty of a warrior to be at the peak of physical fitness at all times, so the plump figure of Leel slightly affronted him. Although, he thought to himself, a man could drown happily in her tits.

It was the third figure in the dormitory that held his eye. The motions she was making as she brushed the long hair of the red-head allowed Xarrith to see tantalising glances of her trim figure through the thin stuff of her shift. As she lifted her arm he could see the perfect silhouette of a small but perfect breast, its up-turned nipple clearly outlined. Where the cloth tightened when she bent, her firm, rounded buttocks showed, the cleft dividing them a darker, wholly enticing shadow. As he watched she stood and for a moment seemed to stare directly into his eyes. Xarrith froze. Her steady gaze seemed to penetrate his very soul as he looked into the infinite depths of those black eyes. She turned away and the spell was broken, but something had changed in Xarrith.

Tasnar heard the hiss of indrawn breath and frowned. He could see nothing in the dormitory that should cause such a reaction in his friend. He took his eye from the aperture and walked the few steps to where Xarrith was standing, clearly rapt, his eye glued to the hole in the wall, and tapped him on the shoulder.

A shudder ran through Xarrith and he straightened slowly. Even in the gloomy light of the passage Tasnar could see the strange look in his eye.

'What revelation have you seen, Xarrith?' he asked curiously.

'Know you those women?' Xarrith knew that Tasnar had met many of the gentry of Qalle.

'Aye. One is my cousin, the one of the long red hair is Princess Leel of Calith.'

Xarrith grabbed Tasnar by the neck of his jerkin. 'The other. Who is the other?' His voice held such a note of urgency and his eyes such a fanatical glitter that Tasnar wondered if the girl were a mortal enemy of Kallinia. Then a more probable exclamation came to him and he began to smile as he gently removed the agitated warrior's hand from his shirt.

'How easily is a warrior conquered,' he murmured sardonically. 'A single glimpse of a pretty bosom and a pert arse and Kallinia is on its knees.'

For a moment he thought he had goaded Xarrith too far and took a step back at the glare of fury and bunched fist that he suddenly faced. He held himself tensed, ready to defend himself and then Xarrith relaxed, his shoulders drooping and his raised hand falling to his side.

'Forgive me, brother, but I beg you by all you hold holy, tell me of her.'

Tasnar shrugged. 'I have not met her but she has the look of the Southern Roads and that people are headed by the House Macarydias. I would hazard she is daughter to the Lord Protector and his wife the Princess Lissa of Argo. This is but a guess, and in answer to your next question, no, it would not be good to go in and present yourself to her this moment.'

Xarrith could not help his smile. 'Even my thoughts are not safe from you, Tasnar.' He once again put his eye to the hole. The unknown Initiate had finished the hair of the plump girl and had seated herself on one of the rude beds, her legs curled beneath her in that manner no man could imitate. Xarrith could see the sweet curve of her hip outlined beneath the cotton of her shift and her position had caused the material to rise up, allowing him to see her legs to the knee.

Tasnar heard him sigh again and grinned. 'Come, O fallen warrior. There is little sport here. It is time we were gone, and besides, I doubt you capable of seeing aught but big black eyes and shrivelled tits.'

'They are not shrive...!' Xarrith caught himself and made a helpless gesture with his hands. 'Enough. Tasnar, if you love me, tease me no more.'

'I think I needs must share your love from this moment. Come on. If you wish, close your eyes and I shall lead you by the hand that you may see your love before you.' Tasnar clapped the bigger youth as high up on his back as he could reach and led the way back to their own quarters.

They trudged in silence along the quiet stone corridors.

'Tasnar?' Xarrith asked eventually when they paused for the Sis Narashan to take his bearings, 'could it be possible to meet them? I mean, is the risk any greater than that which we have already taken?'

Tasnar considered the question carefully. Truth to tell, being found in the company of women would probably be judged less harshly than being found in these passages. It must be known that some of the Acolytes made sport with the Erclis and the Initiates clearly felt there was little risk in sharing each others' favours. If he could catch Silka alone, perhaps...

'I must think on it. There may be a way, but it will possibly not be soon.'

Xarrith growled deep in his throat. 'What you have shown me tonight has been a wondrous revelation and I thank you from my very heart, but by the aching balls of the Prophet, my desire for a real woman is even greater.'

'There is one behind you.' The voice was low but

with a quality that carried clearly in the quiet of the passage.

Xarrith was the first to react, spinning on his heel and falling instinctively into a defensive stance. What he saw caused his knees to buckle.

'It is... you.' The blood ran from his face as he confronted the dream woman who had abducted him and seduced him and who had haunted his sleep on so many nights since.

Tasnar also recognised her from the glimpse he had caught during his earlier explorations. This time she was not walking serenely past him, her gentle face haloed by the light of a hooded lantern. This time she was standing with her hands on her slim hips and a strange light burning in her eyes, a look on her face that would have quelled a battle charge.

Sister Maria said nothing for some minutes, just stood looking at the two appalled Acolytes whilst maintaining her severe expression and gently tapping the toes of one foot on the stone floor. 'So,' she said eventually, 'Sis Narash and Kallinia have penetrated the secret defences of the Citadel. What think you will be the reaction of the Council of Elders when they learn of this?' Her voice was calm and totally without emotion, a thing Tasnar found more disconcerting than if she had been angry. He looked over at Xarrith, but the warrior was on his knees, gulping like a landed fish and he could expect no help from that quarter.

'Is it certain they shall find out, Holy Sister?'

Maria raised her eyebrows in surprise. The reply was impressive for one so young. She had no intention of telling the council, knowing that she would have little chance of saving these two were she to do so. Her main concern was in learning if all the Acolytes now knew of the passages. She had learned almost at once when Tasnar had discovered the secret ways and had been monitoring his explorations closely. It had been her intention to confront him some time ago but on the one time she could have done so, she had pretended not to know he was there and had hurried past to enjoy an assignation with a lusty young priest.

Now she was cursing her hot blood for making her lose her normally iron control. She did not doubt her ability to keep one Acolyte in harness — there would even be delightful bonuses by the methods she would employ — but six of them?

'My duty is to the Holy Prophet of Qalle and to His living representatives. As, I may add Tasnar of Sis Narash, is yours and your duty does not involve lurking in the hidden passages.'

'Forgive us, Holy Sister, but I came upon them by accident and as there is no mention of their being forbidden in the Acolytical Canon, we felt there would be no harm in indulging our curiosity.'

Sister Maria had to fight back a smile at another clever reply. 'Then this is the first time you have come this way?'

'Indeed, Sister,' said Tasnar, the light of innocence bright in his intelligent eyes. 'Though I fear we have come too far and are lost.'

She ignored the lies, considering her options. 'Follow,' she said abruptly and led the way to her own quarters, stepping out briskly. Xarrith, still in a daze from first having been so smitten by the young girl he had briefly observed in the dormitory and then by the encounter with his dream woman, stumbled along behind her and Tasnar, his mind a blank.

Sister Maria opened a door that led directly into her room. Xarrith followed Tasnar in and at once recognised it. He felt his head pounding and his prick swell at the memory. His eyes were drawn automatically to the woman dressed as a Sister elder and he wondered for a moment if he had indeed dreamed the whole thing; surely such a woman who looked so clearly pure and holy could not possibly have done such things to him, could not have implored him to spank her...

He saw that Sister Maria was looking directly at him. Her eyes held his and something in their serene depths told him with utter certainty that she remembered that night as well as he did himself.

Maria cleared her throat and the spell was broken. 'So what are we to do with you?' she mused aloud. 'By my sworn duty, I should bring you before the Holy Father. You both know this, do you not?'

Tasnar licked his lips. 'As you say, Sister Maria, but I appeal to your mercy. Regardless of any punishment that the Holy Father may mete out, it is certain that Xarrith and myself would be sent from the Citadel to return in disgrace to our people. Our lives would be ruined for this harmless prank.'

Maria smiled inwardly. The answer was perfect, but she could not capitulate at once. 'So you are suggesting that my sense of mercy should be elevated above my duty to the Living Prophet?'

'But the Prophet wrote that mercy is the highest of virtues, particularly to the truly contrite,' Tasnar replied, doing his best to look truly contrite.

'Your knowledge of the scriptures does you credit, Tasnar. Very well, I shall keep your transgression from Father Tarrip on this occasion, but only on this occasion.' Relieved smiles broke out on the faces of the acolytes 'But you must agree to submit to such punishment as I think fit, here in my room.'

Tasnar glanced at Xarrith before replying and saw his slight nod. 'Thank you, Sister. My colleague and I are yours to command.'

At the words, Maria felt a surge of excitement, her mind conjuring with the images that immediately filled her mind, the thought of just how she could command these two fine examples of Qalle youth to fulfill her every whim, her every need, her every fantasy. Then another thought struck her; did Tasnar know that his words would have such an effect on her? Surely not. Although his people were famed throughout Qalle as mediators and diplomats, Tasnar could not possibly have the skill at his age to manipulate her. She shook her head to dispel the disturbing idea.

Maria crossed the small room and from a high shelf lifted down her favourite instrument of punishment. Compared to the tokans that Tarrip spent such long hours constructing, this was a very simple thing, merely a rolled cylinder of pliable leather, quite soft to the touch, as long as her forearm and the thickness of three fingers. She liked it because it could bring pleasure as well as punishment and this appealed to her sense of justice. Countless were the times that she had used it to bring a crying, quivering Initiate to a screaming orgasm moments after the girl had been howling in pain. And if there was no girl to be punished, Maria would, in the secrecy of her bed, use it on herself.

Until now, she had not had the opportunity to use it on a member of the opposite sex.

Xarrith eyed the stubby whip apprehensively. He had felt enormous relief when Tasnar had successfully pleaded their case, but knowing that he must now be humiliated — to worry about the pain Maria seemed about to inflict was beneath his contempt — left him uneasy. His entire upbringing had taught him that he and his people were the dominant ones, and now not only must he overcome this conditioning, he must allow a _woman_ to chastise him.

Tasnar had mixed feelings about the ordeal he was to face. He was naturally inquisitive, always seeking to expand his knowledge of all things. And from his observations of the Initiates, who received punishment clearly far beyond anything meted out in the male side of the Citadel, it seemed that punishment could indeed lead to pleasure.

'Remove your garments.' The sound of Maria's soft voice broke him from his reverie. Tasnar sensed that Xarrith was about to protest and quickly began to disrobe, hoping his friend would follow his example and not worsen the situation. After a short pause, Xarrith reluctantly began to tug at his shirt.

Maria struggled to keep her arousal from showing at the sight of the two fine examples of Qallian youth who now stood naked before her. The comparison between their two bodies served to enhance the spectacle. Xarrith, his massive frame and bulging muscles, Tasnar seeming tiny beside him but finely shaped and carrying not an iota of fat. She remembered how much she had enjoyed Xarrith on that memorable previous occasion, but now he was not drugged and the knowledge that this giant warrior who could snap her like a twig was totally under her power was heady indeed. Her eyes dropped to his crotch, admiring the tight bulge of his testicles and the length of his penis. Even in its current flaccid state it was still impressive and the memory of how it had appeared fully erect was enough to start the moistness between her own legs.

'Turn and bend,' she commanded, 'and seize your ankles.' Out of their vision, she was able to take her time in admiring the two pairs of firm buttocks presented to her. Tasnar, she saw, had a behind as slim as an immature girl. She ran a hand over the tight flesh, much firmer and resilient than any girl. A shudder ran through him as she did and she clearly saw his balls tighten in arousal. Knowing they could not see her, Maria opened a fold in her robe and pressed the warm leather of the thick whip to herself, rubbing it along the length of her sex, pressing it hard to her swollen clitoris. For a while she indulged herself, running the end of the whip into her vagina whilst enjoying the sight of the revealed bodies before her. Only when she saw Xarrith shift his feet, perhaps wondering when the punishment was to begin did she withdraw the implement from herself and bring it around with a vicious hiss to impact solidly across Xarrith's bare buttocks.

As the leather bit into his flesh, Xarrith could not prevent a grunt escaping his tense throat. The pain that flared through him was not great, but was made ten times worse by the knowledge that he could not retaliate. The blows rained down and Xarrith began to experience a sensation that far outstripped any pain. To his eternal humiliation, he realised that his body was betraying him.

He was growing an erection.

Maria could not see the shame of the warrior, standing as she was behind him. She was finding the sensation of beating a male for the first time an exhilarating one. To date, she had only ever beaten the softer, more curved behinds of young women and although these experiences had been delightful, this new experience and the certain knowledge of what would soon follow was bringing the Holy Sister to a state of enormous arousal. When beating one (or more!) of the Initiates, it was not only the sensation of power over the victim that aroused her, but the sight of the naked body, the exciting revelation of the vulnerable sex exposed between parted legs, the way the lips of the vagina engorged and reddened, the indication of the first frisson of arousal in the girl as those lips became shiny as her juices began to flow.

The thought of what was between Xarrith's legs was slowly driving her into a frenzy and the tokan blurred and hissed through the air as her blows became harder and faster. The very firmness of the abused flesh served to stoke her excitement ever higher. Women were soft in their erogenous zones and when punishing buttocks or breasts the impact of tokan or hand tended to be absorbed, but the body of this youth had a hardness that caused her implement to bounce from the impact, jarring her arm as she went about her business.

Eventually, Maria was exhausted. The tokan fell from her hand and she flexed her aching arm and shoulder as she admired her handiwork. After his initial grunt, Xarrith had borne his punishment in absolute silence and had maintained his undignified position without shifting an inch. As she studied his now bruised and reddened buttocks, Maria again slipped her hand into her robe. Simply the act of punishing the warrior youth had bought her to the brink of orgasm and now she found herself so wet that she was able to push four fingers deeply into herself. Biting her lip to suppress her moans, she ground her thumb against her swollen clitoris and felt her knees give as the sensation took her.

Determined to bear his punishment as a warrior should, Xarrith maintained his uncomfortable position as he heard the Holy Sister cross the cell. The sound of liquid being poured made him suddenly aware of his own thirst. He was disgusted with himself for being unable to control his body. Bent double as he was, he could feel the rigid length of his penis pressing against his belly. Although hot irons would not have made him admit it to any person, to himself he had to admit that the situation had aroused him hugely. His mind had inevitably gone back to the magical, dream-like night when she had seduced him and his balls were aching even more than his abused behind with the desire to repeat the experience.

Maria drank deeply of the wine before feeling able to speak without her voice shaking and betraying her excitement. She turned again to enjoy the sight of the two naked youths, titillated that soon she would instruct Xarrith to face her, wondering if he would be erect. She could see that his balls were swollen, the sac of his scrotum drawn tight and shiny in the nest of his jet-black pubic hair. She toyed with the idea of having him remain in position until she had dealt with Tasnar, but could contain her curiosity no longer.

'Stand, Xarrith. Stand and face me.'

Xarrith had been almost certain that this command would come and had considered using his hands to cover himself if it did. But that would have shown weakness, shame even.

'At your command, Holy Sister!' His voice was defiant as he stood, turning on his heel to face her and gripping his hands behind his back, thrusting his hips slightly to demonstrate pride in his body rather than shame.

It took all of Maria's self-control and years of training to suppress her gasp, but she could not prevent her eyes widening at the sight. She had known him to be big from her previous experience, but now, his mind not fuddled by drugs and given the extra stimulus of the beating, he was enormous. Tarrip had been the biggest man she had encountered so far, but Xarrith in his current state dwarfed the Holy Father.

The Kallinian saw her reaction and smiled inwardly. It seemed likely that he would soon have his revenge for the humiliation he had suffered at the hands of this woman. In his mind he saw her begging for his attentions, moaning her needs to him as he worked on her fine body. His prick pulsed at the thought and both he and the Holy Sister saw the single drop of clear liquid that suddenly appeared on the plum-sized tip.

Tasnar had been holding his uncomfortable position for a long time now and his back had begun to cramp. He had of course heard Xarrith being beaten and remembered the story of how the Holy Sister had seduced his friend. When the sound of thrashing ceased, he tensed himself to receive his own punishment. When nothing happened and the silence in the cell stretched, he could contain his curiosity no longer and cautiously turned his head. From the corner of his eye he could see that Xarrith was massively erect. Even though he had observed the phenomenon on a number of occasions when the two of them had amused themselves with the Ercli women, he could not but be impressed, even a little jealous, by this current display.

When Sister Maria did not admonish him for failing to maintain his uncomfortable pose, Tasnar was emboldened to turn his head further. Now he could see the Holy Sister, see that her eyes were wide and riveted on Xarrith's sex. From his low eye-line, he could see that her robe was not wrapped fully around her waist as normal. With delight he saw that he could see almost the full length of her shapely legs, and yes, even a glimpse of her pubic hair! He strained to turn his head even further, but the movement was too much for his awkward position and suddenly he lost his balance.

His stumble broke the spell between Xarrith and Maria. The Holy Sister took a deep breath to compose herself. She took in the lean, naked frame of the Sis-

Narashan — such a contrast with the warrior boy — and noted that he too was now fully erect. As Tasnar scrambled to his feet and stood next to Xarrith, Sister Maria decided that his beating could wait. Not only was the ache in her arm and shoulder still fierce, there was a much more urgent ache lower down her body; an ache that must be assuaged.

'Well, Master Tasnar. I find that the effort of disciplining your colleague has exhausted me for the time being. I needs must find another way of ensuring that the lesson of this day remains in your mind.'

Before Tasnar could react or even wonder what form of punishment she had in mind for him, Sister Maria had sunk to her knees before him and enfolded the full length of his prick with her warm, moist mouth. He gasped at he exquisite sensation, and again as he felt her teeth scraping gently along his rigid flesh. With an involuntary movement, Tasnar began to thrust with his hips, pressing himself more deeply into the mouth of the Holy Sister. He felt himself on the verge of orgasm.

Feeling his penis beginning to pulse in her throat, Sister Maria withdrew her mouth, not wanting him to come yet. With finger and thumb she squeezed him tightly just below the glans, holding him until his orgasm receded. She noticed that Xarrith had been unable to resist the temptation of rubbing himself at the sight of what she was doing to his friend.

All thoughts of dominating this woman had fled from Xarrith's mind when she had taken Tasnar into her mouth. He remembered with almost painful vividness the time she had taken him in that manner and was ready to forgo his very birthright if only she would do so again.

The Sister elder wiped her mouth delicately on a sleeve of her robe as she rose from her pleasant task. She stood facing the two youths who were almost quivering in eagerness, their hard pricks standing proudly from their bodies.

Watching their faces, Maria slowly parted her robe, exposing her lower body. She saw their eyes widen at the sight and to her amusement each of them stole a hand to their erections. Wanting to encourage them, she touched herself, brushing her fingers along the slit of her sex, parting the lips that were becoming slick with her own growing arousal.

'Well, Tasnar,' she said, 'perhaps you would do me the honour of returning the favour I did for you?'

With alacrity, the youth knelt at her feet and nuzzled at her sex, drawing in the fragrant scent of her. He felt quite awe-struck as he gently touched her hot flesh with the very tip of his tongue; this was, after all, one of the most holy women in the entire Citadel.

Tasnar felt her shiver as he ran his tongue between the lips of her sex. Perhaps unusually for a man, he enjoyed giving this form of pleasure to a woman. An older cousin, one who had initiated him into the mysteries and pleasures of sex, had tutored him in the convoluted folds and lips within lips of the female fount of pleasure and now he remembered the lesson, using his fingers to delicately draw back the little cowl that covered Maria's clitoris. He was rewarded with a gasp of pleasure from her as he pressed his tongue against her most sensitive spot and when he ran a gentle finger into the soaking depths of her cunt he at once felt the muscles of her vagina contract around the questing digit as the first orgasm took her.

Xarrith was all but shaking with frustrated desire as he watched Tasnar working on the Holy Sister. He was torn between the almost overwhelming urge to bring himself to a climax and wanting to wait in the hope that she would allow him into her body for his release.

Through the haze of her lust, Maria enjoyed the sight of his inner battle, seeing him frantically rubbing himself and then snatching his hand away from that huge member, leaving it jutting out towards her like a beckoning arm. To stoke his fires ever higher, she lifted her robe up her body, exposing her breasts with their stiff nipples to his gaze. She pulled the garment over her head and dropped it to the floor and stood naked in the cell, her legs spread to allow Tasnar easy access to her cunt. Teasing the warrior further, Maria ran her hands over her body, squeezing her breasts out towards him, rubbing the nipples with her thumbs. His groan echoed her own as Tasnar's skilled tongue and fingers brought her to another climax.

She eased her hips away from Tasnar and gently disengaged the arms that he had folded about her hips. It had been a most satisfactory beginning. The two climaxes she had enjoyed she regarded as a pleasant foretaste of what was to come.

'You are very skilled, for one so young, Tasnar.' She smiled down at the youth who was still on his knees before her and stroked his hair.

'Thank you, Holy Sister. Should there be any other way in which I may be of service... and Xarrith, of course, will also be willing to do your bidding I am certain.'

They both looked at the Kallinian. His face was suffused with the effort of containing himself. To Maria, buoyed up by her lust, it seemed that if anything his penis had grown even more huge.

'Well, Xarrith, your companion in crime offers a fine testimonial on your behalf. Speaks he true?'

Xarrith could not trust himself to speak and could barely comprehend her words such was his state. He nodded his head vehemently, understanding at least that now, it was to be his turn.

Maria crossed the cell, glancing at the room reflected in the large mirror. She enjoyed the sight of her own naked body, breasts firm, nipples still erect and the gleam of her thighs, wet with her own juices and Tasnar's saliva below the matted hair of her mons. She saw the two Acolytes whispering together, two of the most beautifully formed youths she had seen. They were both still fully erect, and the sight of those two fine weapons jerked her out of her reverie.

Stooping, she lifted the lid of an ornately carved chest that stood at the foot of her bed. From it she took a small glass bottle in which a viscous liquid moved sluggishly. As she drew the glass stopper, a pungent, musky smell pervaded the cell, an odour that immediately filled the nostrils and invaded the brains of the two eager Acolytes.

'Come, Xarrith. Lie here on my bed.' The Holy Sister had poured a little of the unguent into the palm of her hand. The youth did as he was bid, trembling with excitement, his penis twitching.

Maria could see that he was on the cusp of orgasm even before she touched him and knew that she would have to use all her skill to prevent him coming as soon as she did. She wrapped both hands, one above the other, now slippery with the musky oil, about his prick and began to squeeze. Her hands enclosed no more than half of the length of him and her fingers could not meet about his girth. She dared not rub him but simply increased the pressure on the hard, hot column of flesh.

Xarrith himself had known himself on the verge and felt the first pulse in his balls as her hands enfolded him. His eyes screwed shut but to his surprise the expected release did not occur. Instead he felt her hands tighten inexorably. As the pressure increased, his climax retreated.

Maria maintained the pressure for as long as she could and with her full strength until her hands began to cramp. She felt him relax a little and his erection soften as she forced the blood from the shaft. She maintained her grip until she was sure he was back in control of himself and then released him.

She stood before him, allowing herself to take on the look of the wanton.

'How would you take my body, Xarrith of Kallinia?' She licked her lips, staring into his eyes. 'You would use my mouth, perhaps, or,' pushing her breasts together, 'perhaps place yourself between these baubles?' Maria rubbed her breasts until they gleamed with oil, enjoying the silky feel. Her waist was on a level with his head and she planted her legs wide. 'Or here, perhaps, warrior. Would you like to go where my fingers go?' As she spoke, the Holy Sister peeled open the lips of her sex and pushed two fingers of each hand into herself, pulling the opening wide.

Xarrith stared into her depths and growled deep in his throat. She turned, presenting her buttocks to his view, then bent to allow him to see her vagina from that angle. She pulled her buttocks apart and rolled her hips.

Again Xarrith growled. 'I am at the command of the Holy Sister,' he managed to say. The smell of the musk was affecting his mind, bringing him to a state of heightened awareness. He could hear the blood thundering in his ears, feel his prick hard as iron as he touched it delicately, taking care not to lose control. As the holy woman displayed herself he could smell her musk, mingling with and even enhancing the sensations in his head.

Coming upright, Maria turned to face the figure on the bed. She lifted his hand from his prick, replacing it with her own. This time she dared to move her hand on him, anointing him with the oil and marvelling once more at the hardness and length. Then she joined him on the bed, rolling on top of him, feeling the length of his body, the firm muscles of his chest and belly, pressing up at her. She kissed him fiercely, pushing her tongue deeply into his mouth. His arms went about her, crushing her body to his until she could hardly breathe. She felt the rigid length of his prick trapped between their bodies, felt it hot and moving as they pressed their hips together. Maria lifted her hips to free it and, reaching down between their bodies, pushed it down until it sprang between her parted legs. Now she could feel it rubbing against her cunt and she pushed back to increase the pressure, working her clitoris against the hard shaft and feeling the delightful rasp of his pubic hair against her most sensitive part.

Freeing herself with difficulty from the powerful arms of the young warrior, the Holy Sister sat up, straddling him. She took his prick in one hand, parted herself with the other and began to feed him into her.

She lowered herself slowly, drawing out the sensation. Xarrith's prick seemed never-ending, more and more of it filling her and for a wild moment Maria doubted her capacity to take it in its entirety. Her doubts were ill-founded. She rotated her hips, forcing the last morsel of flesh into her hungry cunt and then simply enjoyed the sensation of fullness that she was experiencing. The huge weapon seemed to reach almost to her heart, it had spread the lips of her vagina as wide as a fist might, forcing her clitoris hard against the bony jut of Xarrith's pelvis.

Slowly, the holy woman and the young Acolyte began to move. Xarrith lifted his hands to caress the breasts that were bobbing above him, drawing a groan from Maria. She responded by quickening the cadence of her own movements. Her buttocks began to slap against the upper thighs of the youth beneath her with a sound that grew in volume and tempo as she strained towards her reward.

Tasnar, all but forgotten by the two main protagonists, had positioned himself at the foot of the bed where he had a fine view of Xarrith thrusting into the cunt of the Holy Sister. The oil she had used mingled with sweat and her own juices to make her taut buttocks gleam, her position drawing them wide to allow him an enticing sight of the chiselled dimple of her anus. His hand began to move faster along his firmly grasped prick as he saw Maria reach around her hip and, to his shocked delight, slip a finger into the forbidden entrance of her body. Both she and Xarrith were breathing unevenly, their movements beginning to lose coordination as they grew closer to their goal.

Moving closer, Tasnar gingerly extended a hand until he was able to touch the hot, slick flesh of Maria.

'May I assist the Holy Sister?' he said softly, stroking her undulating behind, enjoying the heat of her.

'Uhh, yes... Tasnar. Place... mmm... your finger where you... ah, see mine.'

She pulled her finger from her body and before the little opening could contract, Tasnar embedded his own deeply within her. She gasped at the sensation of being penetrated by two males at the same time. This had long been one of her few unfulfilled fantasies, one she had thought she had little chance of experiencing but now it seemed it was about to happen. For a while she savoured the feel, Xarrith's huge prick in her cunt, Tasnar's probing finger in her anus.

Opening her eyes and stilling, for a time, her movements, Maria placed a hand on the broad chest beneath her. Feeling her stop, Xarrith too opened his eyes and looked up at her, a question in his eyes.

'Be still for the moment, Xarrith. Tasnar will join our game.' She twisted her head to look at him. 'There is room for more than a finger, Tasnar.'

Wriggling a little to elevate her posterior and spreading her straining thighs even wider to allow easier access for the Acolyte, Sister Maria, Holy Woman of the Living Prophet of Qalle, Adept of the forbidden Society of T'arn, her cunt impaled on the massive prick of one young Acolyte, held her breath as she waited for another to fuck her anally.

Hardly able to believe his luck, Tasnar manoeuvred himself carefully, threading his way between the sprawled limbs of Xarrith and Maria. Holding his prick firmly, he placed the tip against the tiny target and thrust steadily. At first, the entrance resisted. It was far tighter than the more conventional route but he persisted. With a suddenness that surprised him, the tight ring of muscle yielded and half of his length was inside her. Maria screamed at the sensation and alarmed, Tasnar began to withdraw only to feel the Holy Sister rear back at him, her sphincter tightening about his flesh, holding him. Again he thrust, feeling the unconventional way open to welcome him and with his own gasp of pleasure echoing about the cell, Tasnar embedded himself to the balls in Maria's arse.

Together, the three of them sought a common rhythm. Tasnar had reached around the Holy Sister to feel her breasts, sharing them with Xarrith. She had leaned forward to kiss the warrior, sucking his tongue into her mouth, wanting her every orifice to be filled; used.

Xarrith and Tasnar were each thrusting into her, filling her with an unbelievable range of sensations. Her orgasms were over-running one another, seemingly one single, shattering climax that could only end in death. The screams and shouts of the Acolytes joined with hers, a volume of noise that, it seemed, must reach every corner of the Citadel. Deep within her body, Maria felt Xarrith come, felt the rhythmic pulses of his giant penis as the seed burst from him, feeling red-hot inside her. Tasnar, working still in her rear entrance, soon followed, squeezing her breasts with his full strength as his hoarse cry flew about the ancient room, his hips bucking spasmodically, trying to sustain the incomparable feeling.

For many minutes, the holy woman, the warrior and the mediator lay tumbled on the bed. Looking at their reflection in the mirror, Maria could hardly tell when one body began and another ended.

But slowly she stirred and sat up, freeing herself from the softening pricks.

'My conduct has fallen far beneath the standards the Citadel expects, I fear,' she whispered huskily as she clambered from the bed and retrieved the whip from the floor. 'I must pay for my misdeeds.' She threw the whip to Xarrith. 'I tremble at the thought of what I must endure at both your hands,' she said as she turned away from the Acolytes and bent over to hold her ankles.

The two young men feasted their eyes on the presented buttocks, the still engorged lips of her sex pushing back between them and the gleaming traces of their emissions smearing them.

Xarrith smiled fiercely and gripped the whip.

'Prepare yourself Holy Sister, I promise we shall cleanse you of your sin most thoroughly.'

5.

Tarrip was not happy. This was not an unusual condition for him, rarely was he seen to smile. But today his melancholia went far deeper than the growling visage he normally presented about the Citadel. Not even the thorough beating he had recently administered to plump Leel and the blonde Maris, both of whom hung limp and naked from the Punishment Frame could lift his mood. The Holy Father tapped his tokan morosely against his booted leg, idly looking at the two Initiates. They were secured in sitting positions, arms tied wide to allow him access to their vulnerable breasts, thighs parted by the leather straps that bit cruelly into their flesh, cunts exposed for beating and whatever else took his fancy. The problem was, he mused, that they were not terrified of him any longer — none of them were. Oh, they screamed prettily, tears flowed easily, as leather or rope or hand abused their bodies, pinched nipples, twisted labia, but somehow they seemed to get as much enjoyment from their punishment as he did, which, for Tarrip, removed the sharp edge from his pleasure. Even in the finale, when he fucked them, now they strained eagerly to him as he penetrated cunt or anus or mouth. And they liked each other! In previous years, many of the Initiates had grown to hate each other and had leapt at the chance to punish one another. Well, these still did, he supposed, but they enjoyed being beaten, being made to pleasure each other.

Irritably, the high priest paced the room, his boots tapping on the stone floor. The eyes of the two girls followed his figure, but with a flare of exasperation Tarrip saw them exchange a secret smile, saw that their eyes, although red from crying, were bright at the thought that he would soon continue the punishment. He looked at the two of them, the fat breasts of Leel that could be made to bounce so delightfully; Nephraan, legs wide, clitoris as long as her little finger peeping from the blonde curls, curls that were still wet from her excitement. Suddenly he was tired of her. He clapped his hands twice, bringing two Ercli women into the room, and ordered them to release the Initiates

Tarrip turned his back on the four figures and poured himself a cup of wine. Perhaps he was growing old? The thought was a frightening one. He knew there would inevitable come a time when his formidable sexual powers would fade, but Prophet take it, he was not yet sixty! He turned back to watch as the Erclis released the two young women, watched as the naked forms winced at their hurts, rubbed life back into limbs that had been deprived of blood by the straps that had held them. His prick didn't even twitch.

Tarrip ignored the slightly puzzled look that the Initiates gave him as the Erclis led them from his room, taken with his own thoughts. Pouring more wine, he cast his mind back, trying to remember just when he had felt that his power, both physical and within the Citadel, had begun to slip.

At first, the current group of Initiates had seemed as promising as any he had met. He sucked air and wine through his teeth with an uncouth bubbling sound as he remembered the body of Hysena being stripped that first time, the look of total fear on her innocent face, trying to hide her charms behind hands inadequate for the task. To his pleasure and no little relief, Tarrip felt his penis begin to swell at the memory. His thoughts went inevitably to the next of the girls to have been the victim of his desires. Jagdig! That magnificent body, struggling like a wild animal against her bonds! He hauled up his robe to admire his erection, now as full and proud as it had ever been. Giving an evil chuckle, he slapped it, enjoying the mild pain and the sight of it as it shook.

Swigging back the last of his wine, Tarrip jumped to his feet and hurried from his room. Old? Father Tarrip? Never! A session with Jagdig and all would be well.

As he swept through the ancient corridors, he turned over his options. He would beat her, naturally. Should he order one or more of the Initiates to aid in the task? Or Colya, perhaps? There were so many options...

But to his dismay, as he neared the crude cell in which the Kallinian had been restrained for the past months, he felt despondency once again creep over him. His erection subsided and he realised that even if he were to fuck the girl, it would not be as good for him as it should be. But, he supposed, it would be better than nothing.

As Tarrip was entering the cell in which the warrior girl was forced to endure her miserable existence, another was entering his own quarters. Checking with care that no-one could observe the action, the figure opened the flagon of wine that stood on the table. Had then been a listener, a faint clinking might have been heard as a carefully measured quantity of liquid was added to the wine. The flagon was stoppered and the figure left the cell as quietly as it had arrived.

'Soon,' the figure was thinking, 'very soon now.'

Jagdig could not help the shudder that took her when she saw the figure of the high priest enter her cell. She had known he was on his way as shortly before an Ercli slave had secured her to the structure that shared her rude accommodation. It was not as elaborate as the Punishment Frame in Tarrip's quarters, having the appearance of a wheel with four thick spokes that ended short of where the hub would have been, leaving a gap in the centre of the apparatus. The rim of the wheel was attached to iron bars that ran the width of the cell at waist height. When a victim was strapped in place, her arms and legs held wide, the back of her neck resting uncomfortably against the rim, she could be rotated about her axis, allowing her tormentor to enjoy her from any angle.

The advantage, as Tarrip saw it, was that once his victim was in place, he needed no assistance to move her into which ever position suited, whatever perversion took his fancy. It was just him and the girl. No witnesses.

Tarrip stood before the Kallinian and studied her.

After so many months of almost daily beatings, humiliations, sexual torments, she should have been totally broken, he mused. But somewhere in the depths of those brown eyes, eyes accentuated by the shaved skull, there still burned a spark of anger, a spark that the Holy Father felt could easily blow into a destructive flame should he drop his guard for a moment.

Oh, there had been considerable progress. It was no longer necessary to keep her restrained at all times or drug her when she was to be conducted to the bathing pool. No, all it took was an order from the Holy Father and the attention of a single Ercli; even Jagdig had learned, that the amount of pain she could stand was finite. Now, when an Ercli entered her cell and nodded silently at the wheel, Jagdig would snarl but stand compliantly as the bar between her legs was removed and the arm-straps that prevented her from touching herself anywhere lower than her breasts were loosened. She would stand, silently radiating resentment as she was strapped to the wheel to await Tarrip's pleasure.

The Holy Father pressed down on the rim of the wheel, causing it to rotate between the iron bars that supported it. It had been carefully balanced to match Jagdig's body-weight and unless he restrained it, it would continue to turn for a considerable time, allowing Tarrip to view his helpless prey from all angles whilst he himself was seated before her.

Casting his mind back to when he had first seen her, Tarrip compared the Jagdig newly arrived at the Citadel with the one who was slowly spinning before him now. A combination of poor diet, lack of exercise and the sweat of pain had melted the flesh from her body. Her once-magnificent breasts had shrunk considerably, and as her body slowly turned over and over, he enjoyed the sight of them changing shape, now lying flat on her chest, then falling to almost obscure her face as her body went from horizontal to vertical, then hanging from her chest like exotic fruits as the cycle of the wheel continued.

With his foot he stopped the movement of the wheel,

leaving the girl upright. Even in their comparatively emaciated state Jagdig's breasts did not hang like the dugs of an older woman, nipples pointing towards her waist. These nipples, Tarrip noticed with relish, were even more exaggerated than when her prolonged punishment had begun so long ago.

As he cast his eyes down her body, to his delight (and not a little relief), Tarrip felt his excitement rising, felt the familiar and welcome surge of lust and the heady, sadistic sensation of being alone with a vulnerable young woman, her nude body his to do with as he pleased. He felt his engorging prick rubbing against the soft wool of the robe he wore, and impatiently he hauled the garment over his head and tossed it carelessly into a corner of the cell. Fists on hips, he stood naked but for his high leather boots before the figure on the wheel, penis thrusting eagerly towards her. He smiled the old, cruel smile as he saw Jagdig cringe, pulling her hips back as far as she could into the space where the hub of the wheel would have been. The movement brought her breasts into greater prominence and Tarrip saw that at least some of his efforts had borne fruit; the knowledge that she was about to suffer yet another beating engendered in her not only apprehension but also arousal. He saw the phenomenon that never ceased to fascinate him, that of her nipples growing and stiffening, changing to a deeper shade of brown until they appeared almost black, as big as the tip of his little finger. He watched in fascination as the circle of tiny bumps appeared in her areolae and noted with satisfaction as the speed of her breathing increased, causing her breasts to rise and fall enticingly.

Prick in one hand, tokan in the other, the high priest dropped his eyes from her breasts to her waist. The frugal diet on which Jagdig had been existing meant that each of her ribs showed through her skin. Her pelvis and hips, previously covered by smooth skin, swelling beautifully in muscled curves over hip and buttock, now stood out in stark points of bone, the flesh so tight on her body that they seemed about to break through the skin. As her nipples seemed more prominent now that her breasts had shrunk, so her sex was exaggerated by the atrophy of the surrounding flesh. Her vulva seemed almost pathetically defenceless, the lips naked of hair save for a fine growth of stubble that had appeared since she was last humiliatingly shaved there. Leaning closer, Tarrip could see the tip of her clitoris peeping from under the hood of soft skin that could not begin to protect it.

Staring straight into the eyes of the warrior girl, the priest ground the blunt end of the tokan into the very top of Jagdig's slit, enjoying the shudder that took her body. Releasing his prick, now as hard as he could wish and still holding her eyes with his, Tarrip seized her breast, crushing it in his grip until his fingers had all but vanished into the soft flesh. He smiled his evil smile as he felt the nipple harden against the palm of his hand and heard the girl groan.

'So, Initiate Jagdig of Kallinia, are we to release you today? Are you yet fit for the polite society of Qalle? Can you be trusted to disport yourself in a manner that will reflect well on the Citadel?' With each question he jabbed the blunt end of the tokan into her, crushing the sensitive nerves of her clitoris against the unyielding bulge of her pubis. With satisfaction he saw tears collect in the corners of her eyes but noted that in the depths of those eyes there still burned the vestigial flame of defiance.

He moved the tokan lower, rubbing the ribbed leather along her bare slit, hearing it rasp against the short stubble of pubic hair. That would have to be dealt with first, he reflected. It could rub him raw.

Tarrip stepped back from his victim and used his booted foot to set the wheel turning slowly. As her head descended towards him, the priest pushed his hips forward. Jagdig tried to twist her head away, but she could not avoid the swollen length of the high priest's penis. She felt it rub along the edge of her jaw and ear, hot and loathsome, and then her head was brushing the floor as the motion of the wheel inverted her. Tarrip halted her in that position.

He clapped his hands loudly. One of the ubiquitous Ercli slaves appeared almost before the echoes had faded.

His orders were received with the usual disinterested silence and the figure — a female, he noted — left as quietly as she had arrived. As he waited for the slave to return, Tarrip turned his attention once again to the naked girl suspended upside down on the wheel. Her back was presented to him, her long legs held wide by the restraints at her ankles. The lips of her cunt opened easily at his touch. She quickly grew moist as he toyed with her thick outer lips and he was soon able to run his middle finger into her. Having wetted it thoroughly, he now presented it to the tighter entrance, teasing her briefly by rubbing gently before suddenly forcing it home to the knuckle with a single, savage thrust that drew a satisfying moan from the helpless girl. The crease of her buttocks was at a level with his waist and, moving closer to the girl, Tarrip was able to rub his prick along the valley between her legs.

Jagdig could see nothing but the floor of her cell as she hung from the wheel. Her head felt swollen from the blood that rushed to it when she was inverted and her breathing was hampered by her position. She felt the Holy Father parting her lips and stimulating her with his fingers and the hard leather of the tokan. The pattern was all too familiar to her now. He would tease her, penetrate her, use each of her orifices until she trembled with need and then leave her, having discharged himself, perhaps over her body, perhaps in her mouth. She did not know which finale she found the most repulsive; gagging on that giant prick as he forced it down her throat, feeling and tasting the gouts of sperm as they pulsed from him, or the feeling of the stuff dripping slimily from her skin where it would be left to dry, making her itch, unable to rub it from herself.

The worst part was, of course, that although she hated this man with a burning, consuming loathing beyond any emotion she had ever experienced, she desperately wanted him to give her the release she needed, wanted him to force himself into her body, to beat her and pinch her until orgasm took her.

Through dull eyes, Jagdig saw the inverted form of the Ercli slave girl as she re-entered the cell carrying a bowl. Tendrils of steam rose from it and as she caught the acrid smell from the contents, Jagdig shivered, knowing what she was about to suffer.

In her dormitory, Hysena was also shivering, but for an altogether different reason. That morning, when she was dressing, she had found something in her shoe. Tipping the object into her hand, she discovered it to be a tightly rolled scrap of paper. She looked guiltily about the dormitory, but none of her sister Initiates had noticed. She hurried down the corridor and bolted herself into the garderobe. Curiously, she teased open the note.

'To the Lady Hysena of House Argo,' she read. 'Greetings and Felicitations from two Fellow Students of the Prophet. Know you that there exists a Hidden Way that doth reach from where We dwell to where do You.

'Should it be Your Desire, my Fellow and I would call to pay our Most Humble respects.
Tasnar of Sis Narash
Xarrith of Kallinia.'

There were details as to how she could reply to the brief missive but nothing to suggest how it had got into her shoe so mysteriously.

For the rest of the day, Hysena was in the condition that her old nurse would have described as 'all of a dither' as she went over and over the note and its source in her mind. She had secreted it in a crack in the wall near to the dormitory, not daring to keep it on her as at any moment she might be stripped naked for punishment and what punishment she might suffer should such a message be discovered did not bear thinking about.

Men! The very thought of men, real men rather than old Tarrip was enough to start the juices between her legs and her hand almost of its own accord had crept up under her robe. She read the note over and over, seeking an explanation as she caressed herself. She did not recognise the names, had no way of knowing how they might look and yet these two strangers had caused her to become enormously aroused. Yes, she loved her Sisters and yes, Father Tarrip could raise her to un-dreamed of heights of ecstasy, but Hysena, in common with perhaps all young women, wanted to be held, loved by a man. Preferably one who wouldn't beat her first, she thought in a haze of orgasm. Or not much, anyway.

In his characteristic manner, Tasnar had spent a solid month weighing the risks of arranging a meeting with the Initiates. In the end, he had taken the risky step of seeking the advice of Sister Maria.

Since that memorable encounter, Tasnar had not ventured into the passages. Almost daily Xarrith had pressed for a further exploration but he had so far resisted, remembering how serious had been the Holy Sister when, before they returned to their own part of the Citadel, she insisted they swear that no such exploration would take place. Tasnar might have broken this oath had he not suspected that Maria was as keen as they to repeat the encounter and sensing with a maturity beyond his years that it would be far safer to leave her to make the arrangement. Patiently, counselling Xarrith to do likewise, he waited.

The encounter had taken place on a Holy Day. Tasnar had been half dozing in the High Chamber, eyes shut and mind wandering, trying to ignore the pain in his knees as Father Lisnan chanted the praise in his monotonous voice. Xarrith, characteristically, had chosen to ignore the event, despite it being compulsory, so Tasnar had to endure the dreary hours without the outrageous commentary that his friend was wont to whisper on the occasions he deigned to attend. Not wanting to associate with his peers, Tasnar had positioned himself in the gloom at the rear of the room. He had not at first registered the gentle nudge as an elbow touched his, but a second, more insistent contact prompted him to open his eyes. The figure next to him was fully covered in the ceremonial robes of a Sister elder, the cowl concealing her head. But Tasnar knew at once who was under them. Under the cover of the droning voice of Lisnan and the chanted responses from the kneeling priesthood, she spoke to him.

'You have kept to your oath, Sis Narash.' Her voice was pitched at a level to reach his ears only.

'It has not been easy, Holy Sister.'

'And I surmise that it may have been even harder for one of our mutual acquaintance.'

Tasnar's smile was hidden by his hood. 'The one you talk of is forever hard. Even in sleep his bed-cover resembles a tent and he moans your name as he sweats through the night. There are times when I fear he speculates on using me as you did have me use you.' It was said lightly, but the youth and the Holy Sister said nothing for several minutes as each recalled the time when Tasnar had buried himself deeply within the anus of Maria. She shuffled a little closer until her flank was pressing his. Tasnar felt the heat of her body seep through his robe.

'You are able to keep him in check?'

'For now, Sister Maria, for now. But in all seriousness, I know not for how long. He has seen and tasted paradise and like a haltered stallion who scents the mare, his reason can contain him for only so long before in madness of his desire he kicks down the stable wall.'

'He must not, Tasnar.' Her whispered voice took on a note of urgency. 'A state of flux runs through this Citadel. There comes a time of change and anything importunate may endanger more than you can know.'

Tasnar shrugged and said nothing. He was not overly concerned with the politics of the Citadel and could anyway do nothing to influence them. He only knew that the solution to Xarrith's problem lay in the hands of the Holy Sister.

Maria thought furiously. With an effort, she forced to the back of her mind the thought of Xarrith, naked and rampant, kneeling above her spread legs and open sex.

Much as she wanted him, the planning of years was approaching its cusp and those from whom she took her orders would make their displeasure known in the most overt manner should she endanger those plans for such a selfish and indisciplined reason.

It occurred to her that the Initiates with their nubile, hungry bodies would make a satisfactory repository for the lust of the Kallinian and, having considered the mechanics of the problem, Sister Maria began to whisper to the young Acolyte and unwittingly set in motion a chain of events that would threaten to destroy the very Citadel and all that it represented.

6.

Tarrip poked gingerly at the viscid contents of the bowl, wrinkling his nose at the acrid smell. It had cooled during its passage to the cell and now he set it on a stand below which burned a candle, bringing it to the requisite temperature.

He had turned the wheel to bring the girl upright, wanting her to see his preparations, knowing how much anticipation played on the mind of a victim, wanting her to remember the previous occasions, to remember the pain that she had experienced and was soon to experience again.

The Holy Father ran his hands over the body of the nude Initiate, amused and titillated by the way she flinched. He cupped a breast in each hand, caressing them gently.

'I mourn for you, Initiate Jagdig,' Tarrip said, his voice gentle, 'mourn that you continue to bring these things upon yourself. This magnificent body, wasted here in this cell. These fine tits,' he squeezed them, 'shrinking away.' He took his hands from her breasts and, leaning forward, kissed her nipples, sucking each in turn into his mouth, feeling them swell under his tongue. The priest ran his hands over the conspicuous contours of her ribs, feeling the bony points of her pelvis before reaching behind her to fondle her buttocks. Flattening his palms against them, Tarrip pulled them apart, drawing her waist towards his. The tip of his penis rubbed against her lower belly, the stubble that grew there scratching the glans that bulged out from under his thick foreskin. For a few moments Tarrip revelled in the sensation, taking his prick in his hand and rubbing it up and down Jagdig's moist slit.

'Will you not speak to me, child?' his mouth was close to hers, his voice all but a whisper. 'Tell me how much you enjoy it when I rub my prick against your cunt like this. I know that you desire me and that your desire grows. I feel you grow ever wetter.' The tip of his penis was fully exposed now, and he was rubbing it directly against her clitoris.

Tarrip bent his knees a little, until his prick was nuzzling at the entrance to her vagina. Holding her buttocks firmly, he gently pushed into her, making the thrust last for a full minute, using gentleness as a weapon in contrast to his normal brutality.

It was nearly the undoing of Jagdig. For seemingly eternal days and even longer nights she had faced her torturer, enduring the pain, surviving the humiliation and frustration. This day she had mentally prepared herself for more of the same, and suddenly he was treating her gently. The long, slow penetration took her back to the time she had yielded her virginity to one of her tribal elders, a kindly old man who had been gentle with her, taking account of her tender years and nervousness, who had employed the same slow thrust, ready to stop should she feel any pain. Thinking back to that time when she had no cares and comparing it to the unspeakable things that she had endured during her time at the Citadel, Jagdig nearly broke. She felt the tears start from her eyes and felt the anguished groan of utter despair building inexorably in her chest.

Had he but known it, Tarrip could have won her then. One more soft caress, perhaps a kiss, and her resistance would have finally broken. For once the ability he prided himself on deserted the Holy Father. He failed to see how close he was to victory and instead dug his fingers viciously into her buttocks at the same time slamming his pelvis against her, crushing her clitoris agonisingly between their two bodies.

The scream that came from the Initiate was of anger at the sudden attack, not anguish. At once she felt her defiance flowing back, the flame of her hatred renewed. Inwardly she berated herself for how close she had come to surrender. Suddenly she felt stronger than she had done for a long time, the resolve not to let the fat old priest defeat her as powerful as it had ever been.

Tarrip sensed the change and pulled out of her now sopping cunt. He looked into her eyes and saw that they blazed.

'So, Kallinian. It seems that my patient lessons are still in vain.'

'Aye, priest. But I mind them all and store them against the day of reckoning.'

The Holy Father stepped back, shocked. These were the first words she had spoken in weeks. And such words! He looked warily at the girl. She was still splayed naked on the wheel, helplessly open to his every whim, her bonds still tight and yet Tarrip felt a delicate thrill of fear tickle his spine. There was something subtly different about how her body hung from the wheel. No longer did she look so helpless and pathetic. And those eyes!

Avoiding looking directly at Jagdig, Tarrip turned the wheel until she was once again upside down. He took the bowl from above the candle and tested the liquid within it with the tip of his finger. It was hotter than he would normally use it, almost hot enough to blister, he judged. He stepped behind the girl and looked down between her spread legs. The ragged inner lips of her vagina protruded, reddened and gleaming in evidence of her recent arousal.

'So you still defy me, Kallinian. This is not wise, and now you shall learn just how unwise it is to challenge the High Priest of Qalle.'

As he spoke, he drove three fingers deeply into her anus and spread them within her, dilating the opening. Quickly withdrawing them and before her muscles had time to contract, Tarrip poured the scalding liquid onto her upturned crotch.

Derived from a certain plant sap, lana juice was commonly used to cauterise wounds. It dried on skin like wax but did not flake off, forming a flexible covering that protected a wound until healing began. In the normal course of events, it would drop off of its own accord within a few days. But if it were pulled off deliberately as soon as it had set, it would take with it any hairs that it might have covered.

Jagdig had endured this particular torture any number of times since she had been humiliatingly depilated by her fellow Initiates. Previously, the lana juice had been little more than blood warm and caused no discomfort. It was only when Tarrip peeled it away that the pain came, pain from the hundreds of hairs being torn from her vulva and around her anus. So she was not prepared for the shock of the stuff being poured over her at a temperature so high.

Tarrip smiled in satisfaction as the shrill screams echoed within the cell. His finger still smarted from its brief contact with the juice, and he could only imagine how it must feel on those most sensitive parts of the Initiate, running over her cunt, coating her clitoris, running into the anus he had deliberately opened that her agony might be made greater. He actually felt his testicles shrink and tighten against his body in sympathy.

For a moment the girl's whole body went into spasm as the stuff licked her like fire, the agony so huge that she could not even scream. But then she did scream, over and over, her body shaking and twisting within its bonds, shaking the wheel in its frame and even causing the bars that supported it to twist and bend.

With difficulty because of the twisted frame, the holy man turned his victim until she was upright. She still shook with sobs, her face suffused red and wet with her tears. Her eyes were twisted shut and her lips drawn back from her lips in the rictus of a scream as she fought to ride the waves of pain emanating from her abused parts.

Tarrip had poured himself a cup of wine and he toasted the Initiate sardonically when she eventually opened her eyes. 'Your war cry does you credit, girl. How the enemies of Kallinia would tremble were they to hear you squeal like a throat-slit hog.' His voice was mocking.

Jagdig was still beyond speech but the hatred flashed from her eyes.

Sipping his wine, Tarrip walked around her. As it set, the lana juice became milkily translucent. It formed a covering over her sex, outlining it and showing every contour. He had originally intended to pour some of the liquid over her breasts, knowing that the pain of having the fine hairs that grew about her nipples ripped out could add a further exquisite dimension to her suffering, but his rage at her defiance had caused him to use the whole bowl between her thighs.

He ran his hand between her legs. The lana juice had set and the priest enjoyed the novel feel of a cunt covered by the stuff. The surface had a slightly oily feel and his fingers slid easily over it, tracing the convolute folds.

Between her buttocks he could feel that some of the liquid had indeed penetrated her anus as he had intended, and he wondered how it would feel as he tore it from those sensitive membranes.

The same thought was occupying Jagdig and she braced herself as the Holy Father peeled the edge of the film away from her belly. When he had freed sufficient of it to allow him to grip the edge with the fingers of both hands, Tarrip locked his eyes with those of the Kallinian.

'You shall learn how unwise it is to challenge the High Priest of Qalle,' he repeated.

Even with her newly-recovered resolve Jagdig was chilled to her very soul at the cold hatred she heard in his voice. She set her teeth as the priest began to rip the film of lana from her, determined not to scream again.

At first the sensation was not unpleasant as Tarrip peeled the film down her belly, but as it approached the more sensitive skin when the bulge of her pubis began, the pain of the hairs being torn from her body grew in intensity.

Sadistically, Tarrip worked from the edges of the film, slowly working his way inwards, closing on the soft outer labia and the hood of her clitoris with its mass of sensitive nerve endings.

Jagdig clamped her teeth shut in an effort to contain her screams. The lana came away with a tearing noise that was counterpointed by the heavy breathing of the priest at his task, his face close to her sex, watching intently as more and more of it was revealed. The skin now was smooth and unblemished, glowing pinkly as if it had been beaten, a result of the lana film.

With a jerk that drew a yelp from Jagdig, Tarrip ripped the film from when it had adhered to her inner lips and the tip of her clitoris. The stuff clung stubbornly to her flesh and her lips were drawn out to their full extent before they were parted from the film, a sight Tarrip found inflamed him greatly.

His fingers moved over the folds of her cunt, marvelling at the smoothness and softness. It was completely uncovered now, the lana film dangling obscenely between her open thighs, still attached to the short, sensitive area of flesh that divided vagina from anus.

Moving behind, her, Tarrip once again gripped the lana film. He took a deep breath and with one savage tug, ripped it from her body. Once more, Jagdig's screams echoed from the walls of the cell.

As the priest had intended, some of the lana juice had actually penetrated the anus of the Kallinian, and the savagery with which he tore it from her took the delicate surface of her inner tract with it, leaving it raw and burning.

Coming to his feet with a grunt, Tarrip circled the girl, studying her nude form from all angles. Her face was bathed with sweat, her breath coming in huge gulps as she fought not to sob. The area between her legs still glowed red in stark contrast to the whiteness of skin that had been denied sunlight for so long. Once more Tarrip fingered her sex, parting the lips, rubbing up and down the nude slit, now utterly smooth to his touch. As he worked on her, the Holy Father felt those lips become slippery as her juices began to flow.

Rubbing his huge prick with his spare hand, Tarrip marvelled at the workings of the female body. Despite all she had endured, despite the pain she must still be feeling, she quickly became aroused, her nipples crinkling, her clitoris engorging.

As soon as she was wet enough, he took her. This time there was nothing gentle about the way he penetrated the helpless girl. Standing face to face with her, Tarrip rammed himself into her cunt time and time again, gripping her buttocks firmly, pulling her onto him. He grunted in time to his thrusts, shaking his head when his sweat ran down into his eyes, sending showers of it, rank and stinking, onto her shaking breasts. He felt his climax approaching and quickly pulled out of her cunt, then moved behind her.

Sensing his intention, Jagdig could not prevent her agonised cry.

'No! I cannot.'

She felt the tip of his penis pressing against her anus and tried to clamp her muscles to prevent him entering her there but his strength was irresistible. Tarrip gripped her breasts for leverage, squeezing them in his fists as if he wanted to tear them from her chest, and forced his hips forward, forced his prick ever deeper into her anus.

To Jagdig, her anus already burning from the effect of the lana, it was as if she were being penetrated by a bar of red-hot iron. The pain then competed with the pain she was experiencing in her breasts as Tarrip twisted them savagely. She could feel him sliding deeper and deeper into her behind, filling her until she felt that she might burst. Impossibly, the pain grew as Tarrip began to thrust, his thick, wrinkled foreskin rubbing agonisingly against the already damaged membranes.

Mercifully, Jagdig felt his thrusts grow faster and uneven as his climax approached and her shrill scream mingled with his animal roar as he ejaculated.

The Ercli slave woman summoned to free the Kallinian who hung limply from the wheel noted without comment that the loins of the Holy Father dripped with blood as he strode past her, his head high.

7.

In the High Chamber, Father Lisnan was approaching the end of the Fourteenth Chant of Praise. That meant, Tasnar sighed to himself, there were still seven to go. As the priest paused to sip from the ceremonial cup before commencing the next chant ('That We Praise the Holy Prophet for His Munificence and Eternal Mercy to Those who may have Slighted Us and Whom We now Forgive.' Tasnar ticked it off in his mind), both Tasnar and Maria cocked their heads. The sound had been at the very edge of hearing, but was unmistakable. Somewhere in the Citadel, a woman was screaming.

'I surmise the Holy Father is about his duties,' Maria whispered as Lisnan launched into the chant, drowning the pitiful sound.

'Clearly he is being most diligent for us to hear her from this place.' Tasnar could not suppress a shudder. Even though it had lasted but a few seconds, the plaint had held such anguish that it had touched the peaceful youth from Sis Narash to the heart.

Feeling the shudder, Maria placed a gentle hand on his thigh for comfort. More than Tasnar, she knew that scream. In her opinion, the old priest was losing his mind and his obsession with Jagdig was now far beyond the acceptable even for this place, and she worried that the girl might not survive. She had done what she could, ensuring that the Holy Father regularly received a mild drug intended to limit his excesses, but the results were scant. Not realising she was doing so, the Holy Sister began to stroke the thigh of the young Acolyte kneeling beside her as she pondered in her mind the plans of which she was a small part and that had been running for so many years and were now nearing a climax.

She was brought back to reality when beside her, Tasnar shuddered again. Maria glanced quizzically at him before realising with a guilty moue the reason: her hand, from resting reassuringly on the boy's thigh, had ridden higher and was now resting on what, through his robe, felt like a full erection.

An unaccustomed wave of recklessness overtook Sister Maria. This particular chant required each pietist to face the massive cartouche depicting the Holy Prophet of Qalle and she knew that for the next few minutes no one could see what might be happening at the rear of the High Chamber. Cautioning the startled Tasnar to silence with a finger on her lips, she pulled up the front of his robe.

His prick was indeed fully erect, as pretty as she remembered it from the time a month since in her quarters. Bending forward, Sister Maria took him into her mouth.

She moved her lips up and down the hot, hard column then used her hand to draw back his foreskin and licked delicately at the tight, shiny glans, forcing the tip of her tongue into the tiny opening at the very head of his organ before once more sucking his full length into her mouth, taking all of him until she could feel her lips brushing the wiry curls of his pubic hair.

As she continued to use her lips and mouth on the youth, Maria struggled to pull her robe up from when it was trapped under her knees. Achieving her purpose, she was able to use a hand on herself, squeezing the lips of her sex tightly together before slipping a finger, then another into herself and wishing it was Tasnar's hand then, but their position was such that he could not reach her and in any case, he seemed to be shocked frozen.

Noting that the chant had yet to reach its halfway point, Maria lifted her head from the lap of the Acolyte and, remaining on her knees, shuffled in front of him. She bent from the hips, resting her forearms on the cold flagstones and elevated her posterior, wriggling it in unmistakable invitation.

At once she felt Tasnar seize the hem of her robe and felt the cool air of the chamber on her skin as he raised it, lifting it clear of her buttocks until it caught on the girdle about her waist. Moving her knees apart, she felt his fingers, somewhat hesitant, touch her and had to suppress a gasp at the contact. She felt him opening her and with growing confidence, exploring, sliding into her wetness, gently rubbing her aching clitoris. His hand vanished but was quickly replaced by the hot, bulbous tip of his penis. As soon as she felt him nuzzling at her entrance, Maria rocked back, taking him deeply inside her, her action forcing him back until he was resting on his haunches, cradling her spread hips on his lap.

For a while, the Holy Sister remained unmoving, savouring the feel of his penis in her body. She loosened her girdle and guided his hands up under her robe until they rested on her breasts and then, taking her rhythm from the chanting priests, began to rock back and forth.

At the back of her mind was the knowledge that a single glance from one of the worshipers would be their undoing, and the knowledge added piquancy to the situation, the heady thrill of fear raising all her senses to a thrilling peak.

Maria pressed her hand hard against her cunt, even slipping one finger into herself along side Tasnar's straining prick, stretching her vagina to its limit.

She achieved her climax just as the chant rose to its own finale, her breathy cry lost among the voices of the celebrants. As she came, she felt the jets of sperm bathing her inner parts as the Acolyte pressed into her.

They barely had time to disengage before Father Lisnan at the altar turned to face his congregation. He noted the youth and the Sister elder, both flushed and panting. Clearly they were all but overcome by the solemnity of the occasion, thought the priest, making a mental note to commend them for their obvious piety.

'You mean, you actually fucked her? You fucked her in the High Chamber while all those buggering priests moaned their dirges?' Xarrith wore an expression that ranged from awe to jealousy via disbelief as he strode about his room shaking his head.

'Would I lie?' Tasnar asked, wolfing bread and mutton.

'Only if there were profit to be made,' muttered the Kallinian. 'And she did finger her cunt while you were up it?'

'Aye,' said Tasnar. This was the third time that he had related the story since returning from the High Chamber some hours ago. He watched his friend in amusement, feeding him more snippets of the event, watching his agitation and frustration grow. 'Perhaps, Xari, if you were like me a true Acolyte and attended to your duty, the Holy Prophet would have rewarded you also. Think you; had you been there, perhaps we could again have taken Holy Maria together. This time you could have fucked her tight arse whilst I...'

'Enough! Still your mouth, little man.' Xarrith shook a fist like a ham under the nose of Tasnar, who ignored it. 'It is enough that tonight I must sleep with aching balls and naught to assuage them but my own hand without you mocking me with pretty pictures of what might have been.' He sat on his bed, knees drawn up, chin resting on them. Tasnar struggled not to smile at such a vision of abject misery.

Xarrith sighed elaborately. 'I shall send for six Ercli women. They may serve to take at least the edge from my desires.'

'It is a thought,' said Tasnar, picking shards of mutton from his teeth with the point of his knife. 'When you have finished with them, perhaps you may wish to join me?'

Xarrith's head came up. 'And where go you, Tasnar?' The studied note of casualness in Tasnar's voice immediately piqued his interest.

'Not to meet six women, I regret.'

'To meet one who is as any six others!' Xarrith leaped from the bed, full of excitement. 'Maria has invited us to her room! Why did you not say earlier, miserable slug?'

Tasnar shook his head, smiling. 'Nay. Sister Maria is away from the Citadel this night.'

'Then who? Mind how well I know you, Tasnar. You wear that smile only at the thought of gold or women and there is no gold here.'

Deciding he had teased enough, Tasnar told him and had the satisfaction of seeing the huge Kallinian warrior struck dumb, mouth opening and closing like a fresh-caught fish.

After Instruction, Hysena hurried back to the dormitory, wanting to get there before any of her sister Initiates. The day had been a difficult one for her. She desperately wanted to confide in one of the others about the enigmatic and mysterious note but it had been explicit; she was to tell no one. Following the directions on the note, she had been able to speak to one of the Ercli slaves, saying simply the she wished to see Sister Maria at the Holy Sister's convenience. The tiny woman had simply nodded and vanished in the way they had. At mealtime the Ercli (possibly a different one — who could tell?) had pressed another tightly rolled pellet into her hand.

Fighting back the overwhelming urge to open it there and then, Hysena had almost panicked at the thought of being found with it and in the end had hidden it in the only place she could think of. Under the cover of the table at which they ate, she surreptitiously slid her hand into the fold of her shift and pushed the pellet into her vagina.

Alone in the dormitory, she pulled up her shift and was searching herself with two fingers when she was startled by a voice behind her.

'So. You break the vow of sisterhood, Hysena.'

Hysena turned guiltily to see Maris standing in the doorway, an amused expression on her face.

'Nay, I... I have an itch. The vow is firm.'

The vow the Initiates had sworn among themselves was not intended very seriously. When Leel had suffered a particularly brutal beating from Tarrip and Colya, the other five girls had combined to soothe her, the soothing as usual turning into an orgy of licking and stroking and sucking. When afterwards they lay sated in a tumbled heap, arms and legs and breasts and vaginas mixed indiscriminately, Silka had suggested they swear that, when one or more of them suffered in such a way, the others, regardless of any squabbles that might exist between them, would stop whatever it was they were doing to comfort the victim in the way she wanted. It was rare that the request did not involve something similar to that which had recently occurred. Untangling themselves, the girls had eagerly agreed. Jokingly, Nephraan had added a corollary: as they were now sworn sisters, all their pleasures must be shared.

'All, sister?' Silka had enquired, one eyebrow raised.

'All.' Nephraan had been emphatic. 'When one...feels the need, she must request of her sister help in the matter.'

Now Maris grinned happily at the disconcerted figure who stood guiltily blushing, her shift still held to her waist, pubic hair on display.

'So you have an itch, my lady. I know of this itch as I too suffer from it.' As she spoke, Maris thrust her hand between Hysena's legs, feeling the incriminating wetness of her vulva. 'You would deny there is a certain dampness here? Or that your fingers were hidden in this fragrant sheath?' Maris had worked her finger into the other girl as she spoke.

Hysena did not resist, enjoying the touch but in a dilemma over the note that was (she hoped) still somewhere inside her. Trying to ignore the sensations that Maris's insistent finger was causing, she wondered how she could avoid telling the other girl about the note.

Then it was too late. With a clatter of sandals Silka and Leel followed by Nephraan came into the dormitory.

Gleefully, Maris turned to greet them. 'It has happened, sisters! Our Lady Innocent is caught with the damning evidence clear on her fingers!'

The others gathered about Hysena, delighted that at last they would have the chance to order her to do their every whim.

Hysena tried to protest. 'It is not so. There is an

explanation...'

'Very well,' said Silka, 'we shall hear it.'

'I... had to hide something. There was no other place.' Even to herself, this did not sound convincing.

'And what thing was so valuable as to merit such a sweet hiding place?'

'It is a secret. I may not say.'

The tiny Sis Narashan shook her head slowly. 'There are no secrets between sisters.'

'That is so,' agreed Maris, 'you must say, Hysena.'

'I cannot.'

Silka looked at the others. 'Then I fear we must ascertain the truth for ourselves. Hold her, sisters!'

Moments later, Hysena was grabbed from behind by Leel and felt her legs being lifted by Maris and Nephraan. She could not fight her friends and offered only token resistance as her thighs were hauled wide. Silka folded back the skirt of her shift, laying bare her lower body.

Settling down on her knees between the spread legs, Silka ran a finger delicately along the exposed slit, running it from clitoris to anus and back. Hysena could not help the shiver of pleasure that the touch brought.

'So, my lady. Let us open this pretty treasure chest.' Silka found that Hysena was now too dry to allow her easy access, and not wishing to hurt her friend by forcing her way, she applied her lips and tongue to her sex.

Submitting to the inevitable, Hysena allowed the warm feelings to overtake her. She undulated her pelvis as tiny Silka lapped at her and pulled her shift up her body. Seeing her intention, Maris and Nephraan helped her pull the cloth higher until her breasts were exposed and as one, they bowed their heads to her nipples.

Soon Silka was able to slide her nimble fingers into Hysena's proffered vagina. She had not really believed the story of something hidden and was enjoying the manner in which the other girl was reacting to her ministrations when her fingertips touched something.

'Perhaps we were wrong to doubt you, Hysena. I think I have found the treasure.' Gently she withdrew the small object and examined it in the palm of her hand.

The other three Initiates lowered Hysena to the floor, leaving her somewhat frustrated as she had not reached her climax when Silka had found the note. Now she found herself ignored as her fellows gathered about Silka.

There were just six words on the scrap of paper.

'The Last Tower. The ninth hour.'

Silka frowned and turned the paper over, but there were only the six enigmatic words.

'What means this?' Silka asked, offering the note to Hysena.

The taller girl read the words and frowned in her turn. She had been expecting more explicit instructions. Still, what was there was clear enough. There was no point, she thought, in trying to offer anything but the truth.

'Maris, close the door. I will tell all.'

8.

'I do not know which of them or if any of them will come.' Tasnar spoke patiently as he and Xarrith moved cautiously along the dim passages. He had received, a note from an Ercli which bore the same words as the one Hysena had read: 'The Last Tower. The ninth hour.'

Sister Maria had told him that she would make sure that the Initiates knew of the arrangement, but could not guide them herself as she had business in Calith. For this reason, she had picked the Last Tower which was located in the Initiates' section of the Citadel and was therefore not strictly forbidden to them. Another advantage was that three hundred steps had to be climbed to reach the room at the top and Maria had felt confident that Tarrip would be most unlikely to haul his gross frame up such a difficult route. Particularly when he was suffering from the effects of the powerful purgative that would be mixed into his meal that night.

Panting from the climb, Xarrith looked curiously about the room. For a place that was so difficult of access, it was richly decorated. Fine tapestries depicting scenes from the life of the Holy Prophet hung from the walls and the floor was carpeted with fine wool into which had been woven battle scenes. There were far more candles than a room of this size should merit and as Tasnar lit them the room grew bright as day. There were a few stools and a small table, on which they deposited the flagons of wine they had brought. In one corner was a ladder that led to a wooden hatch set in the stone roof.

'What is this place, Tasnar?'

Tasnar poured himself some wine. 'It is the highest point of the Citadel. Not only does it make a fine lookout, the legend says that should an enemy overrun this place, the last defenders would fight their way here and, rather than suffer the shame of capture and ransom, throw themselves from the tower.

Xarrith snorted. 'That is a false council. A captured

warrior might escape and take his revenge but a corpse can only stink. Were it I who... Quick! To the roof!'

Tasnar was already moving to the ladder. He too had heard the soft sound of footsteps coming up the stairway. Many footsteps.

Sister Maria had not worn the robe that identified her calling but was wrapped in a rough cloak of the kind worn by the peasants of Calith. She slipped unseen from the Citadel and down the broad track that led into the city. As she reached the bottom of the slope she turned to look at the Citadel, its stark outline silhouetted in the moonlight, dominating the horizon above Calith. She saw light flickering from the window of the Last Tower and speculated wistfully on what might be happening behind the stone walls. Gathering her cloak about her, the Holy Sister walked into the city.

Tarrip lay on his bed groaning, arms folded over the bulge of his stomach. Standing over him solicitously was Sister Colya who was trying to cajole him into taking a draught of medicine.

'Holy Father should take even a bit, for the pain.'

Like a recalcitrant child, Tarrip tuned his head away from the proffered cup. Colya's dull wits were not equal to dealing with illness in her mentor. When Tarrip had complained of pains in his belly shortly after his meal, she had searched without success for Maria whose skill as a healer was known throughout the Citadel. She had obtained from one of the cooks a powder to mix with milk that, she was assured, was a sovereign remedy in such cases.

At a loss, Colya reverted to the only solution that she could think of.

'I do something to take mind off pain,' she said in what she fondly believed to be a seductive voice. Being careful not to touch his stomach, she lifted the hem of his robe and took his flaccid member into her mouth.

Tarrip stopped groaning but her efforts produced only the merest stirring from his normally eager prick. Even when she stripped off her own robe and rubbed him with her pendulous breasts he achieved no more than half of his normally formidable length.

'It is a kindly thought Sister,' Tarrip said, looking at her naked form through dull eyes, 'but I fear that even your expert ministrations cannot wake my good friend.'

'If perhaps holy one will take medicine? Then maybe prick will go in here.' As she spoke Colya pulled open her sex, drawing out her long inner lips.

Tarrip's mouth twisted in a half-smile, half-grimace. Truth to tell, he was not very ill. He had had little appetite that evening and had only picked at his food, brooding over his recent problems. Frighteningly, his first reaction when the pains had begun was of relief that he would be able to take to his bed early rather than devise some reason to punish the Initiates.

Moving carefully, he swung his legs off the bed and sat upright. 'Give me the cup.' With a shudder, he swallowed the bitter milk in a single draught. Almost at once he belched massively, easing much of his discomfort.

'Ah. Is working already. Now, I go and fetch naughty girls. Pretty Silka with nice tight cunt and Maris with big, bouncy tits perhaps. We make them squeal and then prick feel better too, eh?'

Tarrip felt his penis twitch at the thought and belched again. 'In a little while, Sister Colya. First, help me to my feet. The night is warm. Perhaps a walk about the Citadel will help.'

Colya nodded her big head in agreement, a relieved expression on her peasant face. 'Holy Father already looking better. I tell cook her medicine does good.'

Tarrip looked sharply at her. 'Cook? You did not get this foul stuff from Sister Maria?'

Colya shrugged. 'Don't know where she is. Is not in room or anywhere.'

A little puzzled, Tarrip threw a cloak over his shoulders. 'Fetch the girls to me in an hour, if you would be so kind, Sister.'

'Maris and Silka, Holy Father?'

'Yes,' The priest smiled briefly. 'The tight little cunt and the big bouncy tits.'

'I go get them ready.' Colya bustled off happily.

The pain was nearly gone as Tarrip stepped out into the warm night, rubbing his hands together in anticipation. He could feel his penis stirring as he planned how he would punish the Initiates and so failed to notice the light burning high up in the window of the Last Tower.

Xarrith and Tasnar lay on the roof hardly daring to breathe. The blade of Xarrith's knife was holding the hatch that led to the room below open a crack. There was nowhere to run. Tasnar had taken a quick look over each of the four walls of the tower, hoping that there might be a ladder or other means of escape, but there was nothing. To one side he could see water from the stream that supplied the Citadel with most of its water glinting in the moonlight, but the drop was formidable. The other sides either connected to the main part of the Citadel or vanished into thick vegetation.

'If it is the Guard, we go with them peacefully,' said Tasnar.

'I am not a peaceful man.'

'Your own words, Xari. A corpse can only stink.'

Xarrith snorted softly, his eye to the crack of light coming from the room below.

Tasnar saw his friend suddenly stiffen and raise one hand, cautioning him to silence. The seconds stretched endlessly as he remained frozen, straining to hear the faint sounds that drifted up from below. Then Xarrith slowly turned his head, alarming Tasnar with the look on his face. His teeth were exposed and the look in his eyes suggested that he was moments away from throwing himself down the hatch and laying about him. He was, the Sis Narashan saw, trembling.

Regardless of the risk of being heard, Tasnar moved to him but before he could advise caution, Xarrith spoke.

'I think I can persuade you to join battle with me,

Tasnar. Look you.'

The youth applied his eye to the crack and looked down. The previously empty room now held five Initiates.

9.

The High Council of the Society of T'arn never met twice in the same place. On this occasion the meeting was held in an abandoned room above a bakery and Sister Maria could smell the pleasant yeasty warmth as she shucked off her cloak and then slid out of her robe. She stood nude and unmoving, arms raised above her head, feet apart, as the impassive guard searched her. The society had been formed four generations ago when war on Qalle was endemic, with every nation involved. Sickened by the appalling loss of life among the cream of the youth of Qalle, tentative messages emerged from Sis Narash directed not to the leaders of the warring nations, but to those who, spies reported, were as disgusted with the continuing pointlessness of the wars as were the inherently peaceful Narashans. A meeting was arranged and from that seed emerged a small group who effectively, in time, took control of Qalle.

The early meetings had not always been peaceful and the spilling of blood was not uncommon as the tribal leaders learned of the existence of the society and attempted to infiltrate it.

Hence the reason that Sister Maria was now naked. Not only, it had been reasoned, could a naked person not conceal a weapon but all council members could see themselves as equal if there could be no ostentatious displays of the sort of finery that was common in the great houses of Qalle.

Maria enjoyed the sensation of the guard probing her vagina and bent down without question to allow him access to her anus. When he had finished, she smiled at him and moved into the room when the other members of the Society awaited her. The guard remained impassive, but then, Ercli slaves usually did.

Tradition dictated that title and position were ignored among members of the upper echelon of the Society of T'arn. There were just eight of them, a representative of each of the six great houses and two who represented the holy orders. All were under forty years of age, it having been accepted that persons above this age tended to be too set in their ways to accept the changes that the society wished to bring to Qalle. At this time there were six women and just two men, not an unusual proportion, as finding genuinely peaceful men among the houses was nearly impossible.

The main weapon employed by the society was sex. The brave pioneers, led by the Lady T'arn of the Southern Roads, had refused to lie with their husbands until a particularly bloody and pointless conflict was resolved. T'arn had been horribly mutilated, branded and then exiled from her people but had lived long enough to set in motion the small group who were to become the Society of T'arn.

Now Maria greeted her peers who sat equally naked in the room above the bakery.

'You are the last of us.' The speaker was a tall, slim woman who represented the Uplands and whose turn it was to preside over this meeting.

'I am the last,' Maria agreed, 'and shall accept my due.' As she spoke she felt the flutter of anticipation. Given that they were all naked and that one of the main points of discussion would be sex, it was inevitable that lust would impinge upon these meetings. Long ago it had been decided that appetites were best slaked before the serious business began. The tradition had arisen that the last to arrive would be put to the mercy of the rest of the group.

Maria looked about the room as the Uplander decided her fate. The two men were already erect and the Kallinian woman had a hand between her legs.

The Uplander came to a decision and rose to her feet. 'We shall each of us beat you in turn. Please part your legs and place your hands on the floor.'

Maria sensed rather than heard the wave of excitement that ran through the assembled delegates. While it was not uncommon for some affectionate spanking to take place during these meetings, for one person to be singled out for such treatment by the rest of the group was unprecedented in Maria's memory. Still, she had come to respect the Uplander as a wise and redoubtable woman and, as she settled her feet wide apart and bent from the waist, knowing how she was exposing herself to the others, Maria guessed that the example she was being made to make would have an explanation. She braced herself as she heard soft footsteps approaching her from behind.

'...and this is the Lady Hysena Macarydias of the Southern Roads.' Hysena bowed, glad of the excuse to hide her blush as Silka completed the introductions. There had been a few moments of consternation when the five Initiates, curiously examining the Last Tower were confronted by Xarrith and Tasnar who had suddenly dropped among them from the ceiling, appearing like the daemons of legend.

Tasnar had been quick to catch the eye of his cousin and had bowed formally.

'I greet my countrywoman. Know that I am Tasnar, son of Tasnar and that I come in peace.' His voice had cut through the confusion of female screams.

'You are welcome, Tasnar, son of Tasnar. I am Silka, daughter of Sis Narash.' For a moment her reply had made Tasnar hesitate before his training took over. He made his bow as deep and respectful as he was able. Only those destined for the highest position among his people were permitted to style themselves son or daughter of the state. Things must have changed in the two years since he had last been home.

The formal behaviour of Silka and Tasnar had the effect of calming the other Initiates.

'Noble Ladies of Qalle,' Tasnar gathered them with his eyes, 'I have the honour of presenting to you Xarrith, warrior of Kallinia.'

Xarrith had done his best to copy the deep bow of his friend, the effort being somewhat spoiled by the glint in his eye and the feral smile on his face. He looked along the line of flustered young women, a sudden vivid memory striking him like a blow when he recognised Maris and Nephraan, remembering how he had viewed them through the spy-hole, each of them naked as they were punished by the fat Sister elder. For a fleeting instant his easy smile slipped and he had the feeling that something was wrong, but the moment passed.

The Initiates blushed deeply as they caught his stare, feeling that this huge, handsome warrior could see right through their shifts — a feeling that caused delicious tingles deep in their bodies.

Xarrith noticed the last of the young women to be introduced and his demeanour underwent a change.

The easy, arrogant smile slid from his face, his eyes dropped and to the amusement of Tasnar who had been watching him from the corner of his eye, Xarrith blushed.

Before him, Hysena stood looking far more relaxed than she felt. When the two Acolytes had suddenly dropped into the room, she had been closest to the door and had been on the point of fleeing through it when the smaller youth had spoken. Being at the end of the line when Silka had begun the introductions, she had had time to compose herself and to study the Kallinian. During her short life, Hysena had had few chances to meet members of the opposite sex and none at all to be alone with any of her own age; she had been too well chaperoned at home and, until now, isolated here in the Citadel. Since her first day at the Citadel, when the kindly Sister Maria had first brought her to orgasm (with, of course, the aid of the Holy Prophet), her sexuality had blossomed. Despite the way he abused her body, part of her held an affection for Father Tarrip as he had been the first man to possess her, but he never featured in the fantasies she conjured in the secrecy of her bed or when one of her sister Initiates was pleasuring her. Instead, she had tried to remember the faces and forms of the young males who had orbited the periphery of her cloistered existence.

None of this had prepared her for her first sight of a

Kallinian warrior. As she struggled to maintain her composure Hysena felt her innards turn liquid and her sex stir. She felt her nipples harden and saw Xarrith's eyes widen as he too noticed the phenomenon. Allowing her eyes to drop from where they had been riveted to his, she was barely able to suppress a gasp as she saw the swelling bulge at his groin.

She was not alone. Smiling wryly, Tasnar saw that each of the five Initiates was staring at Xarrith with raw lust, and any doubts he might have had as to whether the meeting with the Initiates would conclude in the manner he and Xarrith had hoped were dispelled. As he felt his own erection grow, Tasnar drank in the sight of ten erect nipples showing through the thin cotton shifts, the varied shape and tilt of breasts, the swell of hips, the promise of pubic hair that could just be discerned through the material of their garments. And this time he was not separated from them by stone walls.

Forcing to the back of his mind the thought that he might have to spend the evening watching Xarrith having to deal with all five of them, Tasnar spoke into the silence.

'Xarrith, we forget our manners. We must offer refreshment to these maidens.'

With an effort, Hysena broke off her stare and achieved a shaky smile. She saw the direction of Xarrith's eyes and with unrecognised, atavistic instinct drew back her shoulders, thrusting her breasts at him, wishing uncharitably that the ground would collapse under her sister Initiates. She managed to turn her head away from the warrior and address the other youth.

'Thank you, sir. Some refreshment would be welcome.' She had hardly noticed Tasnar, but now she saw the slim beauty of his body, the intelligence on his face and the look in his eye that suggested that while making love with Xarrith would be a wild, animal thing, with this one the experience might be even better. Almost overwhelmed by her conflicting desires, Hysena seated herself on one of the stools.

'Wine for my lady,' said Tasnar, approaching with one of the flagons. 'I regret that my foolish friend neglected to bring cups, so we must do the best we can.'

'It is true.' Xarrith joined in with relief, having been desperately searching his mind for something intelligent to say. 'When Tasnar told me we were at last to meet, so overwhelmed was I that all other thoughts fled from my mind, the thought that I may at last see you face to face rather than... than...' He caught the warning glance that Tasnar was directing at him. Of course he could hardly explain that he had seen her before. The circumstances in which he had done so would inevitably lead to embarrassing revelations.

Hysena smiled and took the flagon from Tasnar. She tried to sip delicately but was not used to drinking from such a vessel nor was she prepared for the harsh taste of the raw red wine it contained. The liquid gushed into her mouth and throat too fast for her to swallow, causing her to splutter. To her tribulation, wine spilled from the corners of her mouth and dribbled onto her shift. More went up the back of her throat to reappear down her nostrils in a sneeze of red droplets, some of which landed on Tasnar.

Coughing and sneezing, her dignity utterly destroyed, Hysena tried to turn away, only to be taken by another massive sneeze most of which this time caught Xarrith. Bent forward, trying to suck air into her lungs, the mortified Initiate heard the screams of laughter coming from the other girls.

'I had heard of the famed hospitality of House Macarydias,' said Maris through her giggles, 'but this is the first time I have seen it demonstrated.'

'Think you we should do likewise and also spit wine at our guests?' suggested Leel to further laughter.

'Nay, sister,' said Nephraan, wiping tears from her eyes, 'it is not a greeting, it is how in the Southern Roads they brand their men.'

Tasnar stepped forward to rescue the flagon from where it lay on its side before it could spill all of its contents. Already a large stain marred the priceless carpet. Worse, some had splashed the hanging tapestries and they were holy things. There was silence in the Last Tower. This was sacrilege.

Tasnar looked seriously at his cousin. 'Trouble may come from this.'

Silka studied the stain that was creeping across the carpet and the marked tapestries. 'More than were we to be caught here?' she asked.

'Possibly not, but dare we risk this?'

On her stool, Hysena wiped wine from her nose and tears from her eyes with her hand. She looked at the others. The mood had suddenly changed. The eager anticipation had fled to be replaced by apprehension. Just moments before she had felt herself to be on the cusp of what promised to be the greatest experience of her life and now, with one careless gesture, she had ruined everything. Just, she thought miserably, as she had done on her very first day here, when her clumsiness had disturbed the Novice Initiate Ceremony.

As she watched, Leel and Nephraan began inching towards the stone stairs that led from the Last Tower. Tasnar was wiping ineffectually at the stained carpet with the sleeve of his jerkin. And she could not bring herself to meet the eye of the warrior boy.

Hysena buried her face in her hands, about to submit to the sobs that were welling up inside her when it seemed that an inner voice began to speak.

'When you came to this place,' the voice whispered, 'you were but a callow child, formed in body but not in mind. In this place you have learned, if naught else, that you can be strong. These here with you now in this room are not your enemies. They need but to be led. Lead them, Hysena Macarydias, lead them.'

Deep inside her, Hysena felt something burn. She lifted her head from her hands and raised her chin. How stupid, she thought, to let such a silly incident spoil such an evening. Standing, she drew a deep breath and clapped her hands. Despondent heads turned to look at her.

'My friends,' she said, her voice clear and steady. When she was sure that she had their attention, Hysena raised her hands to the neck of her garment and, not daring to hesitate lest she lose her resolve, ripped downwards.

Staring at them defiantly, she dropped her hands to her sides and stood before the frozen gaze of her peers. She felt her nipples crinkle as she saw the six pairs of eyes that were riveted to the sight of her suddenly exposed breasts. Proudly, she pulled back her shoulders. It seemed that she could feel her breasts grow warm from the heat radiating from the bulging eyes of the Kallinian and as she allowed her eyes to move down his muscular frame she could not stop the hiss of her breath as she saw the bulge at his groin. Even as she watched it grew; held in check by the cloth of his breeches it seemed to crawl with a life of its own down his thigh almost as far as his knee. Hysena felt the stirring of her sex, felt the secret lips grow and open like petals.

'My friends,' she repeated, 'I have transgressed. Through my carelessness I have sullied these fine depictions of our Holy Prophet. I throw myself upon your mercy.' Matching action to her words, Hysena prostrated herself face down on the stained carpet.

For long moments there was silence in the Last Tower. The four standing Initiates looked at each other in confusion, caught between the desire to fly lest this desecration be discovered and the desire to see where this new direction might lead. All in the room had felt the stirrings of lust ever since they had entered the room. All had experienced the frisson when they realised that for the first time since they entered the Citadel they were with members of the opposite sex without chaperonage. Their eyes flicked from one to another and to the slim figure of Hysena, still prostrate before them.

Xarrith studied her, his mouth dry as he saw the slim figure outlined beneath the thin cotton of her shift. He had been openly disdainful of those in the Citadel who were diligent in their devotions but now as he studied the double bulge of her buttocks, his prayer to the Holy Prophet that nothing else happen to interrupt this evening was as fervent as any that the ancient building had witnessed.

Silka was the first to find her voice. 'Name your transgression, my child,' she said.

These were words that all of the Initiates had heard on countless occasions when summoned before Father Tarrip, the words with which they were forced to condemn themselves from their own mouths, words that inevitably led to unimaginable pain and, often, pleasure. This time there was no Tarrip, there was no Colya. This time there was something better.

'I have despoiled an icon of the Holy Prophet.' Hysena's voice was muffled by her position.

Silka began to circle her friend, in imitation of the Holy Father. 'It is a most serious matter.' She fought to keep her voice grave. 'And what else?'

'I did not attend to my devotions this night.'

'Hmmm.' Silka bent down and put her head close to Hysena's, another faithful imitation that drew a stifled giggle from Maris. 'And what else?'

'I have had thoughts that are forbidden to an Initiate of the Holy Prophet of Qalle!'

Silka stood and faced the others. 'From her own mouth, the Lady Hysena has condemned herself and must be punished. What say you?'

Leel, Maris and Nephraan spoke almost as one. 'She must be beaten!' and dissolved into giggles.

Xarrith exchanged a puzzled look with Tasnar. From their observations through the spy holes they had witnessed the terrible punishments that the Initiates were forced to endure. How could they possibly make a joke about it? He turned his attention back to Silka,

'A beating,' she was saying, 'is meet.' Her voice took on a mischievous note. 'But which of us should administer this condign punishment?' Five pairs of female eyes swivelled to rest on the two young Acolytes.

From where she lay on the floor, to Hysena Xarrith

appeared as massive as a tree. She wriggled slightly, enjoying the sensation of the rough carpet against her bare nipples as she thought of how it would be to place herself over his knees, feel him raise her shift to expose her buttocks. She wondered how his hand might feel on her naked flesh. She pressed down with her hips, rubbing the bulge of her mons against the unyielding floor, bringing a delightful pressure to her clitoris. She looked again at Xarrith and caught his eye. To her delight, she saw his face colour.

Silka noticed and smiled. 'My brother Acolytes,' she said, 'it is not fit that any of us punish this wicked girl. Perhaps you could suggest a solution?'

'I……I,' Xarrith stammered hopelessly. He looked to his companion for help.

Tasnar also had his eyes on the girl on the floor, his mind filled with lustful thoughts. 'I suppose it to be our duty to assist,' he said slowly, hardly believing what he was being offered. 'I take it that in her contrition the Lady Hysena does concede to this punishment?'

'I do so concede!' said Hysena, her voice trembling in anticipation.

Tasnar drew up a stool and seated himself. 'How is this punishment to be administered?' he asked, hoping the bulge in his breeches was not too obvious.

Following his example the others arranged stools of their own in a loose circle about Hysena and considered Tasnar's important question.

Silka looked to the others for an indication that they were satisfied that she should continue as speaker for them. 'The Holy Prophet has said that all must share the sins of the wrongdoer,' she said. 'Therefore, should we all join in the punishment of Hysena, so shall the sin be shared.'

'Aye,' agreed Leel, her eyes bright with excitement, 'and also we must in turn take punishment that the sin be shared.' She felt her nipples crinkle at the thought.

'Is this agreed?' Silka asked.

'Aye!' shouted the delighted girls.

Silka looked, down at Hysena. 'Please stand, my lady.'

Hysena did as she was bid and brushed some shreds of wool from her naked breasts, causing them to bob. She saw that Xarrith was staring open mouthed at them and pulled her shoulders back proudly.

Silka saw the naked lust on the face of the warrior and shifted on her stool as she felt the dampness of excitement start between her thighs.

'Perhaps the Lord Xarrith would commence the punishment?' she suggested.

Hysena smiled her thanks at her friend and with no further ceremony she crossed to Xarrith and draped herself bottom-up over his knees. Even as she settled herself she could feel the hardness of his penis against her thigh and wondered at the size of it.

Xarrith too was aware of his erection, being pressed delightfully by the hot thigh of the beautiful young girl on his lap. For a moment he wondered if this was a dream as he looked about the room, seeing the eager eyes of the four Initiates as they watched. Leel, he saw, had one hand on her plump breast and was squeezing it, Maris and Nephraan were holding hands. Silka was sitting primly upright on her stool but her breathing was quick and her nipples were erect and showing clearly through her white shift. Finally he looked at Tasnar, seated next to him. The smaller youth raised his eyebrows and winked at him. Tentatively, Xarrith raised his hand and brought it down on Hysena's behind.

The blow was not as hard as she had anticipated, but still Hysena squealed as it landed. The hand landed again, harder this time as Xarrith gained confidence and Hysena groaned deep in her throat, pressing her hips down hard against his penis. She wrapped an arm about one of his muscular legs, pressing her naked breast against the rough wool of his buskin, stimulating the nipple.

Xarrith looked up from his work. He saw that Nephraan now had her arm about the other girl and was caressing her breast. The sight was enormously exciting.

And he had another beautiful and apparently willing girl cast over his knees.

Hysena too looked over to Maris and Nephraan and smiled a wanton smile at them. She adjusted her position, pulling herself further across the knees of the warrior, allowing her legs to fall apart knowing what she was exposing to Xarrith's eyes.

Feeling her move, the Kallinian dragged his eyes away from the sight of Nephraan's hand moving on the big breast of the Uplander and his breath hissed in his throat as he looked down. He saw the perfect hemispheres of her behind, the smooth white skin slightly reddened by the gentle spanking he had given her and covered in tiny goose-pimples. That sight alone was utterly beguiling but his eye was drawn inevitably to what lay between the perfect cheeks. The lips of her vagina nestled in the silky black curls of her pubic hair, the cleft slightly parted to allow him a glimpse of the inner pinkness. The gleam of her juices was afforded a nacreous quality by the candles that lit the room and his hand moved as if of its own accord to stroke her there.

Hysena had been expecting another spank and so the gentle caress arrived as an unexpected and wonderful surprise. She moaned and reflexively straightened her legs, lifting her hips even higher and pressing herself onto Xarrith's exploring fingers, feeling one, then another, slide gently into her liquid depths. Her hips gyrated voluptuously as he probed ever deeper, her hand sliding up his leg and along his thigh until she could grasp the impossible thickness of his prick through the wool of his buskins.

From her seat beside the two who now seemed to have entered a private world of their own, Silka had a fine view of Hysena's pretty cunt and of the fingers that were playing with it. She watched for a while, her hand moving gently between her own thighs, feeling the moisture seeping through the cotton of her shift as she pushed a finger into herself. 'I think that is hardly a punishment, maiden.'

Hysena came reluctantly back to Qalle and twisted her head to look sheepishly at her friend. 'That all of my life until now… ahhh… has been spent apart from this warrior is indeed punishment,' she said, her voice unsteady as the waves of pleasure flowed through her being. Xarrith had now found her nude breasts with his other hand and was teasing them alternately. She desperately wanted to free the huge bulk of his penis, to caress it, to take it into her mouth, to feel it filling her in every place and she knew that she would, but also she wanted to postpone the moment, to make it last.

It took a great effort of will for her to take the wrist of the Kallinian and disengage his fingers from her body. She saw the look of dismay on his face and, standing, deposited a gentle kiss on his lips.

'Do not fret, Xarrith of Kallinia. There will be reward, but first there must be punishment.' She smiled wickedly at him. 'Besides, there are five of us and my sisters would never forgive me should I dare sequester you for myself.' With a sweep of her arm, Hysena indicated the other Initiates who were now frankly squirming on their stools in anticipation, inflamed by the sight of Xarrith caressing Hysena where they in their turn wished to be touched. 'The punishment must be shared by all!'

Xarrith came once again to realise that the room held more than just himself and the beautiful Southern Roader and he looked at the four other young women and then at Tasnar. 'So, my brother. It would seem that the Holy Prophet shall this evening test our mettle to the full.'

'Aye, sir.' Tasnar used his thumb to flick sweat from his brow. 'I pray we shall not be found wanting in this task.'

Hysena stood naked before Tasnar. She saw his wide eyes roaming over her curves and could not resist rolling her hips. Then she turned and bent over, placing her hands flat on the floor and moving her feet wide apart.

'Punish me, for I have sinned,' she said, looking at the startled youth through her spread legs.

Tasnar swallowed hard, staring at the gorgeous vision

of the long, bare limbs that were presented to him, drinking in the sight of her exposed vagina, the lips distinctly wet now. He slowly raised a hand and brought it down sharply on her trembling buttock.

Maris and Nephraan took it as a signal that all inhibition might now also be discarded. They reached for each other, moving their stools together until they were close enough to kiss. For long minutes they were aware only of themselves, the sliding of tongues into mouths and hands over breasts, the quickening of breath and the growing lust suffusing their loins. Eventually, they broke. Each now had a hand on the sex of the other and they gently frigged each other and enjoyed the sight of Tasnar spanking Hysena.

'Tis no hard punishment,' Nephraan observed, 'see, he hardly touches her.'

'You are right sister,' agreed Maris. She looked over to Tasnar who was totally absorbed in his enjoyable task. 'Sir!' she called, 'we are used to far firmer treatment — see!' Having gained the attention of the Sis-Narashan, Maris pulled Nephraan over her knees and ignoring the unconvincing struggles of the other, pulled up her robe and began to spank her briskly.

Xarrith had watched the things going on in the Last Room in disbelief. His fingers were still damp with Hysena's secretions and he lifted them to his nose to take in the musky scent of her as he watched Tasnar beat her and then looked over to where Nephraan and Maris were devouring each other. When Maris put Nephraan over her lap and began to spank her, the sight of those long legs kicking, her cunt carelessly exposed, caused something to burst in his head.

He threw back his head and roared. *'Now! Prepare yourselves! Kallinia is upon you!'*

He leapt to his feet and regarded the frozen figures before him, eyes glinting, face creased with a huge grin.

Hysena closed her eyes and was enjoying the building ecstasy as Tasnar had started to caress her between spanks, running a gentle finger along the length of her slit and briefly tickling her clitoris each time his hand fell. When the sudden roar came, she lost her balance and rolled instinctively into a ball, thinking that somehow the Holy Father was upon them. Opening a cautious eye, she saw the imposing figure of Xarrith. Never before had she seen such naked lust. She saw him turn his head slowly, as if selecting a victim, saw the play of the muscles on his arms, the great width of his shoulders and, unable to prevent her eyes dropping, the impossibly huge bulge of his prick which was almost bursting from his buskins. She saw his eyes light on Leel who was cowering on the stool next to his, a combined look of fear and desire on her face. The warrior reached out and plucked Leel effortlessly from her seat.

'Is even a Princess of Calith subject to the wrath of the Holy Prophet?' he growled.

She nodded rapidly, unable to speak for the delicious fear that had turned her insides to liquid. The grip about her upper arm felt like steel and even had she wanted to she would have been unable to resist as the Kallinian tore the shift from her body. She closed her eyes and shivered with delight as she felt him run a hand over her body, weighing her breast and flicking her nipple before cupping her sodden cunt in his open palm. Using just that hand, Xarrith lifted her so that the full weight of her body was supported by the hand between her legs. She felt herself thrown over his shoulder and he wrapped an arm about her thighs to hold her there, bottom pointing to the ceiling, her breasts pressing into his back.

Xarrith paraded her around the room like a trophy, slapping her plump behind as he walked until it glowed pinkly in the flickering light of the candles.

'Who now shall punish this wanton?' he asked of no one in particular.

'I!' Silka called and stood from her stool where she had begun to feel left out of the proceedings, being now the only one not engaged with another.

Xarrith crossed the room with his squirming burden and smiled down at her. The top of her head reached only to his chin.

'With what coin shall you pay for this boon, little sister?' Xarrith asked teasingly.

Silka studied his rugged features and slowly, sensuously, licked her lips. 'I have no coin, warrior, but perhaps this shall suffice'?' she said quietly. With that, she sank to her knees and with trembling fingers, began to unbutton his buskins.

Across the room, Nephraan was now sitting on the lap of Maris, facing the blonde Uplander and easing her shift down to expose her big breasts. Maris shivered as warm lips took her engorged nipple. She slid her hands along the thighs that rested on hers, pushing back the material that covered them until her hands could caress the buttocks of the other girl. Her fingers sought the divide and found it, slick and hot with arousal. Glancing across the room, she saw Silka kneeling before Xarrith.

'Nephraan. Look yonder,' she whispered. Nephraan lifted her head from Maris's breast and twisted to look. She saw Silka undo the final button and ease the buskins over Xarrith's hips and down his thighs. Both girls gasped in amazement at what was revealed.

From the bulge she had been surreptitiously observing ever since Tasnar and Xarrith had made their precipitate entrance to the Last Tower, Silka had known that something huge was hidden beneath the Kallinian's buskins, but she was not prepared for what now confronted her. Her own gasp mingled with those of Maris and Nephraan and she drew her head back at the sight of the monster that sprang free as she pulled down Xarrith's garment. Wordlessly, eyes wide with shock, she reached for it. Her small hand could encompass only half of the girth and when she wrapped her other hand about the hot shaft her two fists covered far less than half of the length.

The room fell silent. Xarrith loosened his grip on Leel who rolled from his shoulder and joined Silka kneeling before him. Her two hands joined those of the Sis-Narashan and even the four hands together still left the huge plum of his glans exposed. As the girls watched in wonderment, a pearly drop of semen emerged from the tiny opening at the tip of the great penis. Silka leaned forward and, extending her tongue, licked it into her mouth. She heard Xarrith groan and continued to lick at him, rolling her tongue over the tight, shiny skin at the tip of his prick and then working her way along his length, drawing back his foreskin as she did, marvelling at the size of his glans. She shuddered at the thought of how that would feel pushing into her and felt the sudden rush of wetness between her legs.

Tasnar had brought Hysena to the brink of orgasm. She was still bending over before him, her legs wide, her delightful bottom thrust invitingly towards him. The slim youth had leaned forward to kiss her between the legs, wriggling his tongue as deeply as he could reach into her vagina, enjoying the way her inner muscles were contracting rhythmically about him. With one hand, her reached around her hip to fondle her dangling breasts and with the other he was struggling to free his penis from the constricting cloth of his buskins. He achieved this just as Silka freed Xarrith's huge organ and, hearing her exclamation of amazement, he lifted his face from between the legs of Hysena and noted with wry amusement that all five of the Initiates were staring rapt at his friend's proud display.

'I had best take my chance before it is gone,' he muttered to himself and took Hysena by the hips pulling her onto himself. There was no resistance and he slid into her in one single thrust.

Hysena had all but lost herself in a haze of arousal. The mild spanking that Tasnar had administered had set her blood singing and being licked from behind was her favourite form of stimulation and this time it was even better than normal, given the piquancy of being administered by this handsome young Acolyte. The gasps of the other Initiates broke into her consciousness and she lifted her head and opened her eyes in time to see Xarrith made naked. Her eyes grew wider and wider and her eyebrows crawled up her brow as she tried to assimilate the vision. Surely her eyes lied! Her knees began to buckle. She welcomed the gentle pressure of hands on her hips and allowed herself to be pulled back, sinking thankfully onto Tasnar's lap. She felt the tip of his prick nuzzle over the lips of her sex, seeking the way into her body, and then the welcome penetration, felt the way being parted and filled as he took her, sliding easily into her wetness. She moved her thighs wider the better to accommodate him and, her eyes still on Xarrith, reached blindly behind her. Finding Tasnar's hand, she guided it to her clitoris and as he began to stroke her, she began to move her hips, pressing back onto him, taking his full length into herself. Looking down, she could enjoy the sight of his prick sliding in and out of her cunt, its lips made prominent and easily seen through the damp tangle of her pubic hair. Almost as if it were happening to someone else, she saw his confident fingers part her to expose her clitoris and felt the exquisite lightning strike as he squeezed her there. Her hands went to her breasts, pinching the nipples, pulling them out from her body. Looking to Xarrith, she saw that tiny Silka was attempting the impossible, trying to swallow the giant member. Even through the gorgeous sensations that were shaking her body she was able to smile at the sight. She felt her orgasm building inexorably within her and moved a hand down to encourage Tasnar to rub her faster and then reached between their legs to squeeze his balls, finding them tight and firm, ready to empty into her.

Hysena and Tasnar climaxed together, their mingled cries echoing about the room loudly enough to draw attention away from Silka and Xarrith.

'So,' said Nephraan, 'our lady of the Southern Roads claims the first reward.' She and Maris were still companionably masturbating each other as they watched, building each other slowly, both imagining how it would be to be impaled on the sword of the massive warrior.

'Aye, sister,' said Maris, working her fingers deeper into the other girl, 'think you that she may pass to us some of that reward?'

Nephraan smiled at the thought and raised her voice adopting a formal tone. 'Madam, my companion and I would deem it a boon were you willing to kiss our cunts.'

Hysena, who still had Tasnar inside her and was caressing his balls and her own cunt, matched the formality. 'I should be honoured, madam. I shall make you wet as the sea and ready to receive the attentions of our new companions.' She gave Tasnar a final squeeze and lifted herself from him, feeling him slide out of her. 'I trust there would be no offence should I suggest that you adopt a more appropriate mode of dress?'

Maris and Nephraan looked at each other and giggled. There was a flurry of limbs and a swishing of cloth. In seconds they were both naked, looking boldly towards Tasnar and Xarrith

Silka, her mouth distended to its fullest extent, had managed to take an impressive proportion of Xarrith's erection into her throat. Tears squeezed from between her tightly shut eyelids at the effort. She felt Leel tugging at her shift, lifting it up her body until it was bunched under her arms and felt her breasts being caressed, the big breasts of the princess of Calith pressing into her bare back. The need to breathe became overwhelming and she reluctantly withdrew her mouth from the warrior. As she did, Leel was able to lift her garment over her head, and now all five Initiates were naked.

Hopping awkwardly as he fought to pull off his buskins, Xarrith drank in the sight. Nephraan was lying on the floor, her legs apart. Hysena was on her knees between them, sucking on the long clitoris, shapely bottom elevated, buttocks reddened from her spanking and her sex gaping and gleaming from the fucking that Tasnar had administered. Sitting on a stool next to them was Maris, her spectacular breasts heaving, their small, pink nipples stiff with excitement. Seeing the eyes of the warrior on her, Maris spread her thighs, letting him see the fine blonde pubic hair and the slit of her cunt. Locking her eyes on his, she slid a finger into herself and heard the hiss of his indrawn breath.

As she fingered herself, Maris saw Xarrith fold a hand about his prick and start to rub. His hand was huge compared to that of tiny Silka, but it did little to make his massive erection seem smaller. Maris reached more deeply into herself adding a second and then a third finger. She saw that the eyes of the Kallinian were riveted to the sight of what she was displaying for him, and her fingers moved faster.

'Fuck me, warrior,' she challenged him. 'Put that thing into me and pierce me to the heart.'

The girl rose from her stool, went to the centre of the room and lay down on her back. Slowly, she opened her legs. She heard him growl and looked at him over the double swell of her breasts. He had released his prick and as he approached her prone form it twitched and pulsed with a life of its own. For a moment he stood over her, a foot either side of her waist. From that angle, he looked unbelievably enormous and despite her need Maris felt her stomach shrink in delicious fear.

Xarrith began to lower himself and to the straining eyes of the Initiate his member became something out of a dream as it came ever closer. Maris felt abstracted, as if this were happening to another girl, not Maris Ap Stavin, daughter of the richest man on Qalle. To her dazed mind she felt herself an observer. It was some other Initiate who felt Xarrith settle his buttocks across her hips, the weight pressing her firmly to the floor so that the tufts of the carpet dug into her skin. It was some other Initiate who felt his hands, surprisingly gentle, lift her breasts and fold them about his penis.

The heat of his hard flesh was searing, the feeling of his thumbs as he smoothed them over her nipples indescribable. He began to thrust, rubbing himself within the prison of soft breasts that he had made. Maris saw the tip of his prick emerge and opened her mouth to receive him.

The room was silent but for the heavy breathing of Maris and Xarrith. The others watched entranced as they saw the Kallinian using Maris's breasts before he partially raised himself and shuffled back to kneel between her thighs.

As he did, Maris raised her knees, spreading her legs and opening herself with her fingers, spreading the lips of her sex like petals. She felt his fingers touch her there, and then the tip of his prick was being rubbed along the length of her slit, teasingly not penetrating and driving her mad with frustration. And then he did penetrate her. Even as wet as she was, wetter than she had ever been, so huge was he that he had to use considerable force to start his prick on its journey. She felt the entrance to her vagina being forced open by the inexorable pressure until she thought it must surely burst and then, with a sudden slippery, gasping rush, he was inside her. Immediately she felt herself more satisfyingly filled than she had ever been, but Xarrith still had more to offer. The dream state continued as the young Initiate felt more and ever more of him press into her secret place. She used her hands behind her knees to pull her legs even wider as she strained to accommodate him.

At last, there was no more. He was fully inside her. Her cunt was stretched to its limit, as totally filled as it would ever be. Maris lay still, unable to breathe, feeling her orgasm swelling to the surface of her consciousness and just as she thought no feeling could possibly be greater than this, Xarrith reared back, withdrawing half of his length, and then thrust into her cunt with all his strength.

10.

Holy Father Tarrip was puzzled. There was no reason why Sister Maria should not be in her room or even in the Citadel, but it was uncharacteristic. However a pleasant stroll had improved his mood and the thought of Silka, with her tiny, exquisite breasts and tight cunt drove the last vestiges of his belly-ache from his mind and he turned back towards his room, impatient now for the time when Colya was due to bring her and Maris to his rooms.

The coarse features of his faithful assistant were troubled when she nervously came to him. She was alone.

'Is no sign of naughty girls, Holy Father,' she told him.

'Then fetch two of the others,' he commanded impatiently. His lust was running high now. 'Any of them will do.'

'I.....I mean, is no sign of any of Initiates.'

'What! How can this be, you idiot woman?' Angry now, Tarrip cuffed her.

Colya fell to the floor, feeling the delicious tickle of fear in her stomach. As she fell, she made sure that her grubby robe rode up, exposing the thick forest of her pubic hair. With Maria and all the Initiates gone, he would have to slake his appetite with her, she reasoned in her simple way.

Not pausing to glance at the woman on the floor, Tarrip strode from the room. Maria and all the girls missing could mean only one thing. She had hidden herself away with them, intending an orgy of her own — and without him!

Tarrip raged through the Citadel. Guards were dispatched to search every corner, only to report back to him, trembling at his wrath as they each in turn admitted failure.

The last of the guards to report squealed as the iron-clad boot of Tarrip thudded again into his buttocks. Frantically searching his mind for something, anything, that might appease his master, he stammered out that he had seen a light in the Last Tower.

'Then search it, imbecile!' Tarrip roared, aiming another lethal kick at the hapless man. In moments, the room was empty as the guards, hard fighting men, scattered like hens before the fox as the priest advanced on them.

Tarrip threw the cup he had been drinking from, shattering it against the wall and further irritated that now there was no outlet for his rage; he noticed the cowering figure of Sister Colya. His face twisted into the rictus of a smile.

'Remove your robe.' His voice held a feral quality of purest evil. Colya was taken by such violent shaking that she could barely comply.

Fear churned in her belly as she watched him select the longest and heaviest of his tokans, and immediately fear was competing with an arousal she had not felt since she was a young girl. She felt a flood of wetness between her legs as he ordered her to lie naked on her back on the cold stone floor. Unbidden, she raised her knees and spread her thighs wide.

Tarrip felt his rage turn to lust as he watched her open to him, saw the swollen red lips of her sex, soaked with her juices, cowering in the nest of her pubic hair. He felt his erection grow thick and firm and, hoisting his robe he grasped it in one hand and with the other brought down the tokan in a full overarm blow that landed with paralysing force on her cunt.

11.

This memory, Hysena was thinking, would remain with her to the very grave. She was sitting naked on a stool, her thighs wide and with Tasnar between them, licking the puffy lips of her sex and swollen clitoris as she watched in admiring wonder the sight of Xarrith pleasuring four Initiates at once. Nephraan was astride his thighs, impaled upon that huge penis. Silka, leaning forward to kiss her breasts, had positioned her hips above his mouth and, between kisses, was breathily exhorting him to push tongue and fingers deeper; from her position Hysena could not see into which orifice she was urging him. Maris had placed his elbow on the floor, raised the muscular forearm to the vertical and lowered herself until his fist and a good length of his arm were hidden inside her. Leel, to Hysena's amazement, had achieved something similar with one of his feet. From the way the plump princess had screwed her face up in ecstasy, she guessed that the warrior was wriggling his toes. As she felt yet another orgasm take her, she pushed Tasnar onto his back and, straddling him, fed his stiff prick into her aching cunt.

This, then, was the sight that met the incredulous eyes of the six guards who had entered the room at the top of the Last Tower, unheard by the busy occupants.

Leel's scream was at first taken by the others to be just one more in the myriad climaxes that had shaken the ancient room during the past hours.

As he felt Leel lift herself from him, Xarrith perhaps sensed that something was amiss. Freeing his mouth from between Silka's legs, he twisted his head and looked up. With a convulsive thrust of his hips he threw Nephraan from him, snatched his fist from the vagina of Maris and leapt to his feet.

'Hold!' called, the leading guard, 'hold in the name of the Holy Prophet of Qalle!'

For a long moment, it seemed that the warrior was

about to throw himself at the six adversaries, but the sight of six crossbows levelled at him caused him to check his instinct. He spread his hands in resignation.

The leading guard nodded in satisfaction. 'A wise decision,' the man said, eyeing Xarrith's erection with frank admiration. 'It would be an ignoble end for such a warrior... and such a weapon.'

As the moment of tension passed, the other guards allowed their bows to droop as they took in the sight of the seven naked figures.

Xarrith turned to Tasnar. 'I am only glad that they did not arrive earlier,' he said, sounding if anything amused at the sudden intrusion. Tasnar was not fooled and could see that his friend was alert to any chance that might present its self.

'Perhaps they may care to join our game.'

Xarrith's eyebrows rose as he recognised the voice of Hysena. As she spoke, the beautiful girl looked the lead guard directly in the eye and thrust her hips towards him, offering her naked sex in unmistakable invitation.

The ploy might have worked had the guard's mind not been filled by vision of Tarrip's murderous rage. And so it was that the five Initiates and two Acolytes found themselves being herded naked down the winding steps of the Last Tower.

'What shall they do to us?' whispered Hysena, walking close to the comforting bulk of Xarrith.

The warrior shrugged. 'You would know better than I. They have dared little against Tasnar and me.'

Hysena ran through her mind the varied and imaginative indignities that had been visited upon her body and those of her sisters during their time in the Citadel.

'We may suffer the fate of Jagdig,' she said, fear in her voice.

Xarrith started at the name. 'Jagdig! Jagdig of Kallinia?'

'Aye,' said Hysena. 'Know you her?'

'She is kin. Distant, but kin. She is here in this foul

place?' He suddenly realised what the thing was that had, from time to time, bothered him. He had seen no one of his people among the Initiates. With growing horror that slowly turned to burning anger, he listened as Hysena whispered to him the fate that had befallen Jagdig.

He had not know her well and had not found her particularly agreeable, but as the full horror of the way the fat priest had used her unfolded, he could think of her only as a fellow Kallinian; a Kallinian in desperate need of help.

'So she is held alone in a deep hole?' His voice was cold and hard.

'The deepest,' said Hysena, shivering at the memory of the place when she had been made to add to the indignities that Tarrip had heaped upon her and ashamed now of how she had enjoyed that part she had played in punishing the girl.

Xarrith gathered his resolve. Looking surreptitiously at the guards, he saw that the lack of resistance had relaxed them and they were more intent on the naked bodies of their charges than any threat they might represent

As the party turned into another passage, there were just two guards ahead of him, the others momentarily out of sight around the corner. Taking a deep breath, Xarrith leapt.

His attack was as ferocious as it was sudden. The two men found themselves seized from behind, a huge hand circling each neck in a grip of iron. Before they could cry out, the warrior had dashed their heads against the stone wall, rendering them instantly senseless. Spinning on his heel, Xarrith turned to face the other guards who were emerging from around the corner with the other captives. Lowering his head, Xarrith charged with a deafening roar, scattering guards and shrieking women alike. He made no attempt to fight, intent only on breaking through them to gain the way back to where he knew lay an entrance to the hidden passages.

Such was the savagery and unexpectedness of his

attack, only one of the guards had the presence of mind to raise his bow. Seeing him, Tasnar lifted his knee and delivered a solid kick to the kidneys, spoiling his aim. The bolt that was intended for Xarrith's heart instead glanced from his side, bloodying him but doing nothing to stop his inexorable charge.

It took seconds. With three of their number, including their leader, down, the remaining defenders had little appetite to follow Xarrith. They had all seen his face.

One ear cocked for the sounds of pursuit, Xarrith fumbled for the knob of rock that would open the hidden door. Finding it, he slipped through and slammed the door behind him, leaning his back against it and taking great gulps of air as reaction set in. He had no light with him, and could only hope he would be able to grope his way to the more familiar passages he and Tasnar had traversed. He felt the wetness on his side, the trickle of liquid running over his hip, and for the first time realised that he was bleeding.

'A scratch,' he muttered disdainfully and, naked and unarmed, hand clamped to the wound in his side, Xarrith of Kallinia set off down the dark passage in search of his kinswoman.

Hysena honestly wondered if the high priest would burst with anger. She was huddled with the other Initiates in his luxurious quarters, still naked, surprised with herself that she felt little fear as she watched Tarrip.

His face beet red, eyes threatening to pop from their sockets, fists clenched so tight that his nails drew blood from the palms of his hands, the priest glared at the guards.

'...and yet one of them still managed to escape you? Not only escape but vanish like a wraith before your very eyes?' The guards shuffled nervously before him, not even daring to glance at the naked Initiates.

'You!' Tarrip singled out the guard captain. 'Tell me of the search you have instigated to recover the Acolyte.'

The guard licked his lips, trying to ignore the pain from when Tasnar had kicked him. 'I...we thought it best to report the matter immediately, holiness. And we did capture the other.' He gestured to where Tasnar lay where they had flung him. With Xarrith gone and knowing what would happen if they harmed the girls, the guards had vented their anger on the hapless youth. He had tried to fight but their numbers had quickly overwhelmed him and they had beaten and kicked him until he was still.

Tarrip looked down at the bloodied form and grunted. 'I can at least question this one. He will know where went the devil Xarrith,' he muttered, kneeling by the boy. He stiffened and slowly turned his head to look at the guards. 'You fools. Can you do nothing right? This one is dead.' He stood in disgust, aiming a kick at Tasnar's body.

Back in his rooms, Tarrip tried to plan. It was many years since there had been anything resembling insurrection in the Citadel; the guards had grown lazy and bored. They had told him that the trail of blood left by the fleeing Kallinian had ended abruptly before a solid wall, and Tarrip guessed that he must somehow have learned of the hidden ways. He was not so foolish as to follow Xarrith by himself and it was unthinkable that the guards could be told of the ways. Where was Maria when he needed her!

Tarrip ordered that the guards patrol the exterior of the Citadel and try to catch Xarrith as he emerged. Six of them he had stand at the door of his rooms. He would take no chances with a loose Kallinian warrior.

Having dealt with that, he could turn to more enjoyable matters.

'Well, Sister Colya, in all my years I have never before been confronted with such behaviour. I do not think the normal punishments will be adequate to appease the Holy Prophet. What think you?'

Colya knew the question to be rhetorical and knew that no answer was expected. 'So,' continued Tarrip who was beginning to enjoy himself, 'we must seek a punishment that is adequate.'

Even this most dire of threats failed to engender much fear in Hysena when he repeated it to the Initiates, most of whom were sobbing, not for themselves but for Tasnar. The guards had dragged him from the cell before barring the door and when Tarrip entered with Colya, she saw that the bloodied body still lay in the passage. Her vagina still ached from his attentions; his seed was still within her. Two hours ago she had been the happiest woman in all of creation and now... Hysena noticed that his evil eyes were hooded, a sure sign that he had some particularly savage punishment in mind and then she did feel fear.

Tarrip ran his eye over the line of naked youngsters, his thumbs hooked into his belt. The punishment he had in mind was archaic and had not, to his knowledge, been employed for many years, having been deemed too barbaric even for the Citadel. If Maria had been present, no doubt she would have found some reason to prevent this and it appealed to his twisted sense of justice that in this way he could hold her at least partly responsible.

'The sins you have committed are of such magnitude that I intend to renew a punishment that has not been seen within these walls since before any of you were born. I intend that you shall remember it until you die.' He enjoyed the expressions that this pronouncement drew. 'Certain preparations need to be made. Until then, you will have time to reflect on the folly of flouting the laws of the Holy Prophet of Qalle.' With that, Tarrip swept from the room, leaving the five of them alone with their thoughts. They heard the heavy thud of the lock and looked at one another.

'Come quickly, Xarrith,' Hysena whispered, 'oh please come quickly.'

Xarrith had found a lantern and with its aid his progress was faster. The only clue he had to Jagdig's whereabouts was from Hysena's statement that she was in 'the deepest' part of the Citadel. He explored each descending stairway he came to, only to discover that they ended in blank passages or empty rooms. The wound in his side had stopped bleeding but now had begun to ache. The amount of blood he had lost was alarming and he was almost despairing at the knowledge that even his enormous strength could not last much longer.

When he did eventually stumble upon Jagdig, Xarrith almost gave in. As he looked in horror at the gaunt, naked body slumped listlessly in its fetters, he was convinced that she was dead. She lay on a pile of dirty straw, her legs extended before her and held wide by chains about the ankles. Despite himself, Xarrith could not prevent his eyes from going to the junction of her thighs and noticing the shaved slit of her vagina. He looked at the rest of her body, seeing the breasts that were spectacular despite the months of privation and near starvation diet. As he looked at them, he detected a slight movement and saw that she was breathing.

He fell to his knees before her and examined the manacles that secured her arms to the slimy wall. They were shut by a simple screw mechanism and it was the work of moments to free them. Moving to her ankles, he was reassured to hear her groan and try to move as she registered his presence. He could not resist another furtive glance at her sex as he worked on the hoops of metal that held her ankles. The fist that caught him under the ear was totally unexpected.

It was not a hard blow but the combination of surprise and his blood loss meant that he was thrown sprawling across the floor of the cell. Shaking his head groggily, Xarrith dragged himself to his feet, looking about him for his adversary. There was no one in the cell but Jagdig and himself. He looked at his kinswoman. She was cursing under her breath, trying hopelessly to force hands that had been all but unused for so long to undo the restraints that still held her ankles. As he watched, he shook his head again, this time in disbelief, his face twisting into a smile of admiration as he watched her struggles. From what Hysena had told him, he knew that this woman had undergone the most terrible tortures and privations over a period of months, that she had suffered at the hands of the fat priest on an almost daily basis and yet the warrior spirit still burned within her.

'Truly you are my kin.' He spoke softly, not trying to disguise the pride he felt.

Jagdig's head jerked as the voice. She had been only vaguely aware that someone had entered the cell, having been sunk into the state of semi-consciousness that had become her existence. Part of her wondered what they were going to do to her this time and another part did not care. There was little left that they could do. It slowly seeped through her battered senses that only one other was present and that this one had freed her arms. Her reaction was more instinctive that planned and she did not expect that her weak blow would bring anything other than swift retribution. She certainly did not think that she would be able to free her legs before she was battered to the floor. His words, particularly the words 'my kin' filtered into her abused mind, and for the first time she looked directly at him.

She saw a tall, muscular figure, naked and covered in filth, one hand pressed to his side. Blood was seeping through his fingers. He was without doubt Kallinian. Her eyes flew wide in disbelief.

'Why are you here?' she asked, half expecting him to vanish leaving her to awaken from a dream.

'To rescue you.'

'You cannot know how good those words sound,' said Jagdig.

Xarrith rubbed his stinging ear with one hand, still clutching at his bleeding side with the other.

'I shall remember not to approach you when you may not be glad to see me.'

'You are wounded.'

'As are you.' He could hardly avoid seeing the countless scars, some new, some almost healed, that seemed to criss-cross the entire surface of her body.

The final chain fell away and Xarrith helped Jagdig to her feet. For the first time in months, she was free of restraint. She luxuriated in the feeling, stretching her arms and arching her back until the vertebrae crackled.

Turning to Xarrith, she bowed and, taking his hand, kissed his palm.

'My life is yours,' she said, the formal obeisance offered by a warrior who had been saved by another.

'I must find means of staunching this wound if it is to be mine for long,' said Xarrith with a wince. Reaction was setting in and he felt a wave of giddiness flow through him and sank on to a stool. He took his hand away from his side and saw that the blood was again flowing freely.

For the first time in months Jagdig was concerned with the feelings and condition of someone other than herself. She saw that her rescuer was all but unconscious, slumped naked and bloody on the very stool that Tarrip used to enjoy her torments. The memory galvanised her. She knew that her kinsman had been in a fight and that he would be pursued. Looking about the rude cell, she remembered how the priest would go to an annexe in one corner, emerging from it not only with yet another implement of torture but also with wine or meat that he sustained himself with (and used to torment her further).

She entered the small room. On the walls were rows of chain and leather fetters, innumerable ranks of tokans of ever more cruel design and other objects that she could not name but which made her shudder. Putting the memories firmly from her mind, Jagdig opened another door. There was wine and water, haunches of meat kept fresh by the cold walls and bags of biscuit and hard bread; food for prisoners. She fell upon a jar of lana juice, shuddering again as the memory of how Tarrip had used even this life-saving substance to cause her unimaginable pain. Could Qalle ever in its entire history have produced such a cruel creature as Tarrip, she wondered as she gathered items with which to treat the warrior.

Xarrith came awake as the nozzle of a wineskin was thrust between his teeth. Instinctively he tried to spit it out but then began to suck eagerly as the rich liquid flowed into his mouth. Too soon it was removed, only to be replaced by another. This time, he tasted water. Stale water, water with the rank taste of a badly cured skin, but still the most welcome drink he had known.

'That is better,' said Jagdig, nodding with approval as Xarrith, becoming more alert, took the skin in his own hands. 'Now I shall see to your side.'

Xarrith grimaced as he felt a damp cloth working on the wound, cleansing away the blood and grime.

'Were you pursued?' asked Jagdig as she bent to examine him.

'The Citadel guard are soft. Not true warriors. I think they have little stomach for battle.'

'Even against a wounded man and a weakened woman?' She began to spread a thick film of lana juice over his skin.

'Even wounded and weakened, we are Kallinian,' said Xarrith.

While the lana dried, the two young Kallinians exchanged stories and gorged themselves on the food they found in the annexe. They found cloaks with which they covered their nakedness and, having armed themselves as best they could from the selection of punishment tools, they set out into the passageways of the Citadel.

At first Jagdig found the going difficult. It had been so long since she had been free to walk that her muscles and bones now protested at the unaccustomed exercise, but after the first difficult minutes her splendid, if currently thin, body began to move more easily and she began to hope that she was indeed free.

'Where do we go?' she asked Xarrith as they made their cautious way through the dusty passages, guided by the flicker of a low-turned lantern.

'Tasnar once showed me a door that leads away from the Citadel. I search for that.'

'Tasnar?'

As they proceeded, Xarrith regaled Jagdig with stories of his adventures with the diminutive Sis Narashan, leaving her to reflect on how different had been her own experience of the Citadel.

'And when we find this door?'

Xarrith turned to look at her. 'Why, then we strike for Kallinia. I know we vowed to stay in this place for three years, but I am sure that my father the king would know of how you have been used. I see us both returning at his side in the full regalia of war. I surmise there is much that he would discuss with fat Tarrip!' The two young warriors grinned at each other in the gloom of the passage.

Xarrith found that he remembered the way to the door to the outside with few false turns, and soon he was operating the hidden catch. The door swung open easily, and the two of them took deep breaths of the clean night air before stepping out of the Citadel.

'Well,' came the voice of Sister Maria from the darkness, 'To where does Kallinia journey at this late hour?'

12.

High Priestess! She was to become High Priestess of Qalle! Her equanimity was usually such that even the most momentous events left her still fully in control of herself, but this time Maria left the meeting of the Society of T'arn in a daze.

The meeting had, at first, proceeded much as usual. The beating that she had received at the hands of the other members of the society had been more ritual than painful and each of them in turn had taken time to caress her in one way or another, arousing her hugely until the last of them, a male, had caused her to lie on her back and then had folded her legs over her shoulders and squatted down on her, his thighs pressing her own against her breasts. After he had given her a few token swats, he had placed his hands on her smarting buttocks and pulled her hard against his straining erection, leaning forward a little to allow himself to slide into her. Maria had found this unusual coupling much to her enjoyment and the others had applauded them at the finish for giving such an entertainment.

'And now, to important matters' the presiding Uplander had said when they had all taken refreshment and seated themselves about the room. 'The experiment to educate and shape the younger members of our society at the Citadel is bearing much fruit. We now have a loyal cadre of the most intelligent and powerful youngsters spreading our message of peace throughout Qalle...'

She went on to outline how the incidents of border violation and raiding had fallen and how growing numbers of marriages between previously warring factions were forging bonds between the great houses.

'However,' she continued, 'there is a power group which, most certainly, threaten us should it be allowed to grow. It must be stopped.'

'Which group?' asked the Kallinian woman.

'The Priests of the Holy Prophet of Qalle!'

Maria was not the only delegate who gasped at those words. As the Uplander continued, she scarcely registered the words that she was hearing; although care had been taken to try and ensure that the members of the church who would mete out the brutal training that was intended to bind the youngsters to a common cause were not politically ambitious, a group had been identified who were attempting to shape the Initiates and Acolytes to their own ends.

'...and this faction is led by none other than Tarrip, the high priest himself,' the Uplander concluded. 'It is imperative that he be removed, quickly.'

Deeply shocked, Maria struggled to find her voice. 'My lady, while not wishing to cast aspersions upon your sagacity, I must express my doubts. Tarrip is a dull and brutal man. Although suited to the position to which our forebears elevated him, I cannot think he possesses either the intelligence or the subtlety to foment challenge upon us.'

The Uplander smiled sadly. 'Indeed he is a savage man, but while he is not, by your standards, intelligent, he is cunning. He plans to cause an uprising against the Citadel itself, an uprising he thinks he can control and put down, thus becoming a hero who would then be in such a position of power that his very word would become edict. What he would do with such power...' She let the thought float across the now silent room, each of the delegates considering with horror how Tarrip would indeed exploit such a position should he gain it.

'Know you his plan?' The questioner was the man who had so recently pleasured Maria.

'Aye. It revolves about the Initiate Jagdig.'

'Jagdig!' Maria exclaimed. 'She hates him with a loathing such as I have never seen. She would kill him gladly even though she knew that her own death would follow. I cannot, I will not believe her in league with him.'

'Neither is she. He intends her as his instrument. His plan is that she escape at a time of his choosing and run to Kallinia. With all deference to our sister from that country...' here she smiled an apology to that woman '... there are still those who resent the new ways and would gladly rise against the Citadel.'

Maria was aghast. 'But... but, few would follow her, just the young and the hot-headed and...'

'And they would be repelled, as Tarrip intends. But then the king, honour bound, must march upon the Citadel, and all of Qalle, thinking the Kallinians were attempting to gain this place, would in turn rise. All for which we have striven would fall.'

The room again fell silent as those within considered such a terrible future.

'What is to be done?' Maria could not avoid the tremor in her voice.

'Tarrip must be stopped. We do not know when he will make his move. The time is not yet ripe for him, but it must be soon.'

'How is he to be stopped? He will be killed?' asked the Kallinian.

'If it come to that, then yes, he must be killed. But that we hope to avoid. It would be enough for him to be disgraced, dishonoured in the eyes of those who support him.'

'How?' the Kallinian demanded bluntly.

Maria saw the eyes of the Uplander fix upon hers. 'It is in the hands of our Sister Maria. Stop him, and his position will be hers. High Priestess of the Holy Prophet of Qalle. The first woman to hold such an exalted rank.'

'But if I must kill him?'

'Then it is likely that you too would be killed.'

Wrapped in her cloak, Maria made her way back to the Citadel, mind a whirl. She knew that she could kill Tarrip quite easily with poison and make it seem that his death was beyond suspicion, but those of the Society of T'arn would know and would have no option other than to ensure that she follow Tarrip into death. It had always been that way throughout the history of the society. Assassination was a last resort, an admission almost of failure...and who could truly trust an assassin?

Eschewing the main entrance to the Citadel lest she encounter Tarrip, Maria picked her way through the night to the secret entrance, easily evading the guards who, scared that somewhere in the darkness might lurk a Kallinian warrior, were calling to each other that there was yet no sign. So engrossed was she with her problem that it did not at first register that light was coming from when no light should be. Quickly she wrapped a fold of her cloak about her head to conceal the white of her skin. Irritably, the Holy Sister supressed the surge of desire that took her as she recognised Xarrith. His companion was nearly as tall but stood gaunt in comparison.

'Jagdig!' she whispered in alarm. Clearly the Society had been mistaken in their supposition that Tarrip was not yet ready to play his hand.

Without thinking, she stepped into the pool of light cast by the lantern Xarrith held.

'Well,' she said, 'to where does Kallinia journey at this late hour?'

Two indistinct heads turned to face her. For a moment the three of them stood frozen, and then the young warrior leapt. He crossed the ground with impossible speed, but Maria was as quick, melting back two paces, throwing the hood from her face that he might recognise her and extending an arm towards him, fingers outstretched.

'Hold, Xarrith!' Her voice cracked like a whip through the silence of the night. It held a timbre of command he could not but obey, and his charge halted as swiftly as it had begun and he stood before her, mouth hanging stupidly open.

'Sister Maria! I, we did not expect...' his voice dribbled into silence.

'You did not expect,' she said, struggling not to reveal her fear. She had not been certain that he could be stopped. 'And your cousin Jagdig, I observe — Xarrith! Bid her stop!' From the corner of the eye that was holding Xarrith's, Maria saw the other Kallinian start for her and she knew that her powers were insufficient to stay one who had such good cause to hate her. To her relief Xarrith turned and put himself between her and Jagdig.

'Xarrith, stand aside.' Jagdig's voice was harsh.

'I will not,' replied her compatriot. 'Holy Maria is not to be harmed.'

Jagdig had allowed her cloak to drop and stood naked. Part of Maria's mind noted that, despite her long incarceration she was still a magnificent woman. Her big breasts heaving with her anger, their nipples stiff in the chill air. Maria could not prevent herself from glancing down at the naked cleft of her sex, stripped of its covering of hair. It seemed to pout invitingly. A drift of breeze brought the smell of her, rank and feral and immeasurably dangerous and, she had to admit to herself, arousing. For a moment a picture of how it would be to have the two Kallinians make love to her together flashed into her mind and she felt the familiar prickle of wetness form in her groin.

'Tarrip is your enemy. I can give him to you,' she said, forcing the image firmly from her mind.

'Hah!' Jagdig snorted, 'he is mine to take, not yours to give, holy woman.' She spat the last two words contemptuously.

'I am his not instrument. I have long planned to rid this place of him.' Maria was thinking furiously as she talked, seeking the words that might placate Jagdig. 'Truly I have used you ill, but that is the way of the Citadel. Be guided by me in this and I vow that your future here will be better.'

'My future here? I shall never again set foot in this place unless it is to destroy it.'

'The stone is not your enemy. It may well be that you could destroy the Citadel, but then the hand of every man of Qalle shall be against you. Are you prepared to be outlawed, Jagdig of Kallinia?'

It was a powerful argument and Maria saw the anger fade to doubt in Jagdig's eyes.

'She is right, Jagdig,' Xarrith broke in.

'Give me but until dawn and I shall deliver him to you.' Maria held Jagdig with her eyes. With her mind she summoned all the skill she had learned under the Adepts of the Society of T'arn and with satisfaction she sensed the indefinable shift within Jagdig's mind as the warrior girl succumbed to her power.

With inner satisfaction, she saw Jagdig relax, felt the anger seeping away.

'That is better. Follow. You shall hide in my room and prepare yourselves for what is to come.'

Maria led the two Kallinians through the dark passages of the Citadel and into her quarters.

'Do not move from this place, no matter what, until I send for you, and then you must do exactly as the messenger says. Be patient.'

Jagdig hardly heard these instructions. She had seen the bathing pool and had already shed her cloak and was anticipating the caress of warm water on her abused body.

Not a word had been spoken in the cell since Tarrip had left. Hysena had her arms about the equally naked body of Maris, as much for comfort as warmth. She saw that the others were similarly comforting each other. The wait was interminable and despite her best efforts, her fear was growing. Hysena could feel Maris trembling within the circle of her arms and she gently stroked her hair, an action that soothed them both, but not enough.

The door to the cell was flung open. Two guards stood in the opening and she could see that more were in the passage.

'Stand forth, Lady Hysena Macarydias of Argo!'

With her heart in her mouth, Hysena struggled to her feet. Biting her lip to stop it from trembling, she stepped from the cell to be surrounded by four huge guards who leered openly at her nakedness.

'Be brave, Hysena!' The call came from behind her as the door to the cell clanged shut.

She managed to keep her head high as they marched her down the passage, trying to ignore the hands that slithered over her bottom and tweaked her bobbing breasts as she walked, turning her eyes from Tasnar, still lying on the cold stone.

When the small procession reached the entrance of the sumptuous quarters of the high priest, Hysena hesitated, only to be thrust stumbling into the room by a firm shove on her buttocks. She held a forearm across her breasts and covered her sex with her hand, unconsciously echoing the way she had stood the first time that she had been stripped nude before the High Priest.

'My Lady Hysena. How pleasant.' By the tone of his voice, Tarrip might have been greeting an honoured guest. She quailed before him, desperately fighting back tears. The priest stood to one side.

The apparatus that had been hidden behind him seemed to hold little to alarm her, and for a moment Hysena relaxed. At first glance it appeared nothing more than a tall, slender stool, set upon three legs and with a pointlessly short and narrow backrest. Then she realised that what she had taken for a backrest in fact pierced the centre of the seat, and was carved in the shape of a phallus. Its purpose was obvious and at once Hysena screamed and tried to run, only to feel the hands of the guards close upon her upper arms like steel bands.

Tarrip enjoyed her helpless struggles and smiled over at Colya who was watching with interest. Tarrip had told her that the prisoners were to be posted, but she did not know what he meant.

The priest felt his prick rise rock-hard beneath his robe in anticipation and savoured the sensation before picking up the stool and holding it before him, advanced on the trembling Hysena.

'Lift her,' he instructed, his voice thick with passion.

Hysena felt two thick arms press into the small of her back as two hands grabbed the backs of her thighs, lifting her until she was horizontal. Looking between her trembling breasts and along the length of her body,

Hysena saw the foreshortened end of the stool approaching as Tarrip, walking slowly to extend the deep pleasure of the moment, moved towards her.

He licked his lips. 'Spread her thighs.'

Again Hysena screamed, high and shrill, as the two guards carried out their pleasurable duty, both leaning forward the better to see her sex as it opened.

Tarrip moved closer, now rubbing the protruding tip of the stool with oil, making it gleam. 'Pull her knees to her chest... no, hold them wide, fools!'

Utterly exposed, Hysena felt cold tears course down her cheeks. Still weakly struggling, she resigned herself to her fate, wishing before all else that this might be the moment of her death. The earlier punishments, all the unutterable pain and humiliation that had gone before, were as nothing compared to this. Before, there had been, no matter how deeply hidden, the knowledge that this unholy priest was the only man to see her shame and that her friends would, eventually, gather about her to soothe and comfort. Now, she was the helpless plaything of not only him, but also a group of slavering guards, for she could not doubt that each of them would in turn do with her as they wished.

A deep shudder took her body as she felt the cold tip of the repulsive thing touch the flesh of her thigh and move along it, leaving a loathsome, slimy trail as it moved towards its inevitable destination. Desperately, she clenched her buttocks and willed the lips of her sex to close. It was hopeless. Even in her anguish Hysena heard the tiny sound as the hard, oily wood rasped against her dark pubic hair, seeking the way into her.

'Such a pretty cunt,' Tarrip murmured, rotating the stool slightly against the softness of her outer lips, teasing them open. 'Such a pretty, pretty cunt.' His voice was a caress.

Hysena felt it easing into her, opening her wider, filling her. She became aware of hands, hard, calloused hands mauling her breasts, pinching her nipples as the thing between her open legs sank ever more deeply into her body.

A groan of total despair rose from her throat as a hard knuckle ground into her exposed clitoris. Even her body was betraying her! With a feeling of utter loathing for herself, Hysena was becoming aroused.

She heard the priest give an evil chuckle and knew that he had noticed. The knuckle on her clitoris was as relentless as the unyielding wooden phallus that Tarrip was working in and out of her vagina. Hating herself, Hysena could not resist responding and she felt herself working her hips, pressing onto the thick wood, almost as she had worked her hips with such abandon when Tasnar had so delightfully loved her scant hours before. The memory was enough to take her beyond the brink of orgasm her scream was of all the emotions; ecstasy and disgust, desire and hatred, agony and lust.

She lay limp in the arms of the guards, only vaguely aware of the wooden phallus as it slid from her vagina.

'See how keen she is!' exalted Tarrip, smiling at the guards and Colya. 'I had intended to punish her, but it seems I must strive harder!'

There was a rumble of crude laughter from the guards. Hysena became aware that, once more, fingers were moving over her sex.

'So, my Lady Hysena,' said Tarrip, pushing two thick fingers into her, 'your pretty cunt shows little contrition for your sins. We must try another way.' He withdrew his fingers and Hysena hated herself again as that part of her brain that was beyond her control mourned their loss. 'Perhaps,' the priest continued, 'Here!' With that, he jabbed his forefinger into her anus.

Hysena squealed and bucked in the grip of the guards. Tarrip worked his finger more deeply into her, rotating it, enjoying the whimper that this drew from the helpless girl.

'Now, hold her firm,' he instructed the guards. Immediately Hysena felt the hands on her flesh tighten, felt her limbs pulled wider. She felt hands on her behind pull her buttocks apart and screamed yet again as the hard nose of the wooden phallus was forced into her anus.

'Now, lift her.' The voice of the priest came to Hysena through a haze of pain. She felt her body being elevated and as she came upright her own weight served to drive the wood into her to its full length. Unseen hands guided her feet to footrests lower down the shaft of the stool, footrests that were set in such a way that if she was to use them to support her body weight and lift herself from the presence that had invaded her anus, she was forced to splay her legs wide, exposing her sex in the most lewd manner. The same hands then bound her wrists and tied them together behind her back.

Then she became aware that the capacity of the stool to torture had not ended, that a mind of exquisite evilness had added a final refinement. Circling the shaft that penetrated the seat of the stool had been set a ring of sharp studs that bit sharply into the soft, sensitive flesh of her buttocks, forcing her to take more weight on her feet. But there were similar studs on the footrests and it was only moments before the pain these caused forced her to allow her body to sink back onto the shaft, transferring the agony back to her behind. The effect was that Hysena found herself lifting and lowering her body in a grotesque parody of the act of love.

Stepping back, panting a little from exertion and lust, Tarrip surveyed his handiwork. It had been many years since he had posted a girl, and he had forgotten just what an enticing spectacle it made. As he enjoyed the sight of her writhing helplessly, lifting and lowering herself, he could see the hard, unyielding wood sliding in and out. Sweat was covering her body, gathering in the valley between her trembling breasts, running over her flat stomach to soak into the black curls of her pubic hair. With her legs forced wide her cunt was clearly exposed, the inner lips pink and spread. He could even see the tip of her clitoris protruding from its protective hood. Tarrip felt his penis grow iron hard beneath his robe. He glanced at the guards, none of whom was old enough too have ever seen a posting. Their eyes were wide and he could see the telltale bulges that distorted their garments.

'Well my brave guardians of the Citadel. Our work is begun. When it is ended, you may take your reward. Now go!' the priest continued. 'The quicker you complete your task, the more time you shall have to enjoy your reward.'

In their haste to carry out these pleasing orders, the guards briefly blocked the door as they fought each other to be the first to fetch the next victim. Smiling his evil smile, Tarrip stepped up to the helpless girl, pulling up the hem of his robe as he did. 'An amusing punishment, think you Sister Colya?'

When she had seen Tarrip lift his robe, Colya had quickly shed her own and now naked, crossed to the helpless Initiate who continued to rise and fall on the posting stool, whimpering and crying. She sank to her knees between the spread legs, the better to see the wooden phallus sliding in and out of her arse. To her joy, she sensed Tarrip positioning himself behind her and felt the prick that had brought her so much joy pressing into her freshly whipped cunt.

They were interrupted by the sound of male voices accompanied by shrill female screams as the guards dragged a struggling Princess Leel into the cell.

The guards froze at the unexpected sight of the High Priest of the Prophet of Qalle copulating with Holy Sister Colya, but Tarrip, hardly breaking his stroke, simply gestured towards the waiting row of empty posting stools.

'You have seen what to do,' he said, grunting as he thrust into Colya. 'Oil the pole and set her upon it.' Delighted, the guards bent to their task.

Slowing his pace, not want to climax with Colya, Tarrip settled into a steady rhythm and enjoyed the sight as the guards attempted to impale Leel on the posting stool. The girl had managed to roll onto her stomach, offering a fine view of her plump bottom, and was trying to press herself flat. One of the guards, standing astride her and facing her feet, grabbed her about the waist and lifted her hips as two others hauled her legs apart, exposing her red-haired cunt and the deeply chiselled pit of her anus. The other, seeing his chance, managed to work the oiled tip of the stool between her buttocks and, thrusting steadily, into her body. Leel stiffened and screeched, but the outcome was inevitable and shortly she was placed, howling, next to Hysena, both of them attempting to find a compromise between pain in their feet and pain between their spread legs, their bodies rising and falling, the thick wooden poles sliding relentlessly within their anuses.

One after another, the posting stools became occupied until Tarrip was able to feast his eyes on the most erotic sight that even he, with a lifetime of perverted memories, had ever seen. Five pretty girls all writhing, crying, pleading, impaled by the thick wooden shafts that held them helpless. By way of variation the priest had caused his guards to position Nephraan facing the opposite way to the others, the pole penetrating her cunt, leaving her leaning slightly forward, her shapely buttocks thrust out as if in invitation, allowing access to her shapely behind.

For the moment Tarrip was contented to watch as the guards, hardly believing their luck, had stripped themselves and were now taking it in turns with the Initiates, mauling breasts, fingering cunts, fucking one for a minute before moving to the next.

To her chagrin, Hysena found that she was actually in less pain when one of the guards was using her, as she was able to use the body between her legs to take the weight from her pained feet. When Tarrip unceremoniously dragged the guard who had been enjoying her helpless charms from her and took his place, she wrapped her legs about the fat priest's waist as he shove his giant prick into her. His size was such that she felt herself lifted until the wooded phallus in her behind was nearly freed, only and inch or two of it now penetrating her. The sight of all the sexual activity about her and the attentions her own body was receiving had its usual affect. Hysena did not fight it, but allowed the climax to build. As the first spasm took her, Tarrip redoubled his efforts, lifting her higher. His bull roar filled the room. Hysena felt the red-hot jets of his sperm squirting into her, and over his shoulder she saw the figure of Sister Maria enter the room.

Tarrip's roar had drawn the attention of all in the room, and for a moment the frantic activity ceased and a brief silence fell.

'Holy Father, what you are about is proscribed and a sin in the eyes of the Holy Prophet.' Her voice, as ever, was soft and penetrating, but even Maria could not prevent a slight tremble of emotion at the sight that greeted her.

Startled, Tarrip turned, still with Hysena wrapped around him. As he moved, the Initiate felt the last inch of wood slip from her behind, and, sensing her chance, she thrust hard with her feet, pushing against the priest. Caught off balance, Tarrip fell backwards with the full weight of the girl on his chest. He hit the floor with a meaty thump, the breath whooshing out of him, leaving him momentarily stunned. As he lay on his back, naked and gasping like some obscene giant fish, Hysena scrambled to her feet and scurried behind the comforting figure of Maria. Tarrip managed to suck breath into his lungs and from his undignified position, looked up at Maria. Although she stood apparently relaxed, her hands clasped in front of her, there was a glitter in her eyes he had never before seen, a look that made him quail. He looked for the guards and saw that they had withdrawn from the cunts of the young women they had been enjoying and were standing like guilty schoolboys before the figure of Holy Sister Maria, their various erections slowly drooping.

'Seize her!' Tarrip had intended his order to be a shout, but it came out as a croak. Only Colya, who had felt slighted and frustrated because none of the guards had fucked her, preferring the more tender flesh of the Initiates, moved. With her hands extended like claws, she grabbed her colleague. Concentrating on Tarrip and deeply shocked by what she was seeing, Maria was taken by surprise and moved back too late to prevent Colya grabbing her robe. The thin cloth ripped and suddenly she was naked.

'Seize her!' This time Tarrip's voice regained some of its power and the guards were galvanised into action. Tarrip was on his feet now, feeling that he once more was in control of the situation. The entry of Sister Maria offered another delightful dimension to the entertainment. 'Which of you wishes to fuck her?' he goaded. For a moment Maria was lost from view as the eager guards jostled around her, taking the opportunity to grope at her breasts and her sex as they restrained her. Tarrip frowned as a strangely fluting whistle momentarily filled the room, a whistle that for its brief duration seemed to fill his brain, but then it was gone and he was able to enjoy the sight of Sister Maria being wrestled to the floor, a guard holding each arm as two others fought to haul her legs apart. His hand went once more to his prick, rubbing it back to erection as the guards held Maria spreadeagled. Tarrip had sunk to his knees and was about to take her when suddenly, impossibly, the room was filled with figures.

When she had seen Maria, Hysena's heart had leapt. She had expected her to be leading a rescue party and her heart sank when she realised that the Holy Sister was alone. She was about to flee when, like Tarrip, her mind was suddenly filled by the strange whistle. Unlike the priest, Hysena did not dismiss it as she had been in a position to see that it was Maria who had given it, and for a reason she did not understand, she somehow knew that it portended something important.

Even long afterwards, when Hysena thought back to those events, she could not say where the figures came from. In moments they had torn the guards from Maria and trussed them with cord.

'Loose them,' said Maria, indicating the Initiates. 'Be very gentle.'

As the figures began to free the moaning youngsters, easing the cruel wooden phalluses from their behinds, Hysena was able to study them. They were Ercli. She watched in amazement as they went about their task, wondering that these quiet, inoffensive people could show such a different side to their nature.

Tarrip came warily to his feet, seeing the girls draw back fearfully as he did. But the Ercli did not. Like most, Tarrip had never really taken any notice of them, certainly he had never feared them, but now there was something menacing in their silence and stillness. Suddenly, they each took a step towards him and involuntarily, he backed away, eyes darting from side to side as he sought an escape. They took another pace, and Tarrip felt terror flood his mind. His hand flew to his mouth but he was unable to prevent a whimper escaping his trembling lips as he backed away, out of the door and into the passage. From the corner of his eye, he noticed a discarded sword and grabbed it with relief. He extended it towards the Ercli, stopping their advance. Tarrip drew air into his lungs, preparatory to a shout that would bring all of the Citadel guards to his side... and a foot slammed into his leg. The intended shout became a scream and Tarrip dropped the sword as he fell. He found himself lying next to the dead body of Tasnar, a body that, impossibly, had kicked him. Gibbering in terror, the priest saw the eyes of the dead youth blink open. The lips moved.

'Forgive me, Father, for I have sinned,' said Tasnar, and lapsed back into unconsciousness. Tarrip broke. Scrambling to his feet he fled down the corridor, dreading the sound of pursuit, but nothing followed him other than the voice of Sister Maria.

'Jagdig is loose, Holy Father. She seeks your company!' Her voice was mocking, echoing along the corridor as Tarrip desperately wondered where he might hide from the Kallinian. He did not doubt his fate should she find him.

13.

Jagdig lay floating on her back in the bathing pool in Sister Maria's room. The warm water seemed to leech away all the hurts and humiliations she had experienced during the previous terrible months. She moved her arms languidly, sending ripples over the tips of her breasts, making her nipples crinkle at the sensual touch of the water. She had soaped herself all over three times before she felt cleansed, and now felt at peace for the first time since she had arrived at the Citadel. With small movements of toes and fingers, she spun herself until she could see Xarrith. When Maria had left them, he had stumbled to the bed and fallen across it in an exhausted sleep and still lay there, snoring softly. Jagdig stepped from the pool and used her discarded robe to dry herself. The air of the room was cold after the warmth of the water and she drew on a dry robe. She found a bowl and, having filled it from the pool, knelt next to the bed. As gently as possible, trying not to wake him, she peeled away Xarrith's robe and began to wash her kinsman. She saw that his wound had stopped bleeding and that the film of lana still adhered firmly to his skin, protecting it from further harm.

As she sponged away the blood and filth from his body, she found herself staring at his genitals. Even at rest his penis was enormous and the sac containing his balls was the size of her bunched fist.

Unable to help herself, Jagdig touched his prick, running a finger along its length, revelling in its silky smoothness, only to snatch her hand back in alarm when it suddenly pulsed and stirred. Guiltily, she glanced at his face. He was still asleep, but now he was smiling. Jagdig looked back down his body and gasped. Even in the moments when she had been looking at his face, his penis had doubled in size. As she watched, it continued to grow, pulsing and thickening. She saw his balls move in their nest of thick curls, the sac seeming to tighten and he previously wrinkled skin becoming taut and Jagdig's hand stole to her sex, already slick with her juices. Staring wide-eyed at the massive erection, she rolled her clitoris between finger and thumb. As her nipples stiffened almost painfully hard, it suddenly occurred to her that this time she would not be halted on the screaming edge of orgasm, that here in the safety of Maria's room, she could at last ease some of the frustrations that had built up over the previous dreadful months.

Whimpering with desire and anticipation, she lifted her leg and straddled Xarrith. Slowly, drawing out the delicious sensation, she lowered herself, feeling him, massive, hard and hot, sliding into her cunt. Squeezing her breasts rhythmically, she sank on to him until she could grind her pubic bone against his, rubbing her clitoris against the hard bone and scratchy pubic hair. She closed her eyes the better to concentrate on the ecstasy of sensation, feeling it build higher within her body as she rocked slowly. With a long groan, she felt the wave of pleasure overcome her, felt the inner pulses tighten her cunt about his cock. Jagdig flopped forward on the supine figure beneath her. She lay unmoving for many moments, savouring the feeling of release and enjoying the feel of the stiff cock, still buried in her body. Then she heard Xarrith chuckle and felt his strong arms embrace her.

'A fine awakening, little one. Were I lifted thus from my slumber each day, this miserable place would become almost endurable.'

Jagdig opened her eyes and smiled into his, inches away. 'Call me 'little one' one more time and you may never again wake,' she said, her voice languid.

She felt Xarrith's arms tighten around her and suddenly found herself flipped onto her back, the weight of his body pressing her to the bed.

'You challenge me?' he asked playfully, working his hips a little, causing her still simmering lust to rise once more.

'To the death!' she replied, pushing up at him, feeling

that mighty prick moving impossibly deep within her.

Xarrith took his weight on his elbows, giving him room to thrust in earnest. Jagdig sought his mouth with hers and wrapped her long legs around him, lifting her knees and crossing her ankles in the small of his back, pulling him hard against her as she once more shuddered in orgasm. She felt him stiffen and then felt his sperm jetting hotly into her and his cry mingled with her own.

For an unmeasured time they lay quiescent, skin on skin, arms about each other, savouring the feeling of warmth and peace; unusual pleasures in that place.

Jagdig had fallen into a pleasant doze and was dreamily contemplating making love again when she felt Xarrith's body stiffen.

'Alert! We are spied upon!' he said, rolling from the bed and onto his feet in a fluid motion. Jagdig looked. Before them stood an Ercli woman.

Xarrith towered over the diminutive figure, magnificent in his nakedness. 'Maria sent you?' he asked her. The woman said nothing, but simply nodded and turned away, walking from the room without looking to see if the two Kallinians were following.

Jagdig and Xarrith grabbed their robes and struggled into them as they hurried after the Ercli. Maria met them in the passage. She hid her amusement as her sensitive nose caught the scent of love that lingered about them.

'You seek the Holy Father?'

Xarrith bowed to her. 'Aye, sister. My kinswoman has much to discuss with him.'

'Where would the most desperate of men hide?'

Xarrith looked at the holy woman. Her gaze was steady and serene. Focusing her concentration, Sister Maria gently laid an image in his mind and saw comprehension dawn on his features.

'The Last Tower,' he breathed, 'where else?' He turned to Jagdig. 'Follow!'

Maria smiled as they clattered away down the passage and knelt beside Tasnar and continued to tend his wounds. They were grievous, but he would, she thought, live.

Tarrip lay panting on the roof of the Last Tower. The climb had almost finished him and only his fear had enabled him to drive his bulk up the winding stairs. He hoped that rather than chase him, Jagdig would have taken the opportunity to make her escape, but in his black heart he knew that this was just a dream. He hauled himself upright and staggered to the edge of the tower. He knew that it would be best to throw himself to oblivion but as he looked down into the Stygian depths, he knew he lacked the courage.

There was a crash from behind him. The priest turned, whimpering.

The moon was high and full above the Last Tower and bathed Jagdig in silver light. The wind had moulded her robe to her body, outlining it and even in his fear Tarrip saw her as magnificent. He could clearly see the cleft of her hairless sex and her nipples, made stiff by the keen wind. She was smiling, unspeaking, moving towards him, arms extended as if to greet a lover. Tarrip retreated. His confused mind was filled with images of her, naked, screaming her agony and desire. He felt the low parapet of the tower against the backs of his calves and could retreat no further. Tarrip blinked. The roof of the Last Tower now seemed to be filled with figures. There was Hysena whom he had so recently buggered with the posting stool, little Silka of the delightfully tight cunt, Maris, Silka, Nephraan. Other faces were from the past; girls and women who had long left the Citadel, some of whom he knew to be dead. At the centre of the sea of faces was Sister Maria, serene and beautiful. She turned to the girls and said something he could not hear but he did hear their laughter like tinkling bells. He leaned back, feeling the depths sucking at him and again came the tinkle of girlish laughter.

Tarrip fell.

And now for the opening of next month's title:

DARKER DREAMS by TESSA VALMUR

PROLOGUE

'It's all up to you. You may have told us how you want your dream to start, but how it ends, well... that's your choice.'

'You're absolutely certain?' Lara asked, dubiously.

The man nodded affirmatively, gave her a reassuring smile and leant back in his leather swivel armchair. Lara took a sip from the cup of coffee cup she held then placed it back on his mahogany desk. She re-crossed her slender legs, smoothed her short skirt over her thighs and looked thoughtfully at her hands resting in her lap.

'Would it help if you had another experimental session?' the man suggested, his tone was smooth and gently persuasive.

Lara had been soft sold plenty by professional gentlemen in the white jackets of consultant doctors. She had spent hundreds of thousands on keeping herself young and beautiful. At twenty six she had a body that any girl would envy. There had been an expression in the last century, something like 'money can't buy happiness'. But back then what could a girl buy? Breast implants, hair extensions, false nails. God how crude the beauty industry was then! Now, thanks to a few subtle genetic modifications to certain growth hormones, a little judicious laser surgery and a life of leisure and pampering, Lara at twenty six, looked like every man's dream eighteen year old girl. A perfect size ten, her narrow waist accentuated her generous breasts that were as firm and pert as a teenager's. Her legs and arms were slim and smooth; her skin a light chocolate brown with a coppery shine. Her hair fell in soft loose curls, the colour of burnished gold; the fashion colour of the moment, the summer of 2027. It fell almost to the swell of her firm and well rounded bottom.

Lara had, thanks to being a member of the super-wealthy, everything she materially wanted, everything she physically wanted... she had everything - except for the fulfilment of her deepest, most secret fantasies. Now, at a price, Doctor Patrick MacKennan of the Dreamscape Institute was offering her a chance to realise her most secret dreams.

'Alright then Doctor Mackennan, you've convinced me. I'm ready and willing.'

'Excellent. Shall we say tomorrow then at two in the afternoon?' the man smiled.

'I'll look forward to it.'

* * *

MacKennan read back through his case notes before bringing them up to date.

'Lara Lustral. DOB 2001, height 1.79m, weight 65.1 kg, social class Alpha 1. Dream test No.1 completed successfully. Client now wishes to experience full dreamscape. I will map and physically stimulate her autonomic nervous system with adrenal synapse focus and induce her desired dreamscape state. The client's first dream tests shows a deep physical and sexual frustration - in her dreams at level one she places herself in demanding physical situations where she is forced to struggle and defeat dominant forces. At level two however she is naturally sexually submissive but even in her dreams her social conditioning makes her reluctant to accept this. I will use electrode impulsing to stimulate her endocrine glands and the L2 computer will exaggerate her dreamscape by neurological messaging.'

Mackennan closed the folder of notes and slid it into a desk drawer. Call him old-fashioned but he found something deeply satisfying about old-fashioned pen and paper. And of course while any Delta class criminal or member of staff could hack into a computer that was programmed in Common Europa language, only a few Alpha class citizens could now write in English.

Lara Lustral was about to have the dream of a lifetime, he mused. Of course, in her dream she would experience whatever she wanted, controlling her dream with her subconscious aided by the computer. However, with her body wired up to the electrode impulser, Mackennan could interfere directly with her dream by stimulating or repressing specific glands of her endocrine system. He could also modify the computer programme to pull her dream in different directions. She would unwittingly be like a swimmer being dragged off course by a strong current of water.

* * *

How to spend the evening before the day of excitement? Lara mused, sipping some champagne and nibbling some delicacies she'd had her housekeeper make for her. She gazed around her apartment for inspiration but none came. She had planned to take a long, hot bath with some aromatic oils; relax then get a good night's sleep. But here she was at nearly midnight, too excited to sleep. She felt like a spoilt kid again, impatiently waiting for some presents to satisfy her. It was a feeling that she had frequently. She'd once overheard one of her servants describing her as a selfish and spoilt little bitch. Lara had to agree with the description but of course she still dismissed the girl.

After hours of daydreaming about what she might actually dream about the following afternoon when she returned to the Institute, she could stand it no longer. Her imagination crowded with delicious sexual fantasies, she rang her chauffeur and ordered him to be ready for her in ten minutes. Half an hour later he had dropped her outside a nightclub where she knew she would easily find some men to satisfy her needs.

'If the alarm goes off get your arse in here,' she warned, in her usual peremptory tone, glancing at the innocent looking ring she had slipped onto one of her perfectly manicured fingers. Her chauffeur nodded.

As was usually the case, the place was pulsing with barely contained sexual excitement and it took Lara no time to size up some men who looked just like what she was after. For the three men, the girl in the snakeskin, figure-hugging mini dress with the mane of golden hair was the answer to their dreams. Within an hour Lara had brought them back to another apartment she kept purely for such assignations. As she left her car in the basement parking zone, one man's arm firmly around her slender waist, she glanced back over her shoulder at her chauffeur.

'Wait for me,' she ordered, raising one cautioning finger to her servant. The smartly liveried young man noted it was the finger with her alarm ring and he nodded.

As he settled back to read a magazine and wait out the night in the car, he glanced in the rear view mirror in time to see the three men and his employer step inside the lift. As the lift doors glided shut he glimpsed a pair of impatient hands push the snakeskin dress upwards exposing more of his employer's shapely thighs.

Lara felt the heady, intoxicating mixture of excitement and sexual need rushing through her as she keyed her pass-code into the door lock and let the four of them into the apartment. It was not the first time she'd brought more than one man at a time back here. In her teenage days she'd been content with a string of boyfriends then as she moved into her twenties she'd sought more excitement. Of course as an Alpha One female, ordinary men treated her with respect and caution. One word of complaint from her and a Delta class man could face crushing fines or imprisonment. Her privileged position in society meant that she could happily play with Delta men then drop them once they'd satisfied her. Once in her domain they would always do as she commanded for fear of punishment at the hands of the élite-supporting, draconian authorities. Nevertheless as a precaution, she had the ring. If she pressed the gemstone three times in quick succession it sounded an alarm her chauffeur carried. Having an armed escort always at her summons gave her the confidence to play the sort of games that some people might describe as playing with fire.

The three men were all young, well built and mildly drunk. They told her that they worked in the construction industry. Lara liked manual labourers like these men; they were generally fit and pleasingly well muscled. Whilst one of the men began to strip off his clothes, his friends eagerly helped Lara shed her dress. In her skimpy underwear, she strutted across to the large circular bed, glancing back over her shoulder to see the effect her near naked body had produced on the three men. She dropped down onto the bed, turned onto her stomach and thrust her bottom up invitingly.

'Come on boys, what are you waiting for?' she taunted.

...to be continued

The cover photograph for this book and many others are available as limited edition prints.
Write to:-

Viewfinders Photography
PO Box 200,
Reepham
Norfolk
NR10 4SY

for details, or see,

www.viewfinders.org.uk

TITLES IN PRINT
SILVER MOON

ISBN 1-897809-50-6 Naked Truth, *Nicole Dere*
ISBN 1-897809-54-9 The Confessions of Amy Mansfield, *R. Hurst*
ISBN 1-897809-59-X Slaves for the Sheik *Allan Aldiss*
ISBN 1-897809-60-3 Church of Chains *Sean O'Kane*
ISBN 1-897809-62-X Slavegirl from Suburbia *Mark Slade*
ISBN 1-897809-64-6 Submission of a Clan Girl *Mark Stewart*
ISBN 1-897809-65-4 Taming the Brat *Sean O'Kane*
ISBN 1-897809-66-2 Slave for Sale *J.T. Pearce*
ISBN 1-897809-69-7 Caged! *Dr. Gerald Rochelle*
ISBN 1-897809-71-9 Rachel in servitude *J.L. Jones*
ISBN 1-897809-72-2 Beaucastel *Caroline Swift*
ISBN 1-897809-73-5 Slaveworld *Steven Douglas*
ISBN 1-897809-76-X Sisters in Slavery *Charles Graham*
ISBN 1-897809-78-6 Eve in Eden *Stephen Rawlings*
ISBN 1-897809-80-8 Inside the Fortress *John Sternes*
ISBN 1-903687-00-4 The Brotherhood *Falconer Bridges*
ISBN 1-903687-01-2 Both Master and Slave *Martin Sharpe*
ISBN 1-903687-03-9 Slaves of the Girlspell *William Avon*
ISBN 1-903687-04-7 Royal Slave; Slaveworld Story *Stephen Douglas*
ISBN 1-903687-05-5 Castle of Torment *Caroline Swift*
ISBN 1-903687-08-X The Art of Submission *Tessa Valmur*
ISBN 1-903687-09-8 Theatre of Slaves *Mark Stewart*
ISBN 1-903687-10-1 Painful Prize *Stephen Rawlings*
ISBN 1-903687-12-8 The Story of Emma *Sean O'Kane*
ISBN I-903687-14-4 Savage Journey *John Argus*
ISBN 1-903687-15-2 Slave School *Stephen Douglas*
ISBN 1-903687-16-0 Slaves of the Circle T *Charles Graham*
ISBN 1-903687-17-9 Amber in Chains *Francine Whittaker*
ISBN 1-903687-18-7 Linda's Trials *Nicole Dere*
ISBN 1-903687-19-5 Hannah's Trials *Stephen Rawlings*
ISBN 1-903687-20-9 The Pit of Pain *Falconer Bridges*
ISBN 1-903687-21-7 The Sufferers *Caroline Swift*
ISBN 1-903687-22-5 Bought and Sold *Tessa Valmur*
ISBN 1-903687-23-3 Slaveworld Embassy *Stephen Douglas*
ISBN 1-903687-24-1 Trained in the Harem *Mark Stewart*
ISBN 1-903687-25-X Dark Surrender *Kim Knight*
ISBN 1-903687-26-8 Into the Arena *Sean O'Kane*
ISBN 1-903687-27-6 The Slave Path *Francine Whittaker*
ISBN 1-903687-27-6 The Initiate *Miranda Lake*

TITLES IN PRINT

SILVER MOON CLASSICS
ISBN 1-897809-23-9 Slave to the System, *Rosetta Stone*
ISBN 1-903687-32-8 The Contract *Sarah Fisher*
ISBN 1-897809-37-9 Bush Slave, *Lia Anderssen*
ISBN 1-897809-39-5 Training Jenny, *Rosetta Stone*
ISBN 1-897809-43-3 Selling Stephanie, *Rosetta Stone*

SILVER MINK
ISBN 1-897809-22-0 The Captive *Amber Jameson*
ISBN 1-897809-24-7 Dear Master *Terry Smith*
ISBN 1-897809-26-3 Sisters in Servitude *Nicole Dere*
ISBN 1-897809-28-X Cradle of Pain *Krys Antarakis*
ISBN 1-897809-49-2 The Penitent *Charles Arnold*
ISBN 1-897809-58-1 Private Tuition *Jay Merson*
ISBN 1-897809-61-1 Little One *Rachel Hurst*
ISBN 1-897809-63-8 Naked Truth II *Nicole Dere*
ISBN 1-897809-67-0 Tales from the Lodge *Bridges/O'Kane*
ISBN 1-897809-68-9 Your Obedient Servant Charlotte *Anna Grant*
ISBN 1-897809-70-0 Bush Slave II *Lia Anderssen*
ISBN 1-897809-74-3 Further Private Tuition *Jay Merson*
ISBN 1-897809-75-1 The Connoisseur *Francine Whittaker*
ISBN 1-897809-77-8 Slave to her Desires *Samantha Austen*
ISBN 1-897809-79-4 The Girlspell *William Avon*
ISBN 1-897809-81-6 The Stonehurst Letters *J.L. Jones*
ISBN 1-903687-07-1 Punishment Bound *Francine Whittaker*
ISBN 1-903687-11-X Naked Deliverance *Lia Anderssen*
ISBN 1-903687-13-6 Lani's Initiation *Danielle Richards*

STILETTO SM
ISBN 1-897809-88-3 Stern Manor *Denise la Croix*
ISBN 1-897809-93-X Military Discipline *Anna Grant*
ISBN 1-897809-94-8 Mistress Blackheart *Francine Whittaker*
ISBN 1-897809-97-2 Slaves of the Sisterhood *Anna Grant*
ISBN 1-897809-98-0 The Rich Bitch *Becky Ball*
ISBN 1-897809-99-9 Maria's Fulfilment *Jay Merson*
ISBN 1-903687-02-0 The Daughters of de Sade *Falconer Bridges*

SPECIAL DOUBLE ISSUES
ISBN 1-897809-06-9 Biker's Girl + Caravan of Slaves
ISBN 1-897809-12-3 Biker's Girl on the Run + A Toy for Jay